PAIN BEHIND BROKEN VASES

AMILIA POWERS

Visit our website at
www.StillwaterPress.com
for more information.

First Stillwater River Publications Edition

ISBN: 9781952521331

1 2 3 4 5 6 7 8 9 10
Written by Amilia Powers
Published by Stillwater River Publications,
Pawtucket, RI, USA.

Publisher's Cataloging-In-Publication Data
(Prepared by The Donohue Group, Inc.)

Names: Powers, Amilia, author.
Title: Pain behind broken vases / Amilia Powers.
Description: First Stillwater River Publications edition. | Paw-
    tucket, RI, USA : Stillwater River Publications, [2020]
Identifiers: ISBN 9781952521331
Subjects: LCSH: Women--Abuse of--Fiction. | Interpersonal rela-
    tions--Psychological aspects--Fiction. | Family violence--Fic-
    tion. | Widows--Fiction. | LCGFT: Domestic fiction.
Classification: LCC PS3616.O88337 P35 2020 | DDC 813/.6--
    dc23

Additional Works by Amilia Powers

Best Selling Author of
Success Manifesto,
co-authored with Brian Tracy

DEDICATION

Pain Behind Broken Vases is dedicated to the Lord. His strength and love has been with me from the beginning. Without His guidance and support I would be lost. He has led me through the darkness and shown me the light. I am forever His…

Amilia Powers

ACKNOWLEDGMENTS

" We live in this world to stand beside one another through life. To lift each other up during difficult challenges and share love and joy during the good times"—Amilia Powers

In memory of my mother Kleoniki Mina for her wisdom and kindness. Her encouragement to never give up and stay in faith. Her words., "Never worry. God is with you every step of the way."

My father Andrew Mina. I thank him for his support. His influence and strong presence who made me feel there isn't anything I can't do in this life.

My son and daughter. Terry Lee Anderson Jr and Kleoniki Irene Anderson for their compassion and love. Who kept a smile on my face and laughter in my heart while I was going through a very hurtful period in my life. Their energy and prayers lifted me and gave me the inspiration I needed to fulfill my dream.

My loving husband Carter Hays. Who I feel a deep sense of gratitude. His strength and commitment helped me stay focused through faith. His unconditional love and guidance encouraged me each step of the way to follow my vision and complete my gift.

For the development of this book. A special thank you to Stillwater River Publications for their assistance and patience. A company who took every word and brought it to life.

Pain Behind Broken Vases

CHAPTER ONE

It was a perfect August Saturday night in South Carolina at the Ocean Side Yacht Club. I always found it inspiring that it looked just like the White House. Tall white pillars, a circular driveway, and gorgeously landscaped. The rose bushes that lined the front of the building had big buds of all different colors. Hedges were perfectly trimmed, and palm trees stood as tall as the club, like soldiers at attention. Each tree had a light beaming from the bottom to the top, which made them look endless, and gave everything a little mystery. The night sky was full of stars that twinkled like diamonds. It was so breathtaking and calm.

My name is Amilia, and I'm a server at the private yacht club. The club is over the top with its luxurious amenities and gorgeous location, along with fantastic views of the ocean. People from all over the country come here for its excellence.

Tonight, there will be a large gala event with an auction, and a live band. Several extra waiters were called in to help with this event because they were expecting approximately two hundred guests. The party starts at 8:30 p.m., and is scheduled to go until 1:30 a.m.

The tables were all set in place; dressed with tan tablecloths that draped to the floor, along with cream-colored cloth napkins, and exquisite solid crystal wine glasses. The centerpieces were in tall clear vases with long-stemmed greenery and white roses. The deep rich colors of tan and cream made the room look stunning. All the different sized candles gave it a special touch. I was captivated by the ambiance.

My boss Pierre is moving about with great purpose, as he always does, making sure everything is perfect. He's really talented and a man I admire greatly. I've worked for him for several years and have nothing bad to say. In the service industry, people can be harsh, but he's fair and just. This clearly works for him and for the club, as the turnover is lower than it would be at other similar venues.

Pierre was walking through the dining room as he called us over to review the plan for tonight, and gave us our assignments. Pierre explained that there wouldn't be any order-taking, everyone would receive the same dish.

First Course: Field green salad with crumbled gorgonzola cheese and vinaigrette dressing.

Second Course: Filet mignon and lobster tail with seasoned potato and sautéed spinach.

The dessert buffet and coffee would be served in the Harvest Room, which would be set up after the cocktail hour was over. Pierre was very firm about table maintenance. He explained the special white and red wines we were serving:

Opus One Robert Mondavi 2009 Cabernet, and Cake Bread Cellars Reserve Chardonnay 2010.

The guests will be arriving in about thirty minutes. I will be passing around hors d'oeuvres with four other waiters. I went into the kitchen to familiarize myself with what I would be serving. The dishes were gorgeous—brown octagons and gold triangles. The chef made vegetable dumplings, Ahi Tuna, duck spring rolls, and Beef Wellington.

Chef placed the sushi in a large boat, and put it on a table in the middle of the room for cocktail hour. It was magnificent. There were candles everywhere. The room was glowing. In the foyer there is a round table with place cards outfitted like the banquet room with an extra-large brilliant centerpiece. It had branches that almost touched the ceiling with bulb shaped candelabras lit up and hanging from them.

The auction was being set up in the VIP Room, which was to the left of the entrance. Several people were getting the auction ready; boxes were everywhere, and expensive items were being displayed, ready for bids.

Once we're ready, we wait, grabbing a quick bite to eat and making sure we are set to give the attendees an incredible experience.

***

Guests are starting to come in and take their place cards. It's almost time to pass the hors d'oeuvres. The guests are directed into the Harvest Room for cocktails by the Party Coordinator.

I wanted to take a minute to look at all the elegant gowns; they were amazing, so beautiful. There was one gown I fell in love with. It was long and black with diamondlike beads on both sides of it, and a small trail that went all the way to the floor. It looked simply fabulous.

This party was instantly different from many others I had worked. One guest in particular stood out. I couldn't help but watch him. Tall, fit, dark brown hair, blue eyes, and ironically what attracted me most was the fact he was the only man wearing cufflinks. I felt myself staring at him. This hadn't happened to me since my husband, but there I was... interested.

In the back of my mind, I'm thinking, *I'm just a server; this guy isn't going to be interested in me.* But upfront, I couldn't help but appreciate his presence. I tried not to focus on him much. There was glitz and glamour everywhere. I caught myself glancing over at him and to my surprise he was looking directly at me. I turned my head, but he didn't. I felt myself getting shy. I laughed thinking to myself, *I'm in a tuxedo just like his.* Funny isn't it.

He pointed at me. I looked to my right, and then to my left. *Me?* He laughed, nodded and said yes, "Come here and take a photo with me!"

I was hesitant at first. I looked around to see where my boss was. I didn't want to get into any trouble. I didn't see Pierre in the dining room. Fraternizing with guests was forbidden. He wasn't with a spouse or girlfriend. When I got in front of him I could feel my heart pounding madly.

"What's your name?" he asked.

"Amilia," I replied. To me, my voice sounded like it was underwater…so distant, so different.

"My name is Luke," he said.

"Luke, I like that name," I replied.

We took a quick picture and then I walked away as the speaker for the event began talking. Luke took his spot at his table and there was an empty seat next to him. I'll admit I was a bit disappointed to see a woman sit down beside him. She was tall and had long brown hair and green eyes. She was well kept, hair done to perfection, even down to its highlights. Her nails were freshly polished. She was elegant…she was not a server in a tux. And I had to wait on them. It was time for me to work.

The two tables I was assigned to were now seated and I went to the bar to get two bottles of wine—one red and one white. Some people began to eat their first course, others chose to dance. The wine went fast.

When I walked up to the bar to get more bottles, Luke was there and he took note of me right away. He leaned in, "Can you step out for a minute onto the back patio?"

I felt my face becoming flushed. I was caught off guard. "I have to finish pouring wine and clearing the first course before I have any time to spare." I replied in a whisper. Then I walked back into the dining room, standing near my tables and waiting for Pierre's signal to clear the plates.

Outside I was calm. Inside I was excited. I didn't know what Luke was going to tell me, but I wanted to hear. But the woman…maybe she was a sister. But me…I'm a waitress, so I shouldn't allow my thoughts to drift too far.

The signal came and I quickly cleared the first course, and then cautiously made my way to the back patio.

Luke walked slowly in that direction and I followed. He casually mentioned how beautifully the night moon lights up the ocean in the dark. I agreed, responding that it was amazing and romantic. Then I shivered a bit from the chill of the night air. Luke instantly took note and immediately took his jacket off, wrapped it around my shoulders, and then he kissed me on the lips. Unanticipated and certainly unexpected, but still warm and inviting. I was shocked, not knowing what to say. I stood frozen for a moment.

Time was lost, only to be found again when my boss's voice broke through, calling out for me. I had to go.

When Pierre saw me and asked where I was, I lied, saying I'd gone into the restroom. Then I glanced over and saw Luke back at his table. What had just happened? I wasn't certain, but I was disheartened when the woman next to him could loudly be heard asking where her husband was.

The night went on. My thoughts of the kiss warmed my heart with excitement. I couldn't believe this could be happening to me. *It was a mistake, I must erase it from my thoughts.* I had to stay focused on serving the guests, of which Luke and his wife were a part. They were sitting at my table being served by me.

When I went to the bar to get another bottle of wine, they were both there, speaking rather loudly. She was wondering why he needed to go outside and smoke a cigar during dinner. She marched behind him as he was going out to the back patio. It really didn't look like Luke wanted to be there. He finally came in for dinner and sat quietly. The guests were having a great time; his wife was dancing with female friends. I didn't see him after dinner, I was too busy. He must have left the room. I didn't say another word to him the rest of the evening. As if the kiss was a distant memory. It was such an uneasy feeling. It wasn't worth thinking about anymore.

At this time Pierre came into the dining room to tell us the band will announce that the Dessert Buffet is being served in the Harvest Room; once they do that we can finish clearing the dining room. I went over to take a peek at the desserts. It looked amazing with everything you could imagine: chocolate truffles, chocolate covered strawberries, lemon tarts, mini chocolate cones filled with whipped cream, and fresh berries. It was endless.

Finally the band made the announcement. Guests were being directed to the Dessert Buffet and putting in the final bids for the items so as to pick them up on their way out. I didn't see Luke and his wife after that. I felt relieved they left. What was I thinking?

We were all tired. It was a long night. We worked as fast as we could to clear the dining room. All Pierre wanted us to do was put the tables in place according to Sunday brunch reservations.

I'm happy we do not have to set up tonight. Half past midnight, we all want to go home. I have a forty minute drive.

The end of the night finally came and I saw Luke one more time. He walked into the banquet room and handed me a note, blew me a kiss, and turned around and left. I had no chance to say anything, and perhaps that was good. I put the note in my pants pocket to read later.

Pierre walked through the room and thanked us for a great job. We punched out and headed to our cars. My mind reeling on how to process the entire night.

***

As I was driving home from the club, I couldn't help but reflect. How grateful I am that my husband and I were able to find a nice home to create a family.

I have a son named Matthew, who is twenty-five years old and lives in Texas. I'm a widow; my husband died of cancer when Matthew was only eight, and ever since then it has been basically just us and our bird, Feathers. He is red in color, with a small beak and a burgundy stomach. Looks like a cardinal from afar. My belated husband bought Feathers for Matthew before he passed.

When Matthew graduated college and was offered a job, I didn't want him to pass up the opportunity. I understood it was in Texas, but I was so proud of him. I didn't want him to feel bad that he had to move. I know he was worried about me being alone, but I assured him I would be all right. Our home is always a source of comfort to me. It gives me a sense of peace. I'm so proud of Matthew, and I know his father is too, cheering from heaven.

When I finally reached home, I pulled into my parking spot and went inside. It felt as if it took forever to drive home tonight. So tired, can't wait to go to sleep. I took a shower and crawled right into bed. I know morning comes around very fast.

CHAPTER TWO

Why does the alarm always go off so quickly? I stretched, thinking about how the hustle was about to begin again. Time for a quick shower; have to get ready to make my way out of the door for the day. It was a perfect day for a Dunkin Donuts trip to give myself a little treat.

I took a sip of my coffee and suddenly remembered—the note. I'd left it in my other pants pocket. Maybe that was a good thing. He was married and I didn't need to risk being involved in a situation like that, plus no fraternizing with members at the club.

Then work was under way, handling the Sunday brunch crowd, which was light, and I was immediately immersed in what I should be—my job. Before long it was two in the afternoon. I was printing my last check for my table when I heard, "Hello Amilia."

My skin tingled before I even looked up. "Luke," I said, stating the obvious.

He looked beautiful in a deep blue button down shirt, rolled up sleeves, pressed denim pants, and square toed shiny black shoes. Now my stomach felt fuzzy too. Why did I have such a response to him?

"Did you read my note?" he asked.

"Not yet, I've been working since seven," I explained.

"Can I have your cellphone number?" Luke asked.

I told him that I didn't have one and I couldn't afford a cellphone at this time and he continued and asked for my home number. Whether it was right or wrong, good or bad, I wasn't certain, but I found myself giving it to him. Internally, I reprimanded myself for the type of trouble that could get me into.

"Can I call you around seven thirty tonight?" he asked. I found myself answering yes before logic could say anything different.

✳✳✳

Reaching home, yawning all the way, I showered, made some dinner, and only then remembered the note from Luke. I went to get it, partly apprehensive and partly curious. *You're beautiful and I want another kiss. Please call me so we can talk.* I couldn't lie to myself about how much I'd enjoyed that kiss. It had been perfect. The phone rang; seven thirty, I noticed.

I got up and answered it, knowing who it was. He began to talk, his words so inviting, warm, and appealing. He told me that he was glad to have met me, that he was surprised and confused about the kiss but he didn't regret it. His voice was like a whisper and I had to really tune in to hear everything he was saying. But I was captivated by every single word, and the goosebumps surfaced on my skin.

But he's married, I thought.

As if he could read my mind, he went on to explain that his marriage was falling apart and he and his wife were splitting up. It had been years in the making. As he explained it all, his voice remained in that same whisper. He talked about his children and how important they were, that he'd sacrificed his happiness to remain a family because he had to for his kids. He continued saying that he came from a broken home and didn't want the same for them. But he wanted to be in love and have fun.

Then he moved on to me. He'd been thinking about me, wanted to kiss me again, wanted to get to know me better. *He can't stop thinking about me*, I thought.

Luke continued on. He wanted to hold someone again, be appreciated as a man, and to—I interrupted him. He sounded as if he was saying things that came to his mind, just to talk. He wasn't making any sense.

"Luke, you're still married. How can we start anything at all right now?" I said.

Now I could admit how unnerving the night before had been, serving them after knowing we'd shared a kiss. I explained it all, glad to have my thoughts in the open, finally gain the courage to spill it out. I wasn't wealthy, I didn't have designer anything.

"Luke, I have a 2001 white Toyota with rusted sides and bald tires," I explained.

Luke said, "Stop please! You have this all wrong. These are her events. I'm not interested in this. She wants all high-end things. This is all stuff, this is not love. I would rather stay home, have fun with my children, and listen to music and enjoy my yard. She can have all of it. I don't need it." His voice was getting louder with anger and hurt.

I replied, "I didn't mean to stir up any harsh feelings. I'm only explaining what I observed. This is an unfortunate position to be in. Luke, have you noticed what I do for a living? I have a small condo with three bedrooms. You have a different life. You say that you don't care about that lifestyle, but you are a part of it."

"I liked you from the moment I set my eyes on you. I do not care about any of that. I have already expressed that to you. I just want a chance to get to know you, love you, and have fun. I'm already making arrangements to move into a hotel for a while until I can figure out what I'm going to do with my girls and my situation," Luke confirmed.

"Yes, I understand. Don't you feel you should establish this first before you take on another relationship, date, or whatever?" I had to say it.

Luke reiterated, "I don't want to lose what I see in front of me. I didn't plan on that happening, it just did. I actually wanted the event to be over quickly so I could go home."

I closed my eyes for a minute. I needed to collect my thoughts on how I was going to reply. I was lost for words. I was a widow. I...I...I—

every reason as to why it made no sense to me. I felt like I was in a fairytale. Wildly romantic things like this just didn't happen to me. I heard Luke talking a bit more loudly.

"Are you still here?" He tapped on the phone.

"I'm here," I said.

Luke then said, "Look, it's getting late, can you call me tomorrow around seven thirty?"

I agreed to do it and we said good night. Before he could say any-thing else, I hung up the phone. What had just happened? It was a lot for me to take in.

I couldn't wait to get off the phone. The conversation was too deep, overwhelming to say the least. I knew Monday was around the corner. I had errands to run, bills to pay, and I wanted some alone time after a busy weekend. My brain was full and tired. I went to the front room, turned off the television, and shut the lights off. I took my robe off and climbed right into bed. No alarm was needed. I was fast asleep as soon as my head felt my pillow.

CHAPTER THREE

I woke up to a sunny Monday morning and felt great. Of course, my conversation with Luke was on my mind. I really didn't know what to think about it. It was so enticing, but it just didn't feel right either. I decided to put it on the back burner and enjoy my day. The beach—that was what I wanted to do today.

After getting ready, I packed my small cooler with some food and a container of iced tea. I took my beach blanket out of the closet and was now ready to go. I was set to do my errands and go to my favorite place, the beach.

After depositing my work check at the bank and going to the post office, I decided to go and check out getting a cellphone. Not because of what Luke had asked, but because of what my son had told me the week before. It would help us stay in touch better and make me more accessible. I really didn't answer my landline all that often. So it did make sense.

I went to the Verizon store. Wow, I had no idea what to do! So many options and plans. I couldn't believe the variety of different cell phones to choose from. My needs were simple—text and talk. It was over-whelming. I approached a woman at the desk and asked her for some help. I told her my budget and she guided me through the process. She recommended a 3G refurbished iPhone, asked me what color, white or black. I chose black. She set everything up for me. I don't know much about tech talk. *I'm grateful for her patience. I have no clue what she's talking about,* I chuckled to myself. I waited at the store until my phone was completely charged.

It came with a car charger, but my car is very old. I do not have a connection for it. I asked her if she had something I could plug into the wall. She replied, "An adapter." We both laughed.

"Yes, one of those." I said. I couldn't think of the word. I thanked her, and all I can say is. "WOW," my first cell phone.

I'm very excited. I can talk and text with Matthew all the time. It gives me a sense of freedom and protection. Having it with me makes me feel as if I'm never alone.

***

The beach on a Monday is great because it isn't usually too busy. I was hungry and eager to eat, and excited to read my book too. The waves lapping, the sun shining, the breeze blowing—it was perfect for me.

I love it here. It takes your mind off the entire world. Sand feels so good on my toes. It feels like a mini vacation, a getaway from my everyday hustle and bustle. I needed this.

Sitting on my blanket and thoroughly relaxed, I decided to make my first call on my new cellphone to Matthew, but I got his voicemail.

"Matt, hi. Guess what? This is from my new cellphone. Call me back when you have some time," I excitedly told him.

I laid back, closed my eyes, felt completely relaxed and almost asleep, but I awakened to a buzz. I looked at the time. I couldn't believe it was six thirty already. It took a minute or two to figure out how to retrieve the message.

It was Matt. *So happy!* he wrote. Before I knew it I was engaged in a text conversation. He wrote that everything is fine. That he loves his job. He met a great girl. Matthew couldn't wait for me to come out and visit. I wrote that I love him and am happy for him. It was amazing, and

Matt's final remark warmed my heart a bit extra: *I miss you and love you!*

I'm so happy I have my phone.

Then it was time to go. Up until that point, I did a good job not thinking about Luke. But now it was within an hour of when I should call him. I wasn't going to. I decided to not answer any of his calls at the house or reach out to him. It was for the best, even if it might not be the right way to handle it. Something puts my stomach in knots. It just doesn't feel right in my heart to step into this situation.

It was a great day, a lot got done. Speaking to my son was the highlight of it all. I pulled out of the parking lot and headed home. Music playing, I was so happy. I needed to make one stop at the gas station on the way home.

I was famished. It was eight o'clock and all I had to eat was a sandwich, and some iced tea. I remembered I didn't eat my apple. The cooler was in the passenger seat. I opened it, took it out, and ate it. So delicious and juicy. It hit the spot.

I wanted a break and to erase the memory of Luke. As if the kiss never took place. When I arrived home I put everything away. Time to shower and prepare for bed, lay out my work clothes, and set my alarm on my new phone for seven in the morning.

I have a very busy schedule this week. It starts tomorrow with my first round of doubles—lunch and dinner shifts. It really is great to have a day off like this. It tides you over until the next one.

My eyes were getting heavier. I crawled right under the sheets and went to bed.

I had stuck to my guns as well, and went about my night like I might normally have. I stayed clear of anything that had to do with Luke.

***

The alarm was ringing. The day began. Even though I had a relaxing day yesterday, I was tired. Maybe exhausted knowing what was in store for me today. I fed Feathers, took a quick pick-me-up shower, brushed my teeth, got dressed, and headed to work. The time got away from me this morning. I didn't have time to make coffee, as if I was moving in slow motion.

When I arrived at work, I punched in and greeted everyone. I poured myself a cup of coffee, it was so good. I put my purse in my locker, checked the board in the kitchen to see what station I had, then started my setup.

As the week progressed, long hours tired my feet. I constantly had to keep a smile on my face with the busy rush of people coming into the club to eat and drink, wanting to be served promptly without hesitation. I just couldn't wait to get out of there.

Finally, it was Friday night. I was watching the clock and it seemed to have stopped. The minutes felt like hours. In the morning, I can't keep up with the time, it moves rather quickly. Go figure that! I looked up at the big antique wooden nautical clock in the dining room; it was made from an old ship's steering wheel.

Eleven thirty. My table hadn't asked to pay. I waited closely until the member gave me the sign to bring him the check. He looked up at me, waved his hand, and I brought it right over to him.

He looked at me and said politely, "I hope I wasn't keeping you. It looks as if we are the last ones here."

With a smile I said, "No, that's fine, have a good evening." Goodness, he didn't say that, really! The busboy finished cleaning the table. We said good night, I punched out, and went to my locker to get my purse. I couldn't wait to embrace the cool summer breeze. You forget what it's like to be human. The thought of another relaxing day off kept me at ease.

For an entire week I didn't hear from Luke, confirming that was a good thing. With all the double shifts I'd worked, I was busy enough to not second guess myself or break down and make the call.

I walked to my car and saw a white piece of paper tucked under the wiper blade. It's Luke. I lit up with excitement. With butterflies in my stomach I reached for it and held it for a moment, took a deep breath, and then proceeded to open it.

HELLO. This is Luke. Do you remember me from last Saturday night? You were supposed to call me when you were finished working Monday night. I just wanted you to please give me a chance to get to know you. I can't get you off of my mind. I tried calling you at home, but there was no answering machine set up. You have no cellphone. Please give me the time of day. I just want to talk.

Sincerely, Luke

Okay, how did he know what car I drive? What should I do? I sat on the hood of my car for a moment. It had been a draining week. Then it dawned on me. Sunday night when we were talking, I gave him the description of my car; make, model, everything. *Well, it's an old car for sure, there isn't another one in this parking lot like it,* I chuckled to myself.

I sat in silence for a little while, listening to the sound of the ocean waves. I looked up at the clear night sky full of bright stars. I asked out loud…"What should I do?" *I can't stop thinking about him either. His note seemed sincere. I really don't know what is happening in his life. Everyone deserves a chance.*

I always wished to find someone special again in my life, a handsome loving man, loyal and smart. Someone who would treat me kindly. On the outside, Luke fit the bill, but it just didn't feel like my wish. Did you ever hear the saying, "Be careful what you wish for?" Well, I felt like I had to be careful.

Maybe I should call him and make a determination about it all. I have Sunday off; perhaps we could go for a drink. The thought gave me butterflies—wait, maybe it was nerves.

There's the thought of different careers, but most importantly, he's not divorced. That is a big deal. Could it be something else? He's a bit pushy, but in a kind sort of way.

I weighed out my schedule, and went into an intensive should-I-or-shouldn't-I internal debate. The debate went all the way to the morning and through my next day of work.

Saturday is usually my longest day. Members love to linger. The bar usually fills to capacity. The kitchen is open until 11:00 p.m. There is a lot of running around. *I have to end my work week before putting thought into anything else. I believe I might be putting too much into a request to talk.*

I pulled into my parking spot. Went into the house. Put my things together for work in the morning, set my alarm, showered, and went right to sleep. I couldn't think anymore. My brain shut down.

I couldn't believe it. My alarm went off but I had it on silent. I was so wrapped up with the note that was left on my car last night I didn't check. The bright sun beaming through my bedroom window woke me up. I jumped out of bed in a panic. I had one hour to get to work and I'm forty minutes away from the club. I had no time to lose. I took a quick shower, brushed my teeth, got dressed, fed Feathers, and ran out of the house.

I didn't have time to put makeup on or fix my hair. I just brushed it and put it up in a ponytail. I got to work, punched in on time, and said good morning to everyone. I had a couple of minutes, so I headed quickly to the bathroom to put my makeup on.

Crazy start to my shift. I hope the rest of my day is not like this. I put my purse in my locker. I feel so wound up I don't think I need coffee. Just some time for my system to calm down.

I checked the assignment sheet to see where I was working and began my day. I took a deep breath, and exhaled.

Pierre came into the dining room and greeted everyone with a good morning. He asked all of us to sit together at one table so he could go over the agenda for the day.

"I have two waiters that called out, so I have extra busboys coming in to help. Work together and do the best you can. I will be here to help with wine and drinks. There are four of you; work in pairs, split the outside dining room in half. We are expecting bad thunder showers tonight, so we are not opening the patio. There will be inside dining only in the evening." He finished and said thank you to all of us.

We have an hour before lunch begins. It felt like setup took forever. I'm not sure what to expect today. Chef came out to the patio to let us know our employee meals were ready. I was so hungry for lunch. I really didn't eat much yesterday. We were talking about this past week, how busy it was with the staff. Now we are short two waiters today.

Break was over so I headed to the patio. Members were beginning to come in. Tables were filling up fast. We did our best to keep up. Words for the day: impatient and demanding. There was no under-standing that we were short staffed. I really believe they didn't even notice us running around. It was so chaotic.

Members were complaining about service. Our boss tried his hard-est to make things right. Buying drinks and giving complimentary des-serts. My inner thoughts were saying, *I didn't want to work dinner if it was going to be like this.*

We finally got caught up with the tables, my partner and I couldn't believe it. We were so happy for the rain. We didn't want to see the patio anymore today. It was already 4:40 p.m., but felt like 10:00 p.m.! It was starting to sprinkle. The patio was already cleared of guests. We had a few more things to do. All the waiters came inside. I noticed the dinner staff setting up.

I approached Pierre and asked him if he really needed me to stay tonight since everyone was here; could I go home?

He said no. "After what happened today, I can't let anyone go."

"Understood, thank you," I replied.

I'm not looking forward to dinner tonight (talk about starting your day on the wrong foot). The sky became very dark, very fast. Inside, the club got dim, as if the lights were turned down. The lit votive can-dles in the dining room magnified a warm glow. It started to rain very heavily. It looked like a movie scene, high winds and lighting.

Dinner ended up being very quiet. The weather must have kept people indoors. It seemed very dangerous to be on the roads. I defi-nitely wasn't complaining about that. Let it rain, that's all I was think-ing.

Pierre came into the dining room and approached each waiter who worked this afternoon. Told us we could go home at eight, after finish-ing our side work. He thanked us for all of our hard work.

Those words, *you can go home*, were like music to my ears. I went to my locker for my purse and punched out. I said good night to everyone and ran to my car. It was pouring!

I was completely drenched. Honestly, I needed that. It felt great. Driving in this weather takes a bit longer. I was just happy to be on my way. I was thirty minutes out of the area and not a cloud in the sky.

By the time I got home—thankfully early, due to South Carolina's unpredictable weather—I was only thinking about one thing: getting out of my soaking wet clothes.

My phone rang and I jumped, completely startled by it. It rang five times before I answered. I stopped and stared at it.

I picked up and—"Amilia, it's Luke; I'm calling to see if you want to get together for a bit, maybe get a bite to eat." (In his monotone deep voice)

I told Luke, "My work schedule is really tight, I've been really busy—"

He cut me off. "Even people with busy schedules need to eat, and certainly deserve a day off too."

I paused in silence for a moment. What I vowed not to share came pouring from my mouth. "I'm off tomorrow," I said.

Luke asked, "Can I pick you up tomorrow at two? We can go to the beach and get some lunch."

The beach made all of my resistance leave. "Sure, but I can meet you," I said.

"I'll pick you up; I insist." Luke was adamant. I gave him my address and he repeated the plan.

After we hung up, I sighed. I guess I was going out to the beach and lunch with Luke tomorrow. I cannot believe I gave him my address; I'm typically a very private person. Well, it's too late now.

Well, Sunday is set. A little nervous; at the same time, excited to be taken out for lunch. I'm starting to get sleepy eyed. I will set my alarm for ten. I don't want to rush tomorrow. Shut off all the lights and went right to bed.

CHAPTER FOUR

Morning has arrived! I'm up before the alarm went off. I couldn't believe it. I opened the blinds in my room. It's a glorious day. The sun is hidden, it won't be too hot. It's just perfect to eat out by the ocean. As the morning moved on, I was looking forward to my day with Luke. I brushed my teeth. Made some coffee, a toasted English muffin with butter and apricot preserves. I said good morning to Feathers. He's very bright today (Scarlet). I went into my room to look for something to wear. My body really ached from working so hard this week.

Shifting through my closet, I went with a floral summer dress with spaghetti straps that I only wore once and my new dark blue shades. Picking out some jewelry, I began to get ready.

In my mind, I'd already begun the competition game, that one where I see every way in which I fall short in comparison to "the other woman." She is very attractive and put together. Hard work was probably furthest from her thoughts.

I'm short, five feet tall and thin, with black hair and hazel eyes, completely different than Luke's wife. Maybe that was good—he didn't have a "type," and if his life with her was rough, that was good, right? Surely Luke wouldn't be interested in someone who was like the one he was leaving.

Not wanting to rush, I moved along. Polishing my toes, blow drying and flat ironing my hair, putting on my lip gloss and powder. I was getting nervous too. I chose to wear my new wedges, and I tied them around my ankles.

It occurred to me that I had no idea what type of car to look for. What did Luke drive? I called to find out; maybe also to make sure he was really coming, although I couldn't say that for certain.

Luke answered his phone, "I drive an SUV, are you okay if I come in for a few minutes first though?"

"I'm not ready for that, I'd rather just go out like we planned," I said. He accepted it, confirming that he really was a gentleman, just as much as he appeared to be a gentleman.

Then I waited, peeking through the blinds until I saw him pull up in his black metallic Denali. I didn't want to appear anxious. I listened for the beep.

I left my place and he got out of the car, walking around to open the door for me, and also giving me a big hug and a kiss on the cheek. He was so handsome and strong.

When I got into the car I was impressed. It was fully loaded and had everything. All the bells and whistles, as they say. I could smell the leather. Then he shut the door and went around to the driver's side.

As soon as Luke was in, he reached over and took a hold of my hand. It felt so strange, but so nice.

I started the conversation. "Luke, how's your day been?" I asked.

"Busy with the kids and running around," he said quickly. "It's nice to have this time with you. How about yours?"

"A hard work week. I'm looking forward to this day off."

He went on to say that he had a perfect place to go eat, a place called Oceanview Terrace, and I was excited. I'd eaten there before and really liked it.

Everything Luke shared seemed so effortless and sincere, and it was strange how the words appealed to what I would most likely respond to. I wasn't sure if it was his instinct or what, but it was so nice. He complimented me, told me how I made him feel so young at heart—like a school boy again. He said he felt so alive, as if touching the earth seemed lighter. I didn't know how to reply to that. He was smiling ear to ear. I held back any emotion. I didn't know anything at this point. I couldn't think further than a lunch date.

By the time we got to the restaurant I was already more relaxed, and definitely less nervous. The place was so beautiful. It had a view of the ocean, was a replica of a large ship, and had a large rusted anchor out front with a large chain attached to it. Seashells and white sand were in the front of the restaurant instead of grass. It was just beautiful, and unique. The plank bridge entrance made it all the better. I truly loved it. We walked inside to the front desk. I was mesmerized; it really felt like being on a ship.

Luke took my hand and asked if I wanted to sit inside or outside. He actually startled me. My mind and eyes were so busy.

"Definitely outside." We followed the hostess to our table and through the dining room where there were small lanterns on each table, and beautiful round windows. The atmosphere of this ship and ocean makes you feel as if you're on a cruise for the day.

Luke pulled out my chair for me to sit down, which made me smile. I felt so special and didn't recall him doing that the night of the gala. Maybe this really was important to him. He was such a gentleman.

The seagulls were in the air, flying around against the bright blue sky, and the atmosphere around us was so appealing to me; the type of thing that made me forget I ever had a care in the world and feel so good about it.

Luke ordered us a bottle of red wine, after confirming if I preferred red or white, and something about the moment was so magical. It just clicked for me in that instant.

"Luke, this is brilliant. I love everything about this place, and being here with you just completes the picture."

Oops! I was horrified that I'd blurted that out, showing how I'd so easily gotten caught up in the moment. I wanted to suck my words back in, but it was too late.

"I couldn't stop thinking about you," Luke confessed.

I clamped my mouth shut and the waiter came back with the wine, saving me from having to respond. He began to open the bottle and then poured for us.

Luke asked me what I would like for lunch. He said he was having the lobster roll and French fries. I'm having a lunch size linguini and white clam sauce. The waiter overheard our order; he asked if there was anything else we would like, and if we wanted to start with appetizers.

Luke said, "No thank you this is fine, Amilia, unless you want something?"

"No thank you, this is great," I said.

Luke reached over the table and took both of my hands and said, "I'm so happy you decided to see me today. I would like to make this the start of something special. I already made plans to move into an apartment with my girls. She won't fight me on it. She has other plans of her own."

"This must be very hard on the kids, not being with the both of you. They are so young, and it will be hard to understand."

"Let's not discuss it anymore today, I want this day to be about you and me together. We will leave that conversation for another time," Luke said.

I couldn't agree more. He was ready to pick up where the conversation had left off, letting me know that he was so happy that I'd agreed to come out with him. They were beautiful words and I felt Luke genuinely meant them. Why me? It was quite literally all so sudden.

I still was mindful of the fact that he was married, even though he had just told me that he'd already started to do the work for finding an apartment for him and his girls.

Our lunch arrived; it smelled amazing. The clams were perfectly cooked, and placed on top of the linguini. I dipped my bread in the sauce. I couldn't get enough of it. Luke asked how was my lunch?

"I love it… delicious, how is yours?"

"Wonderful, it's so fresh," Luke said. "Here, try mine." He cut off a small piece and gave it to me.

"Mmm it's very tasty!" I twirled linguini and clams around my fork and scooped it up with my spoon and gave it to him. He thought that it was fantastic. I didn't know if this was appropriate on the first date, but I felt I should reciprocate.

"The food here is great! Would you like to walk down by the ocean after lunch?" Luke asked.

"Luke, I would love that." He poured us more wine. He asked me where my family lives. "They live in California. I have two older sisters and have a son who lives in Texas. My husband died when Matthew was very young."

"Are you dating anyone?" he asked.

"No, I'm not." The waiter came over and took our plates. Luke asked if he could pay for the check but finish the wine on the beach. Luke assured him he would bring the glasses back. The waiter agreed.

We got up and walked out back and down the stairs to the beach. Luke took off his loafers and set them under the steps. I took off my wedges and put them with his. There was a light breeze; my summer dress was long so when I took off my sandals it was brushing against the sand as I walked. With our wine in hand we headed towards the ocean. He held me so tightly with a gleam in his eyes, like he'd never felt happiness before now.

We walked by a woman lying on her blanket, she had her radio playing love songs. Luke put our empty wine glasses down on the sand, took my hand, and started dancing with me. He looked right into my eyes as my dress was flowing in the wind. I felt like a princess that just met her prince charming in a fairytale romance. It was magical. He held me close, and gently put his hands on my cheeks. Luke kissed me ever so softly.

I whispered in his ear, "Please don't hurt me."

He looked at me and said, "Please give me the chance to prove it to you." He picked up the empty wine glasses and started to head back. Just before we reached the restaurant Luke wanted to sit together on the beach. The way he looked at me took my breath away. He pulled me in tightly, a gleam in his eye and a sexy smile on his face, the sounds of the ocean in the background. Our feet in the sand, and his arms around me. He looked at me and said that he wanted to see me again. There was nothing that I wanted more.

However, he looked down at his watch and that moment was shaken. It was six thirty and Luke had to be home by eight to check on the kids. He works nights and wanted to spend as much time with the children as he could. Time to go.

We put our shoes on and returned the glasses to the restaurant. We walked over to the car; he opened the car door for me. I thanked him for a wonderful afternoon.

Luke said, "Amilia, there will be more times together, I'm missing you already." He took my hand and held me tight. I noticed his sexy Rolex watch. I was so busy with everything around me today it just caught my eye that moment. Big and bulky and it fit him just right. It had a silver band and a navy blue face.

We pulled up to my house. He got out to open the car door for me. Luke held me, and kissed me on the forehead, and told me he would call me tomorrow. I thanked him and told Luke to drive safe. He waited until I got into the house, and then he left.

Now, back at home, and all alone, I thought about how perfect the afternoon had been. Utterly romantic and appealing to my every sense and sensibility. The feel of that last kiss on my forehead before Luke slowly drove off still felt warm. But alas, it was time to get ready for bed. I was on the cusp of yet another busy week. I sat for a moment on the couch. I had butterflies in my stomach.

I asked myself what happened today. I tried not to think about it and just go with the flow. *I can't lie to myself that today wasn't everything I have ever wanted because it was. I have this uneasiness, but I am sure it will go away.*

Around nine o'clock the phone started to ring. I didn't answer it, I didn't recognize the number. I shut off all the lights, got into my nightclothes, set my alarm, and went straight to sleep.

CHAPTER FIVE

Morning hit my eyes. I slept all through the night; I'm so relaxed. I got up and had a bounce in my step. Walked over to the kitchen to put the coffee on, then began to get ready for work. I could smell the aroma in my bedroom. I got dressed for work and poured myself a cup, thinking deep inside.

I still didn't say anything to Luke about having a cellphone. I do not know where this is going, and I still have reservations, even though last night was incredible.

Time is getting away from me. I finished up, checked on Feathers—thankfully he seemed to be all right, and didn't need anything. I picked up my purse and keys and headed out. When I got to the car I saw a piece of paper on the windshield. I opened it:

Good Morning beautiful, it's Luke. I tried calling you last night to say sweet dreams, but there was no answer. I decided to leave you a note, so you know I'm thinking about you. Have a good day.

Luke drew hearts and smiley faces. I thought about calling him from my cellphone, but I just didn't want him to have my number yet. I didn't have time to go inside and make a call. *I will wait to ring him at the club, I have to get going or I will be late.*

Once I arrived at work I went to my locker, put my purse away, and punched in. I said good morning to everyone. It was a fiasco. Busboys were rolling in more tables and Pierre was in a panic, pushing us right along. Repeating and repeating how busy today was going to be. He posted the stations on the board. The day just flew by. We didn't stop.

Taking turns for breaks among the wait staff. Eating when we could. It was a beautiful day, everyone came to the club to eat and hang out. It was ten o'clock before we knew it. My legs were tired, my feet hurt. I didn't have a chance to call Luke today. We finally got the dining room all cleaned up. I punched out and began my drive home.

I got home late, about eleven, and was ready for a shower and sleep. The day had been crazy busy and I barely had a chance to think about Luke, much less call him. Before crawling into bed, I glanced at my caller ID. Five missed calls, all of which were from Luke. The times of the calls were so strange though, because he knew I wouldn't be home. I told him I had to work doubles. We had this conversation on Sunday if I'm not mistaken.

Even though I was tired, I decided to call him back.

Chills running up and down my body. I really didn't want to make the call. I had a terrible feeling in my gut. It feels like alarms are going off, trying to tell me something.

"Hi, Luke," I began.

A tense and firm voice responded. "I would have appreciated a call today," he replied.

"I'm sorry, I didn't mean to upset you," I muttered.

"I called last night too, not a courtesy of a return call until now," Luke replied angrily.

"My day was really busy, I'm sorry, it started the second I walked into work, and tomorrow, it's right back at it," I said.

Luke replied, "Try a little harder next time. "

"Luke that wasn't very nice," I softly responded.

Luke said, "Don't give me the bullshit." I didn't know how to answer that comment. My thoughts were silenced. I was never spoken to that way before. I liked Luke, and I felt it best to stay quiet.

"So anyway listen," Luke said, "Wednesday night the weather is going to be great. Would you like to grab some drinks and go to the beach?"

"I have to work Wednesday night," I mentioned.

Luke asked, "Can you do what you can to leave early?"

I told Luke, "I will do the best I can."

"Baby, I'm sorry about my tone of voice," he said.

I replied, "It's all right, we both are tired and it's late."

"I will see you Wednesday night. Make sure you call me tomorrow on your break, don't wait until the end of the day," Luke seemed to demand. (It felt like this was an order not a request. That I better listen to what he says or else. "Or else" is what made me a bit uneasy.) "Let me know what your boss tells you when you ask him to leave early, all right? Have a good night," Luke said.

"You too," I replied.

We hung up. I was stunned for a minute. *Are we an item and I don't know it*, I thought. I took a shower, got myself ready for bed. Set the alarm. I couldn't stay up anymore, I was falling asleep. I was physically and mentally tired, and now, stressed. By the end of the call I became frazzled. What would Pierre say when I asked him to leave early on Wednesday? Goodness, I had no idea.

When morning came I was exhausted, feeling like I'd gotten no sleep at all. All I could think was, *I wish I could stay home today and relax.* That was not an option though, so back to the grindstone I went, dreams of my wonderful day at the beach last week vivid in my mind.

My phone rang and I looked at the caller ID, it was Luke.

"Good morning Baby," he said. He sounded so happy that I couldn't help but smile.

"Good morning to you Luke." He told me that he just wanted to hear my voice and then gave me the reminder about Wednesday night, telling me not to forget. *How could I forget,* I thought? Then he abruptly said he had to go, and he hung up.

Honestly, I didn't know what to make of it, but I didn't have time to evaluate it either. I had to get to work. I put myself together quickly, and off to the rat-race. As I turned onto the parkway, the traffic was jammed up for miles. I had no idea where the heavy traffic came from this morning.

I'm watching the clock. If I'm late today, I can't ask Pierre to leave early tomorrow. I was getting nervous. I didn't want to get Luke upset with me.

Traffic wasn't moving. I noticed up ahead no one was getting off the exit ramp. I edged the car over two lanes and got off.

From this exit it's about thirty-five minutes to work, with lights. I drove fast. I even went through a yellow light so I could catch the green light ahead. I ran a stop sign. I know that's wrong, but I knew I had to beat the clock. I finally pulled into the parking lot. It was 10:55 a.m. I ran to the kitchen and punched in. I made it without issues.

My boss came in and said good morning. He asked why I was out of breath.

"You look like you ran here from home," he said.

"I'm fine thank you." (If he only knew). He handed me the set up sheet and let me know this was my assignment for today.

"You are working a private party in the Captain's Room. There will be approximately thirty people and Jasper is your busboy. We are very shorthanded today. After you are done serving dessert, Jasper will stay and clean up. You will move into the main dining room and start setting up for the rehearsal dinner which starts at six. Your lunch party begins at twelve thirty. You both have plenty of time to set up. It ends at five.

"The first hour when the guests come in, there will be cheese and crudités. You will serve our house red and white wines. The first course is a mixed green salad. The second course is a choice of two items; a steak sandwich or salmon club, both on sesame toasted wedge, served with sweet potato fries. There will be a small lunch menu at each individual seat with details. During lunch you will serve beer, wine, and soda, plus coffee with platters of cookies."

I was immersed in everything I had to do today. *This is happening a lot now; we seem to be one or two waiters short every event. I wonder what is going on.* Every minute counted, from preparing for the lunch party right through to dinner. It worked out very nicely. Pierre peeked in every so often just to check if I needed anything. He was very pleased. Working double shifts kept me busy—the entire time. Four o'clock came in no time. I hadn't had a chance to call Luke or to talk to Pierre about Wednesday night. I'd been working unusually hard today.

The young lady at the front desk was new. I'd seen her at the club, but didn't know her name. She came into the Captain's Room and told me to come with her, I had a phone call. All I could think about that it was my son, if something was wrong. I asked Jasper to please continue to clean up, I would be right back.

I answered, "Hello!"

"Hey, it's me, Luke." I sighed, he continued. "How's it going?"

"Working Hard," I quickly said.

"You said you were going to call me?"

"I didn't have a chance to speak to my boss yet. I was going to ring you after he and I spoke," I clarified.

I saw Pierre from the corner of my eye walking towards the front desk. I knew talking on the phone wasn't acceptable. He asked me what I was doing. I covered the receiver with my hand.

I lied and said, "I'm giving directions to a guest who is coming to the party tonight." Luke heard the conversation and hung up. I continued to speak as if I was finishing giving directions. "You're welcome," I said, and hung up.

My boss resumed conversation with me. I put a nice big smile on my face while he was talking. He asked how the party was going. I explained the guests loved everything—the service and the food. Jasper was passing by the front desk, pushing the cart towards the kitchen with all the dirty plates and empty glassware. I walked over to him to help.

"Amilia," Pierre said, "now that it has slowed down, can you start putting things together in the main dining room for the party tonight? There is extra wait staff coming in, but they will be arriving late from other jobs. I would like there to have a head start on all the setup.

"The tables and linen are in place. I prepared one setting so the waiters will follow that setup. When the other waiters and busboys start to arrive they will jump in and finish where you left off."

The chef made us lunch. Jasper and I would take turns until the party was completely done, so the guests would not be alone. I asked Jasper if he would like to go first.

"Amilia, you can go first," Jasper suggested.

I thought that was so sweet. "Thank you Jasper that is very nice of you." Once we were done emptying the cart, I went over to the sink and washed my hands, then took my plate of food, a slice of Italian bread, and poured a glass of iced tea. (The chef made this really great pasta penne with broccoli rabe, oil, and garlic; it smelled so good.) I couldn't wait to taste it. I didn't have anything this morning. We were so busy, so I was grateful for such a delicious lunch. I ate the entire portion and I walked back into the kitchen to pour myself some more iced tea.

I noticed the kitchen staff devouring the pasta really fast. I quickly grabbed a big bowl, and filled it with pasta for Jasper. I put it to the side with some Italian bread. Jasper walked into the kitchen with a tray of dirty glasses. Looked at me, and said there was no food left. He had this puzzled look on his face.

"Jasper, no worries, I put food aside for you." He smiled. He was so glad. I told Jasper go ahead and eat now. "I will stay with the guests. There isn't anything else to clean."

"Great, I will start the setup in the main dining room."

As I was polishing the silverware, my boss walked in. It was a perfect opportunity to ask him a question. "Pierre may I ask you something?"

He answered, "Of course, what is it?"

"I need to leave early tomorrow night."

"No problem you're always here, you always work very hard. Please remind me; I get very busy, and I will forget."

I couldn't believe his answer. "Thank you so much. I appreciate the time off." All of my nervousness for that kind response? Pretty ridiculous.

Then, before I got too wrapped up in something else, I snuck back to the kitchen to call Luke and let him know. He was happy, and I actually was too, but maybe for different reasons. All I really wanted was a great night's rest.

By ten thirty that night I was home, and my phone was ringing. It was Luke. He told me that he'd pick me up at nine the following night, and that was it. He hung up. *I don't understand what is happening right now. Maybe it's because I'm new in the dating scene, and I need more time to adapt.*

Time for me to shower, get some sleep, plus I couldn't wait to get all cleaned up. I felt disgusting after working all those hours. My skin felt so dry. I put some chap stick on my lips and applied moisturizing lotion. My body has been taking a beating from the heat and sun lately. I brushed my hair and teeth, put on a nightshirt, set the alarm for eight. I didn't have to be at work until ten and went right to bed. It was as if my brain stopped working.

I popped up at about 4:00 a.m. from a bad dream. I dreamt that Luke and I had a big fight. He was hitting me and he wouldn't stop. Luke was slapping me in the face repeatedly and holding me by the collar of my shirt. I couldn't get loose no matter how hard I tried. I was screaming and hoping that someone, anyone, would hear my cry out for help. He threw me to the floor, looking over me with a clenched fist.

I got my bearings and went into the kitchen to get a glass of water. I needed to shake myself off. I was sweating profusely. It felt so real. It is so hard to explain. I went to the bathroom and splashed water on my face, patted myself dry. Took a deep breath and exhaled slowly. My heartbeat was racing, and I wanted to calm down.

I went back to bed and tried to go to sleep. It took a while before I was able to doze off. I finally fell asleep, and my alarm went off. I'm so tired. I reached over and shut it off. I slowly got out of bed and moved around. I *needed* coffee this morning. I put a pot of coffee on and said good morning to Feathers. Changed his water and gave him fresh food. I went into the front room. I opened the blinds to let the sun shine in.

It was going to be a beautiful day, there wasn't a cloud in the sky. I looked up and sent a prayer out to my son. (Good Lord, keep Matt safe and happy Amen.) I could taste the coffee and it smelled so good. I went into the kitchen, took out the largest cup from the cupboard, and poured myself a cup. It was delicious.

I washed up and got dressed for work. I'm leaving a bit early today, but I just need to get going and do something. I was still shook up from my dream last night. I drank the rest of my coffee. Took my purse and locked the door. As I was driving to work, I was thinking if my dream was trying to tell me something. I just wanted to keep myself busy and not focus on this, or it will start making me nervous.

When I got to work the kitchen was quiet. All you could hear were sounds of pots and pans. I greeted everyone. I was there twenty minutes before clock in. I put my purse away. The chef was very kind and offered me a corn muffin, I graciously said thank you. I really wasn't hungry though. I sliced the muffin in half and toasted it and added some butter.

My boss came into the kitchen. "Good Morning Amilia!"

"Good morning Pierre," I said back. He told me I didn't have to stay for dinner setup. That I could leave right after lunch was finished. (This means I will be home earlier than I thought.) I thanked him. He made sure to mention to be here ready to work tomorrow, that it would be very busy.

My first thought was to call Luke to tell him, but this would be my opportunity to relax before he picked me up. I wanted to clean up a bit, change my sheets, vacuum, do the rest of my laundry, and I needed to tidy up my bathroom. I decided not to call him. I finished my muffin and had some cranberry juice. I punched in. I began to set up. I felt like I was retrieving some lost energy. The day started to look brighter and brighter. The other waiters started to come in.

They asked me, "Are we late?"

I laughed! "No, I'm early, coffee is ready. The chef made it not too long ago." They thanked him.

I went to the front desk to see what the reservations were like. It was a very slow day. We didn't have any large tables. I didn't know how my boss was going to split up the dining room in terms of stations. We still have the outside patio. There are four of us, and two busboys.

Pierre came into the kitchen and hung the station sheet on the board. I was so excited to see that my station was inside. I didn't want to work out in the sun today. It really wears me out.

Lunch went rather quickly. There wasn't much action. I had three tables that sat just about through the entire lunch period. It took a few minutes to clean up. There wasn't much to do. I couldn't put anything away; the other waiters were still working.

I went to Pierre's office to say good night and thank him once again.

"Thank you Amilia, I will see you tomorrow. Have a good night."

I was home around five. I put my things down on the couch, changed my clothes, and went right into cleaning. I removed my sheets, I vacuumed and dusted. I took a shower and blew out my hair straight, I like it down. I put my makeup on. I love this new lip gloss I bought. It looks so fresh; it matches the toenail color I have. Then I picked out a long flower summer dress with straps.

I decided to paint my toenails. While I was waiting for Luke I was dancing around the house, listening to music, putting on perfume, and growing more excited for tonight. At eight my phone rang; it was Luke. He wanted to know why I didn't tell him that I had gotten home early.

"We made plans for nine," I said.

When I got home was irrelevant he said. "I don't appreciate that shit," Luke blurted out.

"I had housework to do," I said.

He didn't care. He was angry and told me that I should have told him. He'd been sitting in his car like an idiot. The fact that I would have had no way of knowing that didn't matter to him. Then he snapped again, "Are you coming out or what?"

I started to feel my dream was trying to tell me something. Warning me to be careful of what I'm getting myself into.

My heart is frightened. This is an awkward position. I must go.

I said I'd be right there and then hung up. My heart was pounding and my toenail polish wasn't quite dry yet. I grabbed the hairdryer and quickly went over them. Now I was rushing around like I messed up. I took a sweater from the closet, put my shoes on, locked up the house, and approached his car. He didn't get out to open my door for me. Luke had an aggravated look on his face.

"You really know how to ruin a good night," he spat.

"I didn't do anything deliberately." I was justifying something I did not understand.

"I'm not stupid, you were just being nasty," Luke countered.

This continued all the way to the beach, where he pulled into the lot, turned off the vehicle, and hopped out to get a blanket and a small cooler. I got out and then he grabbed my hand, squeezing it tightly, and I didn't dare say a word even though it hurt so bad. I was so relieved when he finally let go. I took my shoes off and carried them, following behind him. I looked out at the ocean, trying to see the waves that I could only hear in the darkening sky.

Luke asked if I wanted a glass of wine, and I replied that I did. Truthfully, I was happy that he seemed to have calmed down, because I didn't understand why he was as angry as he'd been. It had been a misunderstanding at worst. *Maybe a lack of communication, and maybe he had a rough day*, I thought.

Luke started in with his slick words again, enticing me with their sweetness. The words were reminding me of just how much I really did long to have someone in my life again. He told me that he'd been so excited to see me that he got to my house early, just to be ready. When he'd seen that I was there he was surprised. Then he pulled me in and kissed me, and I accepted it.

After our lips parted and he moved away, he continued on, telling me that I didn't understand how he thought about me all this time, every minute of every day he said. I couldn't quite grasp that level of intensity, but managed to thank him for making me feel so special, telling him that I thought of him, too.

Really, I was grateful for the attention and glad to be out with him, especially at the beach. I didn't recall telling him that it was my favorite place to be, he seemed to instinctually know it.

Then we both grew quiet, and I looked over at Luke, noticing how quickly he was drinking. And I was pretty certain he'd drank a bit before even picking me up. I'd smelled that distinct scent of alcohol in the car.

Out of nowhere, he said, "Next time I ask you out, don't be a bitch, just let me know what time you are getting off of work."

I was offended. "Luke, it's late and you've had enough to drink. I should really get home." I stood up, and he did, too. He pushed me very hard and I almost fell over, but I regained my balance quickly, thankfully.

Then he flung the blanket around, whipping sand into my eyes. After that, he picked up the cooler and started to walk quickly toward his SUV. I tried to clear my eyes from the sand as fast as I could. I quickly picked up my sandals and followed. I could tell he was really drunk now and I didn't want to get into the car with him, but I had no choice. I didn't have my phone on me to call my friends for help. I also didn't have any money; my house key and purse were in the SUV. I didn't want to be left at the beach. The mood he was in now, anything could happen. If I said the wrong thing I would be left there.

He unlocked the door, and before I even got completely into the SUV he sped off and the door shut with such force. He drove aggressively and sporadically, swearing and complaining at other drivers on the road, weaving in and out of lanes. I couldn't wait to get home, and squeezed my eyes shut with each swerve he made in his car.

Finally, I arrived back in front of my home—grateful to be in one piece. He slammed on his brakes, which left skid marks on the pavement in front of my house. I was tossed forward into the windshield. I unbuckled my seatbelt right away and leaped out of the car. We didn't say anything to each other. He drove off, fast and reckless, out of the parking lot.

It had been a quiet ride to say the least, and all I could think of was that I was grateful to get out of the car. We didn't even say good night to each other. I just hurried into my home, key in hand, glad to have my front door between us—locked and secured. I was distracted with anxiety for what was looming on the horizon.

What was I supposed to be feeling? I knew that I did not like the way I felt at that current moment. I was really upset—with myself. The next day was going to be a big day, and I was not looking forward to it.

Standing in the bathroom, I stripped off my clothes and turned the water on, eager for it to heat up and wash away the anxiety, not to mention the sand. Once I finally got in, I breathed in, enjoying the reprieve. My thoughts slowly cleared a bit and I realized that I'd barely eaten that day; just a corn muffin, cup of coffee, and some wine. Not a good diet, but not as bad as the anger that I was carrying for myself.

I thought, *how could I let someone treat me this way?* There was no one to be mad at except me. Harsh and true words directed at the source of blame—me. I thought it would be different. What started off as a love story pained me dearly.

My emotions are all torn up. I don't know if I should cry, scream, or both. I feel my heart was taken by words of poison. I wish I could understand what is going on with him. There are obviously a lot of underlying issues that are deep. From the tone of his voice I should have put my foot down and said, "Tonight is canceled." Luke was already angry about who knows what. He's been drinking. I like him but he doesn't talk to me about anything. I'm hurt and upset. I feel he is taking all of his frustrations out on me. I can't believe how hard I'm crying. My hands are shaking. I was so afraid. I must calm down. I went to the kitchen and washed my face and took deep breaths.

Walking into my bedroom I sighed. The bed wasn't even made. My phone was beeping that the battery was almost dead. I plugged it in, made my bed, and slid into the fresh linens. I've always loved the way that felt. Surely it would help me sleep, and finally I drifted off despite myself. Then at 3:30 a.m. precisely, my phone began to ring and it woke me up with a start. But I didn't answer. I unplugged the phone and tried to find that place of sleep again.

CHAPTER SIX

Before I knew it, it was eight, and this time I was awoken by my alarm. Despite the sporadic sleep, I didn't feel tired, but I still felt very upset at myself.

I was filled with this madness of energy. I pushed back the curtains in my room. I went into the living room and pulled up the blinds and opened the windows to get some fresh air into the house.

I looked out the front window and I saw a large bouquet of flowers on the porch. They were placed on the small round table I have outside. I opened the front door to bring them in. I put them on the side table in the living room. They were beautiful. All different color roses: yellow, white, red, and pink, with baby's breath and greenery in a crystal vase. There was a note in the arrangement. It was handwritten by Luke.

Good Morning Amilia,

It is Luke. I'm sorry about last night, this is really not me. There are a lot of things going on and I should not have acted like this towards you. Please forgive me. Give me another chance. Please call me when you get this note.

Sincerely, Luke

I had to think about this for a minute; maybe I should call him. He must be going through a lot with his wife and the kids. It's probably too much to handle.

I went to my room, plugged the phone back into the wall, and with perfect timing, the phone started to ring. It was Luke.

"Hello," I said. Luke began right away, with the same lines that seem all too familiar. I should hear him out. He wanted another chance to make it up to me please. And…when is the next time he could see me again?

"I work a lot, you know this," I reminded him.

To Luke, time didn't matter. He'd see me whenever he could. "Call me when you get out of work."

"Okay, Luke. I will ring you tonight. The flowers are beautiful. Thank you. I have to get going and get ready for work." After we hung up I couldn't help but wonder why I'd ever agreed to it. I was not too excited to see Luke.

Last night was still freshly seared into my mind. All the emotions— *I don't believe he even realized his actions. I know he feels it didn't go well, I received flowers. I guess I will have to see.* But for now, time for another day at work to begin. I'm happy there's not excessive traffic, but my thoughts are nagging me. In my gut I knew it—Luke was not for me.

Trying to shove it from my mind, I pulled into the club to start my work day. Punched in and ready to begin my day, I walked over to the floor plan, disappointed to see that my tables were outside that day. It was so hot, the heat always wears me down so fast.

I said good morning to everyone and greeted the chef. He was outside enjoying the view of the boats from the balcony. He said hello to me. Although I feigned happiness, I knew that people could see something was a bit off. The chef asked if I was okay, to which I made up a bogus excuse.

"No, just deep in thought," I said. Then he asked if I'd had a great day off, to which I offered a, "It was great, thank you."

He told me to be on my toes today. "It's going to be a crazy day."

"OK," I stated. *How ironic was that statement,* I sighed to myself.

The banquet manager was on duty today. Miles came out to the patio and said good morning. He wanted to make sure we had our assignments and told us that Pierre would be in this afternoon.

Chef came out to let us know lunch is prepared for us to eat. We have a half hour before guests begin to come in, and we need to get to our stations. It is going to be very busy.

I was starving. I didn't have much of anything to eat yesterday, and nothing that morning. I went into the kitchen and took a cheeseburger and put lettuce, tomato, and red onion on it, and picked at some French fries. I poured some cranberry juice and went to the back of the main dining room to be alone to eat. I didn't feel like having small talk with the other waiters.

As I was eating, I texted Matt. I told him I miss him and love him, hope that he has a blessed day.

I know I told myself I wasn't going to think about what transpired last night, but sitting here collecting my thoughts, I can't help it. It was nice that he apologized to me though, and is going to try to make it up to me I guess.

Break time was over. I finished my entire plate of food. I took my plate and glass to the dish bin, and went outside to the patio. People were starting to pile in for lunch. I can't believe that the members want to sit in this heat and eat. I can feel the sweat drip down my back.

I wiped my forehead all day. I drank water every chance I had. Being out here is too much for me.

It became hotter as the day moved on. Lunch out here completely died down rather quickly. I went inside so I could breathe in the cool air from an airconditioned room; it felt so good. I was a bit blinded by the sun and had to regain my focus. The bar was packed. There were only five tables finishing up lunch.

Miles approached me and asked me to shut down the patio until the evening hours. I could take a break and be back around five. I was happy about that.

I wanted to get my hair done today since I had all this time to spare. I went to the back of the kitchen and called the salon to see if there were any available appointments. I asked to speak to Bianca; she is a friend of mine, and works at the salon. She just so happened to have a cancelation, and told me to come right over.

I punched out, grabbed my purse from my locker, and headed out. I couldn't wait to see her. My hours give me little time to pamper myself.

When I arrived there I went in and gave Bianca a great big hug. I was so happy to see her. She asked me how things were going, and I told her about Luke and what happened last night.

Bianca replied, very concerned, "Listen, be careful, and watch yourself. No one should treat you this way, it doesn't matter what is happening in their life…"

"Bianca, he asked me to give him another chance. I like him, and I want to see where it goes," I explained.

Bianca replied, "Please give me your cellphone, and I will put my new number in it for you. If you need to call me for anything please do it."

"Bianca, I'm sure I will be all right, trust me. Thank you so much for being a good friend. My hair looks terrific. I have to get back to work. Thank you for squeezing me in." I hugged Bianca goodbye, paid her, and left.

I noticed on my way back to the club that the clouds were getting darker. I didn't listen to the news this morning. I didn't know it was going to rain. I put my hair up in a ponytail, drove back to the club and punched in, put my bag in my locker.

Mandy saw me come in, waved me over to the front desk, and handed me a note. She told me Luke called six times in one hour. She asked me if everything was all right, Luke sounded very angry.

"Do the bosses know?" I asked.

"No, but does he understand not to call you here? That it's not allowed."

"I will tell him again, thank you for covering for me."

"No worries," Mandy said.

I walked to the back of the kitchen to call Luke. He answered, "Where the hell did you go? I've been calling you back to back."

"I went to get my hair cut Luke, I can't receive phone calls here at the club, it's not allowed; this is not my home."

"Call me when you get out tonight," Luke said. "I will come over to your place." He didn't even say goodbye. Just hung up.

I'm not getting it, why is he checking on me? Or maybe he wanted to say hello. He didn't give me a chance to ask him anything. Well, I still didn't tell him about my cellphone. It would be easier for him to get a hold of me. I just don't know, it doesn't feel right.

I had to get back to the dining room to work. Dinner looked slow. It started to rain very hard. The patio chairs were falling over from the wind. There were several cancelations.

We were setting up for dinner in the main dining room, but the reservations became lighter.

Miles came into the room and said, "We do not need all the waiters on tonight; due to the weather, there aren't many reservations." He asked who would like to go home.

"I would, thank you," I stated.

Miles asked, "Anyone else?" Two others raised their hands. "Ok, good night to all of you, I will see you tomorrow."

I called Luke. He answered. "Hello!"

"I'm leaving now, dinner is very slow because of the weather."

"Ok, drive safe, and I will meet you at your house." I'm so happy I cleaned up my place, and everything is put away.

CHAPTER SEVEN

I got to the house and Luke was sitting in his car waiting for me. He turned off the engine and got out right away, walking over to me and instantly embracing my stiff body. Then he kissed me, softly and tenderly, until despite myself my stiff posture loosened, enjoying feeling good. Then he picked me up and twirled me around.

That was all it took to wipe out my day's worth of incessant gut instincts.

"This is a nice greeting," I said with a smile and a laugh.

Luke took my hand softly and we walked up to the house together. I opened the door and let him in, locking the door behind us. He wanted me to show him around.

"I was going to freshen up a bit first, but if you want a tour, I'll give you one," I relented.

We were in the living room, straight ahead is the kitchen. Luke loved how spacious the kitchen is. The dark brown granite countertops and light cabinets. I had a grin, and began to mention the best feature for me is the ice machine on the stainless steel refrigerator (he laughed).

We walked down the hall. I showed him the first bathroom with a whirlpool tub; he liked it. I have three bedrooms. Straight ahead is the guest room. It's average size, decorated in pastel colors, rich blues and white, lots of pillows and a big white comforter. The drapes are long, they touch the carpet.

We went further down the hall and my room was at the end. I have my own private bathroom. I decorated it like it was out of a magazine from Italy. Long burgundy drapes, and a tall black framed mirror with an Egyptian plush rug with tassels. Burgundy comforter with a gold pattern design. I have a queen lounge chair in the corner of the room. I can say my room is beautiful.

Luke said, "Wow this room is amazing! Your own private suite. I love the bathroom. Where is the third room at?" he said.

"Come, I will show you," I replied. I pulled back the curtains on each side of the hidden entrance, and placed them on the hooks. On the top of the stairs there is a large open room. There is plenty of closet space and a vanity bathroom. A big king size bed and a flat screen TV mounted on the wall. The room was decorated in light green cream colors with a light brown carpet.

Luke said, "Your home is beautifully done, I like it so much. It's like a show piece."

"I don't know about that, but I really love my home." I beamed.

I asked Luke if he ate. He answered that he was fine; he told me he brought a couple bottles of wine and glasses with him. He had to go out to the car and get them. I told him that I have wine glasses here.

I turned on the TV and put some soft music on (my son calls it elevator music). I lit some candles to make it relaxing. Luke came back in. I told him I was going to take a quick shower and be right out.

I grabbed my purse, hearing my friend Bianca's voice in my head. *Watch out for this guy.*

***

Back from my shower, glad for the reprieve from him and some time to clear my head, I was greeted with another smile and more compliments on the home. I noticed that his words were not steady. It was easy to tell that the glass of wine in his hand wasn't his first of the evening.

Luke suggested that I join him on the couch and I did. In a second flat he began to pull at my hair, pinch my breast, and became an out of control octopus.

I immediately stood up. "What's going on?"

He confessed, growing innocent again, and saying he'd had a few too many drinks and didn't want me to be uncomfortable. Then he asked me to sit down again. Confession time—he mentioned that he was having a hard time with the wife in his efforts to get sole custody of his daughters.

"I thought you said she didn't care about the kids."

All Luke indicated was that it was time for a change of subject. Fine, whatever. I began to enjoy the relaxing sensation that the wine gave me, and I was on my third glass, more than what I'd usually ever have. I was officially dizzy, in a happy way.

We cuddled and laughed and kissed, played around. But it was getting late, and I had to get up early.

"Do you want to spend the night?" I asked. It wasn't about intimacy so much as it was about how much he'd had to drink. He agreed. (I can't let him drive away in the condition he's in. I like him. I'm worried about his safety and others on the road.)

I blew out the candles and turned the TV off, then we made our way to my room. I noticed his stumbling and was grateful that he fell asleep almost the second his head hit the pillows. He was *tired*, and I was too. It was one in the morning.

Unlike an alarm clock, I was awoken by a fierce shake on my arm. Luke was yelling and his voice was so loud. I tried to get my eyes open all the way to see what was going on! He was holding my cellphone and wanting to know about it. He went through my bag, snooping around.

"My son thought I should get one so we can communicate better," I said, waking up in a very unpleasant way. My gut already tense.

He was mad that he didn't know about it or have my number. To Luke, everything was a game with me.

"I didn't know where we were headed in terms of being together," I said. It was true.

He began screaming at me to stop the bullshit and treating him like an idiot. The short tirade was followed up with an accusation that I was dating someone else.

"I'm not dating anyone! You have this all wrong!"

He shouted that I was a fucking slut and then he grabbed the phone and smashed it against the wall.

I was so scared! I wrapped my arms around my knees, which were bent to my chest, and I hid my head. I was frightened.

He kept cursing and screaming, "Fuck you and your phone!"

My entire body was shaking by this point and I was numb. There was nothing I could say and I chose silence.

Finally, he was dressed and stormed out of my house, swearing the entire way and slamming the door for emphasis. Only then, alone and shaken, did I begin to cry. And I cried hard. Finally, fearful he'd come back, I got out of bed and went to the front door to lock it. I still had a few more hours before I had to get up. When I went to lay back down I was so mentally drained that everything was blurry.

CHAPTER EIGHT

I forgot to turn the alarm back on after I lay down. I woke up late, took a quick shower, and began to run around, getting ready to get out of the door. In a panicked state, I left a message for Pierre, the club manager, saying I was going to be late. I hung up and went out the door. There was fortunately a break in traffic; I ended up being only six minutes late. Not too bad thankfully.

Rushing over to my locker I put everything into it and bolted into the bathroom to tidy myself up and put some lip gloss on. When I got back out I took a deep breath. Time to get focused. (I cannot believe how hard he threw my phone; all I could hear in the dark was the pieces hitting the floor one by one.)

Pierre was in the dining room, commenting that he couldn't understand my message at all. I explained that I thought I was going to be late today, the highway looked backed up, but I was able to get here on time. He shrugged his shoulders. The busy day was all that he had on his mind. I was equally thankful for it, as it would be a good way to keep my mind off of Luke. I felt so shattered with everything; not surprised, but completely devastated.

Before long, it was staff lunch time. I wasn't hungry, really, despite the chef making us mushroom ravioli. More than that, I just wanted peace and quiet, no conversation. I decided to eat out in the main dining room.

I glanced up and saw Pierre walking toward me, a quizzical look on his face. He wanted to know why I wasn't eating in the break room with the other staff.

"I needed some time in peace. I was thinking about my son. I also dropped my phone and I need to get another one. I do not have any insurance on the one that's broke."

His eyes were sympathetic and he commented that he hoped things would get better, and that maybe the carrier could offer some help or suggestions.

I offered a forced smile. "I know it's just a phone. It was my first one and I was getting used to it. Thank you."

He left, I finished, and went to put my plate away and add some more lip gloss. It didn't help me feel better, really. Then I thought about Pierre. He'd been kind, but there is a strict policy about fraternizing with guests at the club and I didn't want to let on too much, as Luke has friends as club members. Plus, how would I explain accepting the way I was being treated without feeling like a fool? And looking like one, too!

Lunch was busy, and fast, which I was grateful for, but again, I was thrown off balance when the hostess handed me a note after my shift. She told me that Pierre had answered the phone and someone had wanted to speak with me. He'd taken a message and told the hostess to give it to me only after lunch was done. My face must have shown my concern, because she added that I shouldn't worry, that he wasn't mad. Be aware of it; don't let it happen on a regular basis.

I'm so grateful Mandy was working the front desk. I can always count on her with kind words to back up anything that is going on. We started working together about the same time.

Slowly, I opened the note: *Please talk to me. Call me back. I'm sorry. Luke...*

I crumpled the note and tossed it. However, I knew...the fact that I was having problems was most obvious. I'd been asking to leave work earlier than ever before and I'd changed. Despite trying to hide it, I couldn't see how my outside could mask the changes and turmoil that were happening on the inside. I just couldn't cope.

Volunteering to take off due to a slower than usual dinner shift, I quickly gathered my things to go, and saw Pierre watching me. He came toward me and I felt like a lead weight was in my stomach. My mind already racing for excuses to explain without really saying anything at all.

He was so kind, directly telling me that he knew something was wrong and that his office door was open for me to talk any time I wished to.

"Thank you Pierre. That means a lot to me. I'll keep that in mind." But I knew I never would. It was too embarrassing, too hard to even say out loud. My pride wouldn't allow for it. Then he wished me a good night and said that he'd see me for Sunday brunch.

I smiled and left, deciding to make my way to Verizon. Hopefully they could help me with my phone issue. There was a note under the windshield wiper blade on my car. I was so hurt by his words I really didn't want to read any more notes.

Dear Amilia, please talk to me.

I know what I did was wrong. I didn't have a right to take your phone and smash it, or call you names. I want to make up for the damage I caused to your home and replace your phone. Some of your actions remind me of my ex-wife. She lied and cheated to get what she wanted and I'm still living through the cycle in my mind. I know this is no excuse to treat you this way, my heart is so angry. Please accept my apologies.

Love Luke.

I folded the paper and put it into my purse and got in the car, still planning on going to Verizon and hoping to stop thinking about Luke. I didn't want any more of this craziness to absorb my day.

✳✳✳

A very anxious me was glad to see the same woman who helped me pick out my phone was here today. I offered the only explanation my dignity would allow, and said that I'd dropped the phone and didn't think it could be repaired. I asked how I could go about getting another one.

Her voice, soft and kind, explained how another shipment of the 3G phones would be in the following week, but she could put my name on a callback list to let me know when they arrived so I could pick it up. That was the best they could do for me and I had no other options, as the other phones were several hundred dollars and required contracts. I didn't have that type of money to spend on my phone. Then I left and went home.

The ride home was so agonizing, filled with me condemning myself that maybe the entire situation was my fault; that if I had just told him about the phone none of that would have happened. Whatever it was, though, and whatever hindsight determined to be accurate, was really irrelevant at that point. I didn't have a phone.

And again, when I got home and pulled into my driveway, I saw the flowers there that were going to make up for everything and earn him a second chance. Each rose had a note on it that read: *SORRY.* I couldn't help but chuckle at the irony of how much roses cost more than my cellphone. I opened up my door and went into my home, took my shoes off, and brought the flowers in. One by one, I placed them on various tables around my living room.

I went into the kitchen and sat with Feathers for a moment. I wanted to avoid what awaited me in my room—picking up the pieces of my shattered cellphone. Not to mention the hole in the drywall from the phone's assault of it. What am I thinking to allow this kind of man in my life, giving me roses to apologize for his volatile outbursts that always cost me my happiness and increasingly, my sanity?

Then the landline rang and I glanced over at the caller ID. It was Matthew, my son.

"Hi, darling," I answered. His voice was filled with concern and an instant bombardment came out, asking me if I was okay, where I'd been. Why hadn't I answered his text messages? "I'm okay." Now I was lying to my kid? I was not okay, really, but I kept complete composure.

"My phone broke, and I can't replace it until next week. I'll text or call you as soon as I get it. But on a better note...how are you?"

He went on to share all the wonderful things that are happening in his life. He'd just moved in with his girlfriend Rachel, and he has a job he loves. Things are going very well for Matthew; I am so happy for him.

"I miss you!" I blurted.

He told me that he missed me too, and wanted me to come and visit him sometime soon. I promised to figure out a time when I could make it. I told him I couldn't wait to meet Rachel.

"I love hearing your voice and please give Rachel my regards. I love you Matthew."

"I love you too Mom, have a blessed night."

Matthew definitely lifted my spirits. With a dose of his infectious happiness there wasn't anything that could wipe the smile off my face. I knew I was blessed. I got to the task at hand of cleaning everything up, took the vacuum out of the hallway closet—I could hear all the small pieces being sucked into it. After I was done there was plenty of time left in daylight. I then decided to take an adventure to one of my most favorite places—the beach. I needed to press pause on life.

I packed my small cooler with a sandwich, yogurt, and a thermos of iced tea. I put on my shorts and tank top, slipped into my flip flops, picked up my keys, and headed out the door.

I wanted to call Bianca to tell her what transpired, but I refused. I didn't want to hear I told you so. All I longed for was a reprieve, a slice of bliss in a life that was getting crazier by the second. I never called Luke back. After the wonderful conversation I had with my son I couldn't stand to ruin it with the sound of Luke's voice.

I started to feel alive, I had so much energy. I lost myself for a minute as if I was living in a fog and I couldn't focus. He threw me a curveball. I was still shell shocked. I had my window down listening to music. I put my big sunglasses on. I was enjoying my ride to the beach, and then, oh my goodness what is that noise?

CHAPTER NINE

My car began rattling and it grew louder. I became very worried. I had to switch lanes and get to the shoulder of the road so I could pull over. There I was staring in disbelief at the steam coming out from under the hood of my car. I put my flashers on and waited for help to come, because I couldn't call for it. There was nothing for me to do, it just required patience and the annoying sound of a hazard signal clicking in predictable intervals.

A half hour went by, no help. I admit it; I was beginning to think that no one would help me out. Just then, a nice lady about my age dressed in a business suit pulled up behind me and asked if she could help. She introduced herself as Leslie. I explained my situation to her and she asked if I could remember anyone's telephone number. She recommended I call the police but I didn't want to make a spectacle. I told her I was actually hoping that the Help Truck that services cars that are on the side of the road would come. I see them all the time, just not today unfortunately.

There were only two numbers that I knew by heart, Matthew's and Luke's. Did I take the stubborn route or give in and call Luke for help? Sadly, I didn't really see a choice, as Matthew was far away.

"Yes, there is someone I can call," I said. She handed her phone over and I dialed Luke's number, my mind working in overdrive to hopefully think of any other number I might know so I could just hang up.

"Luke, hi—" He asked where I was, as he'd been leaving messages all day long. "I'm stuck on the highway, my car overheated and a nice person stopped and let me use her cellphone."

He asked where I was and I explained that I was on Ocean Boulevard, halfway to the beach, and my house. Then he said he'd be there in about twenty minutes.

I thanked Luke, and then I thanked Leslie. She mentioned staying until my help arrived and I told her I'd be okay. Then she left and I waited, eating my yogurt and drinking iced tea, and wishing I could get some reprieve from the heat. I was scared and nervous.

The twenty minutes felt like hours. Luke pulled up, and the tow truck was right behind him. Luke walked over to me and gently kissed me on the cheek.

"Thank you," I said.

He instantly apologized again, reminding me that he would always be there for me. Then he said to take anything important out of my car and put it into his. His friend was the tow truck driver and he'd take it to a shop that Luke trusted. How could I argue? I really didn't know what to do. Then he said he'd take me home.

"Thank you, Luke for everything."

I had both of my house keys on my key chain. I took one off the ring and handed the rest of the keys to Luke. I grabbed my belongings, and got into Luke's car with him. I'll admit it, I was grateful for the air conditioning. He asked if I was ready to go home and I nodded my head yes.

On the way home Luke told me that he would like to put this behind us and start over. He was kind at the moment. Luke seemed as if he genuinely cared about me and my wellbeing, and felt bad for hurting me. How could I resist to at least being open to a chance? He offered to drive me to and from work until my car was fixed, asked me if he could take me to dinner the following night.

"It will be an early dinner," he said, "I have many things to do in the evening. Is two o'clock all right?"

With a voice that was so genuine and sweet sounding that I felt myself feeling relief, that it had finally sunk in that he had to stop being so volatile, I said yes.

Personally, I was glad that I didn't have to work the following day, as I didn't want Luke driving me there. I just didn't. He explained how he had things to do that evening and he'd come over to my house the following afternoon.

Then we were back at my house. He kissed me on the forehead and I got out of the car, hearing him call out that I should just wait and see...that things were going to be different.

"The flowers are beautiful," I called back. Then he waited until I walked in before he left.

✳✳✳

My house was so hot, my goodness. I turned on the air conditioner in the kitchen and in my room. It was going to take a bit to cool the house down for sure. In the corner my bird sat in his cage, happily making noise and pecking at his toys. I refilled the water dish and began to unpack my beach bag. I sure hadn't made it far that afternoon.

And as the day went on, I showered and relaxed, enjoying the solitude and quiet, and finally double checked that the front door was locked before I went up to bed. The day was done and I was glad. Something about my house at that moment gave me such comfort. I glanced around at everything, feeling the love in it and grateful for what I did have. The day had ended in kindness, which was just what I needed.

This new feeling of contentment almost didn't seem real, like a fairytale love story. I'd had my reservations about Luke all day, but when he came so quickly to rescue me I knew that he must care and that was the easiest feeling to go with before I drifted off to sleep that night. I was too wiped out to think of anything else and I had no alarm clock that needed to be set for the morning. Life was good.

✳✳✳

Morning came and my eyes fluttered open. I got up early only to close my eyes again for a couple more hours. I felt so calm and rested.

I began to get ready, thinking about Luke arriving at two. I wanted to look good for him so I took a long relaxing shower and then blew out my hair and styled it in a high ponytail. That always looked good on me.

I wasn't sure what to wear. I hadn't bought anything new in a long time. I did have a summer dress that I'd never worn before. Maybe that would be perfect. It was light blue and white striped with small cap sleeves, and a shoelace on the top part of the dress. I put it on and it looked great. I took out a pair of sandals. They were cork wedges with white cloth over the front of the open toed shoe. Yes, I felt wonderful and it was going to be a great day.

I went to the kitchen, poured some coffee, took out my nail polish, sat down at the kitchen table, and polished my toes. I looked at the time and still had a half hour before Luke would be there. The excitement was building.

When he said we'd go out for dinner I assumed it would be an early dinner, which was fine. All I knew for certain was that I wanted to see him. A few minutes before his arrival, I slipped my shoes on carefully over my dried toenails and waited. Luke didn't like to be kept waiting. Was I nervous or anxious? I went over to the front window to see if he was outside, there was no sign of him yet.

Luke must be running late, and I was starving. I went to the kitchen, took out some muenster cheese and crackers to start nibbling on, and poured myself a glass of cranberry juice while I waited. I needed something in my stomach before I got sick.

I looked up at the kitchen clock; it was now three thirty. Still no Luke. I walked over to the window, looked through the blinds, and looked up and down the parking lot to make sure he wasn't out there waiting for me. I finally decided to take my shoes off and turn on the TV. I also called him to find out if he was okay. It wasn't like him to just not show up. His phone went right to voicemail.

Admitting that my night wasn't going to be what I had planned, I sighed and went to my room to change into a pair of comfy shorts and a t-shirt. I wasn't sure how to feel about everything. The reality was that Luke was not divorced yet. Sometimes I found ways to deal with that and other times it overwhelmed me. The thought of him having dinner with his family bothered me, but I knew it shouldn't. It was selfish, but at the same time he went out of his way to help me.

Dinner for one, I thought. I was getting hungry. Finally I made some chicken and potatoes, put it in the oven like a roast, stared at my phone occasionally hoping that it would ring. It didn't. Still no call from Luke.

When dinner was ready I decided to eat in front of the television. I needed a distraction to help me pass the time. After I was done with dinner I put everything in the dishwasher, wrapped the leftovers, and then headed back toward the living room. I am not sure why, but I decided to look out the front window one last time. I was upset and disappointed and not sure how to come to terms with that. Then I thought about work the next day and his promise to pick me up for it. Could I really rely on him for that?

I needed a backup plan so I called the club. Thankfully Penny was there. I got along well with her. I was so relieved when she answered and said she'd be glad to pick me up in the morning.

She asked me, "What's going on?" I told her I would explain everything at a later time. I asked her for her cellphone number to write in my book. In case of any changes, I would be able to reach her right away. I thanked her for everything. One problem solved, but what about Luke?

CHAPTER TEN

Grateful for Penny's kindness, before even going to bed I made sure my alarm was set and my clothes were laid out. I wasn't going to keep her waiting. When morning arrived, I stretched and yawned as I got ready. It hadn't been the most restful night. I tossed and turned with Luke absorbing all my thoughts. I just couldn't shake the uneasy feeling I had about him.

Dressed and ready with time to spare, I fed Feathers and put a pot of coffee on then I went to see if the paper was delivered. I opened the front door to grab the newspaper and I jumped when I heard a loud beep, then another, and another. I looked and saw Luke coming down the road, along with someone else who was driving my car. They pulled up in front of the house and a smile came across my face. I was so happy to see Luke, and how strange that it was more intense than my happiness at seeing my vehicle fixed.

I flew off my porch—you would think I had wings. Luke got out of his car and I hugged him tightly, melting right into his body and extended arms. He smelled so good. We kissed and he kissed me again on my forehead. I sensed that he was really glad to see me as he didn't let go for a couple of minutes and he kept whispering in my ear how he missed me. Then it would be followed up with a kiss.

"I miss you, too!" I said. "Luke, you are so wonderful. Thank you so much. I never would have expected…I was so…" I had so much to say and none of the words were coming out. I asked him what happened. I began to mention he'd promised last night we would go out.

He assured me that when he promised to do something, he does it. He said that he'd never promised that he would be here yesterday, maybe that's how I interpreted the conversation, and we'd talk about it another time, as I had to get to work and he had to go. His friend walked over to me and handed me the keys to my car. I thanked him.

Luke got back into his SUV and put his hand on his mouth. He sent me kisses and left with a casual comment about calling later that evening. I waved to him as he drove off.

I ran back into the house, grabbed my phone book to call Penny to tell her I have my car, thanked her, told her I wouldn't need a ride after all, and I would explain everything later. (It was better, actually, as I had to be at work an hour earlier than Penny and being late again was not a good idea.) Then I took off, feeling the rush of making my way to the club by nine o'clock.

My emotions were running wild. Should I mention to Luke how upset I was? I decided it was best to keep that to myself. After all, he'd made up for it today with the delivery of my car. He'd kept that promise. It was a blessed morning. It was terrible that I felt even a touch of my own madness. I felt so selfish. By the time I arrived at work—with even a few minutes to spare—I realized that I hadn't even remembered the journey or a single other car on the road. I was that lost in thought.

Instead of walking into the building I decided to walk around back and sit for a while before my day began. There was a beach chair that wasn't put away last night near the back steps, so I made myself comfortable and watched the waves crashing intensely on the sand and shorelines. The wind was rather strong this morning. I let my hair down and it felt great to be free, even for a moment. I loved it.

Pierre came out back and noticed me. I turned my head to him with a smile, my hair whipping against my face. He looked worried and asked if everything was okay.

"Good morning Pierre, everything is fine. I had a few minutes and love listening to waves."

He nodded, but alas, my brief moment of bliss was over. It was time to punch in and get ready for lunch. Only three of us were on, a small number for a busy day. I mentioned it to Jasper, and he nodded his head but couldn't hide the concern in his eyes. I put my purse in the locker, clipped back my hair. Put on a pot of coffee for the staff. We began our usual set up for lunch. I went to the front desk to look at the reservation book for any special table requests and it looked like a very light crowd today, but with this place you can never be too sure.

Penny came into the dining room and I gave her a huge hug, so grateful for her friendship. We talked a bit and I filled her in on how Luke hadn't come over last night after all, but did show up with my fixed car this morning.

Penny said, "Amilia I'm not impressed. He seems to have a control thing. He always wants to know where you are what you are doing. If you're busy he gets angry, and he hangs up before I can say another word."

"There was so much that happened in such a short time, lots of highs and lows. This was all true, of course, but Luke's life is complicated. I know it will get better. I'm sure of it. He showed me how much he cares about me. I appreciate you being by my side Penny. I really feel like it's going to be okay," I shared.

Her reservations were noted and then tossed, just like I'd done with all mine. She had to get back to the front desk.

Then I went into the kitchen and called Luke quickly to thank him again. I got his voicemail though. I left a message and then turned around to Chef calling out my name. He'd made bacon and egg sandwiches for the staff. He wanted me to let the entire staff know that breakfast was ready. It was so nice to be spoiled by Chef's cooking, because he was great.

With my sandwich in hand, I couldn't wait to eat. It looked really good. The smell of bacon can go right through you and burst open all your hunger senses. I just felt so happy and good, and I wanted it to remain that way. My thoughts were good, and I didn't want anything to invade them, so I didn't go to the break room with everyone else to eat. I poured a cup of coffee and went in to the banquet room alone to eat. I just finished as people began to come in and were seated at my table.

Time to work.

As the day progressed, it dragged on. I thought it would never reach three o'clock. Unfortunately, I only served four tables in my station today. Finances were heavy on my mind. Penny came into the dining room with good news—I had received a call that my phone had arrived early. I was so happy. I wouldn't have to wait until the end of the week. I gave Penny a big hug and thanked her.

I'm off tonight, and this would be a great opportunity to get a pedicure since the salon is in the same shopping center as Verizon. My tables had all left.

I helped Jasper quickly bring everything into the kitchen and put it away.

With work all done, I punched out. I took off to get my phone and a few other things. As I walked toward my car, I saw Luke pull into the parking lot. I raised my arm and waved, smiling, and moved quickly towards his car. Before a hello or anything he asked me where I was going.

I explained I had the night off and I was going to go get my toenails done, maybe buy something nice, and hopefully get a new phone. He began to say he liked me the way I was. I didn't have to impress him. I didn't have to be like his wife. Nice words, but I wanted to do what I had in mind.

Then things got interesting. He told me to go with him, he was going to pick the girls up from school and then drop them off at the sitter's house until their mother got them. Wow…that was a big step. It gave me hope that his crazy life and situation might actually be tapering down and then we could focus on being a couple.

I waited in the car while Luke went in to get the girls. As they walked out I marveled at how cute they were. The oldest had her hair in pigtails with big pink bows and a pink summer dress with a white poodle on it. His youngest was wearing a floral dress that tied in the back, and had her hair in a ponytail. Then he put them into the car and made sure they were buckled in, and they looked at me with wide curious eyes and smiled.

I realized how awkward the situation was. I smiled too.

"Hello sweethearts, don't you both look lovely today." They said thank you in unison.

Luke looked over at me and took my hand, commenting that he wanted me to meet his family so I could see how much I meant to him. To prove what we had going was serious. I melted…just a bit.

A short while later the girls were dropped off at the sitter's house, they were very happy to see her. They were yelling, "Julia, Julia!" Luke spoke to her for a few minutes. He kissed each child on the forehead, handed Julia their bags, and shook her hand. When Luke got back in the car he didn't waste any time getting to the point. He wanted us together.

"Luke, this is kind of sudden. Where are you staying? What's happening with the kids?"

It was then that he asked if he could come over tonight and spend the night. We could discuss everything in depth. My mind was racing with excitement, hesitation, and every emotion that fell in between.

I automatically said, "Yes, of course." It was already six thirty by the time he dropped me off at the club so I could get my car.

"I'll probably be home around eight Luke. I want to go and get my phone," I said. I felt myself slightly tense, not sure how he'd respond, and he surprised me by pulling out a hundred dollar bill and handing it to me. I heard myself saying he didn't have to do that, which was ridiculous, because I wouldn't need a new phone at all if he didn't break it. *And if you'd just told him about it*, I thought.

"Please, I insist. I will never do that to you again." I nodded and we agreed to meet back at my place in a few hours.

Then he mentioned taking a shower if he got there first. "How are you going to get in?" I asked.

His confession startled me. He told me that he had an extra set made when he'd had the car fixed. Then he added that he'd just forgotten to give the extra set of keys to me. Was that normal? Obviously not. I knew in the back of my mind he knew what he was doing, but there wasn't anything I could do about that now.

I responded with a nice thank you and instructions for where the towels were. I hadn't had a man stay with me since my late husband. It was hard to allow anyone in my life, I loved Nicholas so much.

I miss him every day. He was a man of kind words, compassion, and love for everyone. His laugh was one of those laughs that was contagious and his joy would radiate through you. So *handsome* and tall, six foot two, with dark hair and dark eyes. I would have to stand on my tiptoes to give him a kiss. He's very missed by Matthew and me.

Luke told me to be careful driving, and to call him on my way back. I gave him a kiss on the cheek, then we left. I was determined not to do anything to upset him tonight because we were on the cusp of a big step, and a key to the house was a natural progression…I guess. I still couldn't help the uneasiness I felt in the pit of my stomach having Luke alone in my house.

CHAPTER ELEVEN

When I walked into the Verizon store the sales lady noticed me, waved me right over. She asked me to wait one minute, and she would get my new phone. She told me that it was charged up and to follow her to the register to cash out. Her expression was understanding, and it helped me feel less embarrassed about the entire situation. I was so grateful for her kindness, to be certain. I left, feeling better having my phone . I called Luke to let him know that I was on my way back home. When he said that he was there waiting for me, it startled me.

Up until that moment, I hadn't really thought about it fully, as it had happened so fast. I'd never had a man stay at my home since my husband Nicholas died. Having him in my home without me there was unsettling too. My house was filled with memories of Nicholas and Matthew, things that were very important to me. I'd loved my husband so much, and it was that reminder that made me ache and feel this strong uncertainty if I was ready to have another man in my home. I really was not sure.

What if he was going through my things? I couldn't stand the thought of it and I pictured all the bins full of loving memories that I'd always kept. I was a private person, liking to have things that were just my precious memories, meant for me and me alone. Some of those things were in those bins—they represented the past but would always be a part of who I was.

After a drive home that seemed to take an eternity, just like the lunch shift had, I finally got there. Luke was in my parking spot and I had to drive over to the other side that was meant for visitors. It was so inconsiderate.

I felt the need to take a deep breath to calm down—bite my tongue—which was something I never had to do with my husband. They were two different men but I couldn't help but compare. Nicholas had been such a loving and giving man, treating me so gentle. The thoughts that bombarded my mind were intense reminders of how much I loved and missed him.

I unlocked the door and let myself in. Luke was sitting on the couch watching TV. I leaned in and gave him a kiss on the cheek. He was having a glass of wine. There was a platter of cheese and crackers he put together for us, and he had a glass of wine ready for me.

"Glad to see you're comfortable. Did you find everything you needed?" He acknowledged he did, and I said I was going to take a shower and be done shortly.

Feeling refreshed and ready to relax, I made my way into the living room. Luke and I did a small "cheers," and he nestled me in near him.

"Tell me about the rest of your day, how did it go?" I asked.

I learned more than I could have imagined with his answer. It had been hectic, as he'd been going back and forth between a hotel and his sister's house. The kids were scattered everywhere, and things were insane. I felt bad for him but his last words startled me like an ice cube being pressed against my warm skin might.

"It would mean a lot to me if you can get to know the girls and we can all live under one roof."

My heart was racing, the sound like a drum pounding in my ears. "What are you thinking, all of us staying here?"

That was indeed what he was thinking and he added that we could possibly find a different place, too.

"How about your ex-wife? What is her take on these plans?" Questions were rolling off my tongue as I tried to buy myself time to process his suggestion gracefully. I didn't want any blowups.

Luke said she was going to give him custody of the kids, as she wasn't equipped to handle them by herself.

"Would you like to bring them over for dinner tomorrow night? I just have to work the morning shift."

He loved the idea, saying it would be the perfect way to see if they liked it here. And how they might feel about living here.

Wow, what is happening?

"What do they like to eat? I'll have to go shopping and get a few things," I suggested.

Luke began to pour another glass of wine, he then refilled my glass and shared that he didn't mind going to the store and preparing the meal while I was working. He could pick up the girls after that and meet me back here. Then he asked me what I thought.

"It seems like a great idea," I said. I was on my third glass of wine, though, so I was feeling rather agreeable.

He laughed, and smiled, and leaned in to give me a kiss. I kissed him back, and felt this intense passion between us. It became very hot, very quickly.

He took off my nightshirt, grabbed my hand, and guided me to the bedroom. He pulled my shorts down and quickly took his clothes off, not allowing me to indulge in the opportunity. There we were, clothes flung all over the room like we were teenagers. With Luke's hands around my waist, he pulled me tightly to him. Our bodies felt like one person breathing. He felt so good, and it was made even better by his great muscles. He was so sexy. I slowly moved my hands up and down his strong arms, then ran my fingertips over his chest, tracing it and memorizing its sculpted detail. His kisses were so intense. Between the wine and the excitement, I was eager and dizzy. All my guards were lowered.

He let me go for a moment and pulled down the covers of the bed and we both slipped right between them. He moved me and touched me in all the right ways, reminding me of what I missed so much in my life. His words. His actions, his confessions of love; it was amazing, he was amazing. How could I have nearly thrown this away? Screaming sounds of happiness.

Even after our satisfaction we couldn't catch our breath. I slid down beside him and cuddled in very closely. He kissed me on the lips and said good night. We both fell soundly to sleep and I slept so soundly, so peacefully, only awakening to his watch alarm going off.

"What time is it?" I asked, rubbing my eyes and still feeling the after effects of my amazing evening. He kissed me on my forehead. It was seven thirty. He had to go get the kids and then go to work. I smiled, touched that he offered to start the coffee for me too. As he was getting ready to leave he told me to have a good day and that he loved me. Then the door slammed shut before I could even respond.

Only then did I realize how much my head was pounding. Too much wine, and too much information. Too much to process eloquently. But it was time to get up, so I took a couple Tylenol and hoped the java would jolt me awake.

I cleaned up the living room. I put the wine glasses in the dishwasher. I threw out the empty bottle of wine and leftover cheese and crackers. I changed the sheets on the bed. The coffee smelled great. I couldn't wait to have another cup. I know that's not the ideal thing to do, but I hoped it might dissolve my headache faster. I gave Feathers fresh water and food.

It was time to leave for work. I brushed my teeth and went into the shower. It was great. I lathered up and stayed for a good fifteen minutes.

I'm really excited to see the girls tonight. I think Luke means what he says now, that things will be different. I got out of the shower and dried off, and began to get dressed. *He gives me a warm fuzzy feeling all over. He said he will be back from picking up the girls around five.*

I brushed my hair and put it up in a ponytail. Applied some lip gloss and mascara. Took my purse and keys, and locked the door behind me.

I looked around the parking lot, puzzled. Where is my car? It took me a few seconds, and I remembered I parked it in the visitors' lot… I really had much too much to drink.

CHAPTER TWELVE

On the road to start my day, my mind was already racing to the night, and what it would be like. I had no idea what to expect and my hands shook from the intense energy surging through my body. I had to take a breath and relax. Then my phone rang. I glanced over at it.

Luke said, "Hey." I was surprised to hear from him. He told me he wanted me to know that he was thinking about me. That was sweet. I smiled from ear to ear.

"I'm thinking about you, too," I confessed, my entire face becoming flushed. He continued to tell me to drive safe and that we would see each other later. He ended by saying, "Bye-bye baby," before he hung up. The rest of the ride to work was nice. This sense of hope and happiness was present, and I felt like nothing would take it away.

When I walked into the club Pierre came right up to me and told me that he was short of help for a dinner banquet. It wasn't a request to stay so much as an expectation—one which he had the right to have, as I was always reliable, if nothing else.

"Okay," I said, already dreading the call to Luke to explain that I wouldn't be back home until seven thirty or so. He was going to be furious, I just sensed it. So I delayed it, and I punched in, and put my things away. *I'm so relieved the Tylenol kicked in and my headache is gone.*

The Chef called everyone to the counter for breakfast. Coffee was ready. I took a glass of juice, a plate of food, and went to the back room of the kitchen where the chef usually eats, and sat down.

I ate my breakfast in no time flat. I was starving, and a bit nervous to make the call to Luke. I knew there was no time but the present to get this off my mind, I had to. The longer I waited the worse the response might be, not to mention inconsiderate. That anxious feeling was in my stomach.

He answered and my voice sounded strangely calm and cheerful as I explained everything, apologizing repeatedly. I was so happy when he was calm and understanding. This was definitely not the answer I thought I was going to get. He said that the kids were with him and he had a lot to do today, and would have dinner ready for me when I got home. He said he understood, that my job is demanding.

That was it. We hung up, and I was so relieved. Things really were changing for the better, and faster. Knowing this made it easier to navigate my day. I kept moving along, thinking about going home to Luke and the girls.

By the time the rest of the staff got there, I already had everything nearly set for the banquet, happy this was a simple party. I love when the event is a buffet, and all I have to do is table maintenance.

Pierre came into the dining room and gave us our assignments. He explained what the sequence of the party would be. The host will make a speech and then welcome everyone to the buffet to eat. It will go rather quickly.

Soon the line at the buffet was moving along. People went up for seconds. We couldn't clear their plates fast enough. I loved the fact they went and got their own drinks. That meant less running for all of us. We worked extra hard, though the two waiters who were assigned to the buffet had a difficult time to keep up with replenishing the food.

The guests were finally slowing down going to the buffet, and I was able to catch up with my table service. They were already asking for coffee. I totally forgot about setting up the coffee station. I went to the kitchen, the coffee was ready.

I heard the Chef whistle behind me. He looked at me and said, "I got your back."

I smiled with a big grin, and thanked Chef. "You are so kind, thank you for everything." Chef made me feel warm inside. I never felt this with him before. *Maybe he is just being nice, that's all.*

I took two coffee pots in the dining room, one decaf and one regular. I handed the decaf to the other waiter and asked him to follow me so we could get the room done. I couldn't resist the dessert table.

When the party left I helped myself to a bite size éclair, and a macaroon cookie. It was delicious. The waiters brought in the leftover desserts. I cleaned up the coffee station. Pierre came into the dining room and thanked us for a job well done. We all said good night.

"Amilia!"

"Yes, Chef?" I answered. He handed me a small container with éclairs and macaroons.

I asked Chef, "How did you know those were my favorites?" He told me he saw me take them through the kitchen window.

"You are very kind, thank you," I told Chef. I felt my whole face become flushed. I punched out, went to my locker, took my purse, and headed to the car.

I took out my phone to ring Luke. I was letting Luke know that I was on my way, but he didn't answer. So I just hung up. I'd be home soon enough—and even early. I drove home with excitement to see him. He'd be surprised I was home earlier than what we discussed.

When I pulled up to the house I was stunned (not even an adequate word for it, really). A U-Haul was parked out front and I looked around, not seeing Luke's SUV anywhere. I had my space to park though.

I got out and ran up the stairs to the front door. It was wide open. Boxes were all over the porch and inside the house. I quickly slid them out of the way so I could shut the door at least. I went into the living room and saw the girls sitting there, hugging their teddy bears and watching TV.

"Hi, girls," I said.

They smiled shyly, and said, "Hi," back. I looked around and didn't see any signs of Luke. Then I heard his voice. He came around the corner, calling out for me.

"Yes," I said. "I moved the boxes from the doorway so I could shut it." He asked me to follow him and I did, wanting to put my purse in my room anyway. My head was racing and I had no idea what to say. What was going on, I wondered. I went upstairs to find Luke, and saw him putting the girls' clothes away in dresser drawers in one of the rooms. My face must have shown that I had no idea what was going on.

Finally I just blurted it out. "What's going on?"

His confused look confused me even more. He asked me if I didn't remember our conversation last night, about all of us being together under one roof, and me being in his life forever. And all of my things from in the closets and drawers were thrown about. It looked like I'd been ransacked and robbed. I was sick to my stomach, almost literally.

Yes, I remembered, but to me that didn't equate to what I saw happening at that moment. There was nothing finalized in our conversation that meant "come move right in tonight!" He apparently made this decision on his own. Then he dismissed me to go tidy up and help him organize all these things. He needed me by his side.

I said, "Luke, first things first, this is going to take time. Did the girls have dinner?" Why that was all I could ask is beyond me. Maybe I was in shock.

He just said no. I thought about Matthew and what he would say, and I thought about me too, wondering how I'd managed to allow this to happen. In my home—my sanctuary—I suddenly felt like I didn't have any control.

I had to get focused. I took the girls upstairs and helped them get comfortable into their nightclothes. I asked them what they would like for dinner.

The girls answered, "Chicken fingers, French fries, and pasta with to-mato sauce." *That's not a big request, I can bread the chicken, and make some fries with the few potatoes I have, and burgers for Luke and myself.*

I began to make dinner. He never did get to the store, but who would have time doing all this? Now I wish I'd worked late. He came down with a bottle of wine in his hand. He uncorked it, poured a glass for him, and then one for me.

Luke said he was going to take a shower, and that was it, he left the room, which left me with a very unsettled feeling. The girls wanted to watch TV and sat on the couch as we flipped through the channels and came across Dora, and they screamed for joy. I went upstairs and brought down their teddy bears. I went into the kitchen and continued to cook. Luke finally returned. We were all ready to eat and had been waiting for him. Table was set. I poured the girls a glass of milk. Luke came into the kitchen and poured a glass of wine, and walked out of the room.

"Luke! Aren't you going to eat with us?" I asked. Then I noticed his face. He was upset, but he turned around and walked back and sat down. Then he grabbed my hand and squeezed it, so hard that my fingers stuck together. It hurt a great deal. But I didn't want to startle the girls by letting them know that I was being hurt. He proceeded to comment that he would have asked for a child's meal if he wanted one. Afterward, he released his grip.

I lost my appetite and massaged my hand, which hurt so badly, and pretended nothing was wrong. I pushed my plate forward with disbelief. I helped the girls cut their chicken so they could finish their dinner and made it fun for them.

The end of dinner couldn't come fast enough. I didn't even know what I would say to Luke if I could speak freely. I took the girls upstairs to brush their teeth and wash their hands. I went downstairs to get their blankets and bears. He was just sitting on the couch looking at Facebook from his phone.

"Are you going to come and kiss the girls good night?" I asked. He just got up and didn't say a word to me.

After they were tucked in, I said good night to the girls. They said good night in their soft voices. I went downstairs to clean everything up from the dinner. I had such a lump in my throat from trying to contain and hold back my emotions. I wanted to scream. I wanted to cry. But mostly, I didn't want him living here.

I noticed my plate of food was missing and thought that he must have been hungry and ate it. It didn't matter, my appetite was long gone. I took a sip of my wine and went about the tasks at hand. I opened up the cupboard where the garbage is and took it out to put the last bit of scraps into it. The bag was full and, I decided to take it out plus I could use some fresh air to clear my thoughts.

I walked past Luke in the living room and opened the front door. He didn't even acknowledge me at all. I was very confused as if I was his personal maid. I closed the door behind me and as I was walking down the front steps I stopped and noticed to my left there was food on the ground. This was odd. I took a closer look and it was my dinner. I couldn't believe it. Luke threw my food on the front lawn. Why would he do that? What had I done to deserve this?

I'm not sure what is going on or where he is mentally. It was unsettling and frayed my nerves a bit further than they already were. I didn't know how to handle this. After I threw the garbage out and went back inside, I thought the best thing to do was not say anything at all. As if I never saw it. I believe he wanted an argument and I wasn't going to give him the satisfaction. I just let him stew over it.

I came into the house. Luke didn't say a word to me and he took a deep breath. I said, "Luke." He looked up at me as if he was ready to do battle. "I'm tired. It's late and I'm going to bed. Why don't you come in and get some rest?" He wasn't expecting that. He cleared his throat and said he would be there in a few minutes.

I smelled like a deep fryer. I couldn't wait to get out of these clothes. I changed, washed my face, brushed my teeth, and got ready to slide into bed. No alarm, because I didn't have to work tomorrow.

But what about the kids? What time did they get up? This was an unfamiliar environment for them. Would they want me to help them? He didn't mention anything about their schedules.

When Luke came into the room I felt him pull back the covers and slide in. He pecked me on the cheek and whispered a good night to me. I didn't reply. I've never known how to address anything that might escalate into something else, and Luke gave me that unsteady feeling about approaching him with anything "sensitive" in nature. So I closed my eyes, and prayed for guidance and peace. Soon enough I was fast asleep.

CHAPTER THIRTEEN

I woke up early in the morning, the bright light beaming down on my eyes. It felt so warm. Luke was still sleeping and I reached over for my phone. It was only six o'clock. I should have gone back to sleep, but thinking of the kids—not to mention everything else—made me wake up quickly. I went to the bathroom, splashed water on my face, pulled back my hair in a ponytail.

I made my way to the kitchen as I thought about what I would feed everyone for breakfast. I only had Frosted Flakes and some hot apple cinnamon cereal. That wasn't much variety, and did small kids even like that? It had been a long time since Matthew was as young as the girls.

My thoughts couldn't avoid thinking about what had happened yesterday. It was overwhelming. I wasn't expecting everything I walked into last night and keeping myself together about it might be a struggle. What would the day bring? I started a pot of coffee.

As I was taking two cups out of the cupboard, I looked down and saw the littlest girl, Alicia, looking up at me. I jumped with a gasp. She had startled me, but my reaction made her laugh. I laughed too.

"Good morning, Alicia," I said. Then she started to cry and pointed to her bottom. "It's okay. Let's go get you cleaned up, okay?"

She nodded her head. I ran the bathwater just right. I went to my bathroom and got some bath soap; it made plenty of bubbles. I didn't have any toys for her. I hadn't had small children in the house since Matthew was little. I remembered Matthew's rubber ducky in his room. It didn't even squeak anymore and the memories it brought out were nice. It was nice seeing a little girl enjoy it. And she was excited to have it. She was very cute.

I stepped out of the bathroom and saw the oldest girl, Victoria, making her way toward the kitchen. We said good morning and thankfully she was happy with the cereal I had. I got that ready, gave her a teaspoon, and went back into the bathroom to make sure Alicia was okay. She was having fun, but I had to get her out and ready for the day. I unplugged the drain, dried her off, and helped the girls get dressed. I brushed their hair and put them both in pigtails. Alicia had a small bowl of cereal; she is not a big eater.

By that time Luke was up, ready to start his day and enjoy some coffee. He didn't even say good morning. He went his way to get ready, leaving me to make sure the girls were ready for school.

I remembered their backpacks. I said, "Luke wait!" I ran upstairs to get them. I didn't mind, because honestly, I needed some alone time to process this abrupt and unexpected shift in my life, in my home.

He gave me a kiss on the lips and thanked me for all I was doing. "Have a good day girls!"

My nurturing side came out—I want everyone else to be all right and loved. "Since I'm not working today, I'll do what I can to put things in order for you."

He smiled. He didn't know what he'd do without me. Then the "I love you" came as he walked out the door and shut it behind him.

I looked around at the physical evidence of my sudden life change. It had literally happened overnight. We'd never sat down to have a heart to heart about what I needed to address: the way he treated me. And while he said he wanted us to be under one roof, he never allowed me to explain. And no, I wasn't that drunk that I'd forgotten. He'd just assumed that it would be all right. And why wouldn't he, I let him.

Negative thoughts flooded my mind. I really disliked the moods he sprung on me out of the blue. *Maybe he's just going through an*

*emotional change as he tries to figure out how he is going to manage
with the girls.*

It went on and on. Sick of the thoughts, I went to take a shower.
My bathroom was a mess and it looked like a bomb went off in my
entire place. So much for a day off, because what I had to do would take
up the entire day, and that might not even be enough time. I dried off,
put on some comfy clothes, brushed my hair back into a ponytail,
poured a cup of coffee, and sat for a minute. It was so good.

Everything happened so fast. I needed to catch my bearings. *Not
sure where to start, maybe with the girls' room. They should feel good
and secure, all this change wasn't their fault.*

Then Feathers squawked, reminding me that he needed attention
as well. I'd never introduced him to the girls the night before and had
been too scattered with the madness to even consider it. I forgot he was
in the house.

I poured myself another cup of coffee. I needed that additional
pick-me-up. Can't believe I'm saying that, but that's what it is right
now. I brought my cup of coffee with me.

I looked around. It's not that bad. I picked all my things off the floor
and put them on the bed in my son's room. I went back upstairs to see if
I left anything behind. Just a couple pairs of shoes; brought them down
with me. I began hanging my things in his closet. It took some time to
do this. I lined my shoes on the bottom neatly. I went back upstairs and
drank the rest of my coffee, which was cold, but I was thirsty.

I fixed Victoria's bed and changed Alicia's sheets and pillowcases, and
allowed the bed to air dry, then put everything in the wash. I sprinkled
some baby power on the mattress to soak up where it was wet. *I will have
to put plastic down when she sleeps until she gets used to the house.* I
folded the remaining clothes and put them away in the drawers. I put fresh
towels in the bathroom so the girls could wipe their hands, set up their
toothpaste and toothbrushes. I know it's not comfortable to live out of a
bag. I vacuumed and now the room looked great. I took my cup from the
dresser. Brought down the vacuum, and the next stop... my bedroom.

I started by fixing the bed. Straightening out the bathroom, there
were boxes of Luke's clothes and daily things he uses for the bathroom.

I put them in the drawer under the sink. I wasn't using that drawer for anything.

I have two dressers in my room. One tall dresser with five drawers and one regular size dresser with six drawers. I emptied the tall dresser and put all of Luke's clothes in there. His undergarments, socks, pajamas, and t-shirts. I put the rest of his clothes on hangers and hung them in the closet. I was getting rid of one box at a time.

There were four boxes in the kitchen. I opened and glanced to see what was in them. There were photos and things the children made. I put those boxes in my son's room in the corner, so they wouldn't be bothered.

There were three boxes in the living room. One very big box when I opened it. It was stuffed with big coats, heavy sweaters, and light jackets. I couldn't lift the box. I took the items out and hung them in the hall closet to the point of being stuffed. I couldn't hang anything else in there.

Finally, I was done, and put the last two small boxes in the back of my—make that our—closet. I didn't even bother to open them up. All I wanted to do was crush down the boxes, get them into the dumpster, and then find something to eat.

I wished he hadn't been so rude to toss my hamburger out last night, because I would have loved it. I was starving. Instead, I found enough lunch meat to enjoy a sandwich. Ham and cheese with lettuce, tomato, and mayo. I had one small bag of Lays potato chips left. I ate so fast; this was the only thing I'd eaten all day.

After I was done, I began to clean the kitchen, just finally getting to the breakfast bowls. When I was done I was in need of another shower. I couldn't wait. I wanted to freshen up and look good for when Luke and the girls returned. Plus, it being hot outside, I decided to turn up the AC a bit more so it would be calming and inviting and perfect when they got home.

CHAPTER FOURTEEN

Luke walked in the door. It was strange to not hear a knock and hear a key opening it instead. He turned around the corner and offered a casual, exhausted sounding hi.

"Hi, where are the girls?" I asked.

He said they were with their mother and then he took his shoes off, tossed them, walked toward me, and gave me a soft kiss on the lips. Only after that did he seem to notice the big difference in my place, and commented that it looked great.

"It took all day, but I did it. I put the boxes with your photos and personal things in Matthew's room. No one will bother them there."

He thanked me again and went upstairs, commenting on how great the girls' room looked too. As for me, it was time to shift the laundry. It was strange but it made me happy—my washer and dryer, that is. They were tucked away in the closet of the kitchen, hidden from sight and highly organized. It felt so good to be organized.

Then he was back, wine in hand. I was beginning to think that a wine bottle was permanently attached to him. He commented that I was going to love the wine he'd gotten, it was his favorite. I picked it up and the label read: Ruffino.

"Sounds great," I said. Then he took it from there and asked me to come sit with him in the living room so we could relax and enjoy some quiet time. And we did, and it was great, until we each had a few glasses of the definitely delicious Ruffino.

He started to get loud. Talking about his ex-wife not knowing how to take care of the kids. How she took advantage of him. The way she was living for free.

"You have the kids don't you, so we can start fresh, right?" I thought it was a kind thing to say. *It's what he's been saying all along. Luke doesn't like to tell me what is really going on. Just like he never told me he was moving in with the kids without discussing it with me thoroughly. He took it upon himself that I would be ok with it. Maybe I should stop being such a pushover and stand up for myself for once.*

He started yelling, cursing me out, so irate. I felt my heart shrivel, and my soul cower at his wrath.

"What the fuck do you know? You're a fucking bitch that only thinks about herself, get away from me, and go to your room. You're a stupid bitch!" Luke slurred out.

And I listened. I took my glass of wine and went to my room. I dimmed the lights and sat in silence, justifying him again. *He's having a hard time with their breakup. It's not me. This is his problem and I shouldn't let this consume all my energy.*

I finished my wine, put the glass on the nightstand, and went to brush my teeth. It was only eight. I wasn't tired, but I wasn't looking for a reason to fight, either, so I changed and went to bed, setting my alarm for the morning. Luke never came to bed. He was gone when I got up.

Glad for a distraction, I got ready for work. In the car, all his cruelty relived itself, yet again, through my thoughts repeating his spiteful words. He was so mean to me. My life was filled with craziness now. I was doing the best I could do, but it was not good enough.

Then his apologies that didn't match his actions followed. Things will be different, you will see, give me a second chance please. Those words made me feel on top of the world, filled with hope and promise that I might find love again. I felt special and when he was gentle, there was nothing more beautiful. I couldn't believe the rollercoaster ride I was on, filled with so many highs, lows, and emotions.

Maybe his future ex was giving Luke a hard time? As the saying goes, you lash out to the ones you love most. That thought startled me, and I realized that I did not even know what I was thinking. All I was doing was making every excuse possible for him treating me badly. *Don't think about it anymore*, I thought. I was at work, time to start the day.

Pierre walked right over and said there was only a single luncheon scheduled for the day. Three waiters could go home.

"I'll go," I volunteered. It would be nice if Pierre called us to give us this option over the phone. It takes time to drive here. I said, "Good-bye and I'll see you tomorrow."

I punched out and glanced at my phone. There was no call from Luke yet. I guess he needed time to sort things out. *I will just pray that this shall pass, and things will get better.*

I noticed that Chef wasn't there, and it disappointed me a bit, but then I remembered that he'd given me those pastries the day of the banquet. I'd forgotten all about them. I left them in my car due to all the commotion. I will throw them out when I get home. Then I thought of what I should do...grocery shop, keep cleaning, talk with Luke. Every option was running through me as if I had so many choices, but none made sense. Peace was what I was looking for. So I went home.

My drive was a silent one, lost in thoughts and unsure of what to do. Finally I got there and when I glanced at my front door, I decided to go walk over to the fountain instead and sit there for a bit. I always found peace near the water. The mist was lightly dusting my face. It felt so good and pure. I did not want to enter my own home.

I looked up toward the sky and asked the good Lord for direction. This was truly a mistake, allowing Luke in my life. That was what I thought. Sighing and uncertain of how to correct such a huge error, I got up and went back to my car to get the container the chef gave me. I almost forgot to throw it out again. The cookies were all molded to-gether from the heat. I walked over to the dumpster and threw it out, then went into the house.

Suddenly the cleaning that I didn't want to do seemed like a good way to spend some time, and hopefully offer another distraction. I put a pot of coffee on and took the laundry out of the dryer to place it on my bed. Afterward, I picked up where I'd left off.

My groove had been found, as I enjoyed the coffee and bringing order back to my small, lovely home. But I was starting to get hungry and my options were limited. After a debate and hoping my fridge would magically produce something different for food options, I went with two soft boiled eggs, some toast with butter, and apricot preserves. Not gourmet, but good.

Satisfied enough that my stomach stopped growling, I went to my bathroom to brush my teeth, finished a few more projects, and decided to indulge in a nap. It was four thirty in the afternoon. I closed the blinds and turned down the air conditioner.

Only then did I really consider that Luke hadn't contacted me all day, but I was tired enough that I must have dozed off. I was startled awake with a light tap at the bedroom door.

"Hi Amilia," Luke said.

"Luke, hi," I didn't move much from where I was sleeping. I noticed he had flowers in his hands, but he was holding them behind his back.

Another compliment on my domestic skills came from him. "This house looks amazing," Luke said. Then a comment about how I was supposed to work that day. Why wasn't I there?

For some reason I felt the need to explain. "There was a mistake in the schedule. The party is next week, not today. I needed a little fresh-me-up so I came in to lay down for a bit," I said.

He sat down on the bed. I sat up, and Luke pulled me toward him, pressing my head to his chest. He explained once again how sorry he was and how he didn't know what comes over him at times. He just got so wrapped up in anger that he lost control. Then he showed me the flowers, his way of saying, "I'm sorry." It's pretty sad when you know why you're getting flowers as a gift.

"They're beautiful," I said. That was my answer. Not as excited as I used to be receiving them.

Luke had planned to make me dinner. He'd bought steak, potatoes, asparagus, mushrooms, and onions. My mouth salivated. I hadn't
had a great dinner for such a long time, it seemed; aside from what Chef
made at work, of course.

We went into the kitchen, and I put the last flowers he'd gotten me
in the garbage, as they were now dead, and replaced them with the
fresh ones. This was a horribly sad visual to see from something so
beautiful. One apology from hurt, to another one from painful tears.

Instead of just letting him do it all like he said he would, I had to
offer. "What can I help with?" I asked. He said I could help with setting
the table.

As I did I smiled, truly feeling cared for and appreciated for the
kind gesture. "This really is a wonderful surprise," I had to say.

I flipped through the stations on the TV and found a soft jazz station. Then I opened the wine per Luke's request and poured us each
a glass. When I handed Luke his glass he was grinning widely, suggest-
ing that I needn't fear pouring more wine in his glass. I did it, but I
didn't want to. Partly for selfish reasons—dinner smelled great and I
was so hungry for it.

Luke opened the oven to check on the potatoes and a strange
thought crossed my mind. *I love my steak medium-rare, but I wasn't
about to say that in case it led to another fight.* It would be fine the way
it was, even if it was still mooing, or more like steak jerky. Then we
toasted, "To a new beginning." May LOVE be with us forever. Our
glasses clanked and I smiled, thanking him again.

I hate these feelings of uncertainty, I thought. Then I said a quick
prayer. I was praying often these days. Then it was small talk, cautious
and light, nothing that could possibly turn serious. My efforts did not
quite work out.

"So, how was your day?" I learned quickly. Work was tough. Luke
had a lot on his mind; what happened between us, the kids, and his
divorce. There was just too much running through his mind that day.
Then he asked about me.

"The same with me, minus the divorce. I'm trying to understand
as much as I can," I said.

He didn't acknowledge that, and commented that dinner was ready. That was a good thing, right? He filled up our plates and we sat down. It was picture perfect.

Luke asked how my steak was and I said, "Great, thank you." Truthfully, it was too well done, but he wouldn't have known, because he hadn't asked how I'd like it done. Not unusual at this point. Nothing seems to be going right. Then he got up to get the wine. Another glass for him, filled up to the rim.

"So, you said the kids will be here tomorrow. We should talk about their schedule," I said.

That didn't appeal to him, as he wanted it to be just "the two of us" that night, no talk of kids and other things. It would normally have sounded nice, but I needed to understand what was going on, especially when kids were involved.

He got up and walked over to the TV, changing the channel to an oldies station. Then he walked back into the kitchen, took my hand, pulled me out of my seat, and we began dancing. Luke held me so tight, it was so romantic. I loved every minute of it. Even though my memory of all the events that took place reminded me often this was far from a dream. This was the kind of moment I dreamt of. I was trying so hard to make this work. We didn't speak much at all, just enjoyed each other's company. Then we sat down and continued to eat the rest of our meal; more food, and much more wine.

I was getting lightheaded, but wow we were having fun. Dancing and laughing like two kids. Kissing, touching, and holding hands like it was our first time. I just wanted him to love me endlessly.

He would grab the back of my hair and kiss me passionately. We were so hot and steamy; my body felt hot next to his even with both air conditioners going.

Then his phone started to vibrate on the table—loudly. It changed in an instant. He picked up the phone and looked at it and answered it with an angry voice.

Even if he didn't love her, the way he talked chilled me to the bone. She wanted the girls to stay another night so she could take them to the fair. He shouted at her, telling her to fuck off, no way. She had to stick to the agreement. She could go fuck herself. It went on and on. Then he hung up, despite her still talking on the other end.

I didn't know what to do, but I knew that the magic of the night was likely lost.

"Are you all right?" I asked softly. I wanted to show I cared, but could any words or gestures really do that? Plus, he'd had a few too many drinks in him.

He told me to shut up and not ask anything about that bitch. Then he walked into the living room and sat on the couch. I changed the channel of the TV, turned up the lights in the kitchen, and blew out the candles. I began to clean our plates and put things away in silence.

Luke was in a complete rage. I was tipsy, and I didn't want to say anything to spark the fire he had going already. He was like a time bomb, ready to explode.

He was obviously still hurt over the breakup. I thought, *This is too early for us to be a couple. I don't think this is the time.* As I was washing the dishes, Luke came in and poured another glass of wine. I could feel the tension when he came into kitchen and his brooding silence scared me. It was terribly uncomfortable. But I remained quiet.

He went back to the couch and began texting. I had no idea what to do so I put the wash into the dryer. Then I crept to my room to change into my pajamas.

As I got ready for bed I could hear Luke's voice. He was practically shouting. It was at me, telling me to come and sit by him. I did, but we didn't speak. To stay busy, I started switching the channels to see what was on the TV. He looked over at me and asked how I'd liked dinner. I could barely understand him through his slurred words.

"It was wonderful, thank you again," I said in sheepish way.

I don't think he realized how many times he asked me that same question, and I gave him the same answer. Then he'd say I should go get some more wine, but I didn't want anymore. I was just coming down from being dizzy and having my wits about me which seemed vitally important at that moment. Eventually, I picked up my wine glass from the kitchen counter and brought it over so he'd stop asking.

Luke was so angry about what had transpired in his life. He couldn't get over it and I saw that so clearly during those times when the wine dropped his defenses and let the anger pour out. Luke got up and couldn't even keep his balance. I hardly understood anything he was saying.

Finally he said he was tired and going to sleep. I told him that I'd be there in a bit, I had a few things to clean up. I knew he wasn't tired, he was drunk, and it was my greatest hope that he'd be sound asleep by the time I got into that bed. I set my alarm, I said good night. With that being said, I could feel somewhat normal. It didn't matter if he heard me or not. This was for my own sanity.

CHAPTER FIFTEEN

I woke to the alarm, my room dark from the blinds being closed tightly. There were no signs of Luke, and I laid there for a bit, stretching and thinking about everything.

Alas, it was time to get up. The house was so quiet, and I assumed Luke must have snuck away. I opened the blinds, and it was another glorious day. I went to the bathroom, brushed my teeth, splashed cool water on my face. Luke must have put the coffee on, because the inviting scent of it filled my nose as I made my way to the kitchen.

Before I got to the kitchen I heard, "Good morning, Amilia," come from the living room. I looked over and saw Luke there.

"Good morning, you're up early," I commented. I noticed he was browsing on his phone—again. He nodded. "Thanks for starting the coffee," I added. He nodded again.

There wasn't much conversation to be had so I went to give Feathers some fresh water, and then called out in a loud voice about how nice the day seemed like it was going to be. All he mentioned was that he guessed it would be.

What could I say? He was like a negative energy battling the sunshine, and my hopes for a nice day. It seemed necessary to try and engage him though, so I asked if he wanted to join me on the porch for coffee. He chose to stay in the living room and I sensed it right then and there—he was still sore about last night. I struggled against my instincts, just wanting things to feel good—even though I didn't do anything. Really!

So I skipped the beautiful morning weather and brought coffee to the living room to sit by Luke, who stayed on his phone and watched the news, which he turned on when I went in there.

One cup down in relative silence. I filled the second cup and went to get ready for the day. When I came back Luke looked at me and it was almost like the first time we'd seen each other, and he told me I looked beautiful. His strong and sexy voice made me blush.

"Thank you," I said. Then there was silence and the moment was gone. He turned back to what he was doing and I went and grabbed my forgotten coffee cup.

I wanted more. I couldn't stand it. What was going on? I had to clear my head and find out. I grabbed my keys and went up to Luke, giving him a kiss, and bidding him farewell. I wasn't sure if he really listened because he didn't respond. Then I walked out the door. It was time for me to go to work.

My thoughts were flooded. I had to pay the bills, and I was nervous to evaluate everything. I'd taken more days off than I usually would. That had to stop. Luke wasn't responsible for me paying the bills, I was. And something inside of me cautioned me to be attentive to this. I'd even put my bill folder in the trunk of my car, not wanting my new roommate to look at them. I felt very private about it all.

Not being used to having someone else in the house was tough. It would take me time to trust him. It likely would not have been an issue if he wasn't so volatile in his emotions. He was up and down constantly, not allowing me to truly relax. If there is one thing you should be able to do in your own home, it's relax and have peace.

✳✳✳

I walked into work, ready to start the day again. I smiled at Chef, feeling excited about the warm coffee and toasted bagel that awaited me. I'm not sure what my expression was but Chef took note of it, asking if I was okay, or if something was wrong with Matthew.

"He's great, everything's good," I said.

Chef commented on how he hadn't seen me smile in a long time, mentioning he was here for me if I needed him. It was a good offer, but my situation with Luke wasn't one that I could share. It startled me that it showed in my facial expressions too.

My phone was still in my pocket and it buzzed.

"Luke, hi," I said, forcing a cheery voice. It was in vain, because I got reprimanded. What was wrong with me? Why didn't I call when I got to work so he knew I was all right? How come I never answer my phone? "When I'm at work, I can't," I emphatically said.

Wrong response, because I had. He sounded crazed and eventually hung up, leaving me feeling lousy and distracted at just the wrong time. When you are a waitress you must have your head in the game; your tips depended on it, if anything.

I slipped away, wanting to regain my composure. I went to the front desk for my assignment, and was glad Pierre was late. He had the ability to read me quite well, and while it normally didn't matter, suddenly it did.

But my assignment would keep me busy. A party of thirty people, and I had a lot of work to do quickly. I got to work—preparing the settings, baskets of bread, polishing glassware, and all the other details.

Jasper came in and said, "Good morning." I told him to grab the bagel and cream cheese I put aside for him before he jumped in, we are going to be very busy with this party. He thanked me.

I looked to see if the birthday cake for the event had been delivered. Deep in thought, I didn't even realize Pierre had walked in the room until he said hi.

I smiled and greeted him; he thanked me for not waiting for him and jumping in. This made me feel secure here; I was getting nervous leaving early this past week. Pierre left the room, but moments later returned and asked me to display the cake on a small table in the room. This was what the host wanted, he apologized for not having it on the assignment sheet. I told him not to worry.

He gave me the rest of the details for the event, and then I carried on with my day. And it was quick and busy, which was good. The host was so happy. I took a step back and watched the love she has. It gets so tiring not knowing how to feel. I would love to feel like that.

I noticed Mandy come into the room, and she approached me with a large smile of happiness, like a bouquet of flowers. She asked me quietly if I had a moment.

"Sure what's going on?"

"Come follow me to the front desk."

"What is it?"

Mandy told me to walk over with her to the front desk, and she would show me. I didn't know what to expect.

Mandy picked up a long white box from the desk and handed it to me. I opened it up. There were a dozen dark red roses with baby's breath—so beautiful—as well as a stuffed animal, a soft beige puppy with floppy ears, a small tail, and a black little nose. Such sweetness in a bag.

Mandy commented, "Someone really loves you."

I smiled ever so slightly. "Mandy can I leave this here with you until I finish work?"

"Yes! I don't mind at all."

"Thank you," I said.

Mandy was right. It should be exciting to get flowers, but the reasons behind it were growing old. I didn't even get a chance to walk away from the desk when my phone started to vibrate in my pocket. I looked to see who it was, and it was Luke. I walked quickly to the kitchen, and answered. His voice radiated right through me, it was so deep. I cleared my throat.

"Baby!" he began.

"Hello Luke, thank you for the beautiful flowers and the cute puppy."

"You're welcome. What time are you getting out tonight?" he asked.

"About four thirty, I do not have to work dinner tonight," I said.

Luke responded, "I have a lot of things to attend to, and I won't be home until late."

"That's ok Luke, I will see you later. I have to get back to work."

Luke seemed in better spirits than this morning, but I didn't care what he had to do, nor did I ask. He returned with, "Bye baby," and hung up.

I don't have the excitement in my heart. I hear his voice, and I fight the hurtful words.

By the end of the event, the host pulled me aside and gave me an extra tip of one hundred valuable, much needed dollars. She was so grateful for the service she received. I thanked her graciously. Jasper and I cleaned up fairly quickly. Pierre came in and thanked us for a job well done. We thanked him as well.

As Jasper and I walked through the kitchen to put the rest of things away, Chef called us over. He saved a plate of food for the both of us. We thanked him. I was so hungry.

I asked Chef, "How did you know I was hungry?"

Chef grinned and replied, "I just do," as he walked away.

"Jasper this turned out to be a great day," I proclaimed. Jasper was so happy I grabbed him to help me. He punched in just at the right time. I love working with him. We went in the banquet room to eat our lunch, it was delicious. We finished our entire plates. I was famished. I felt like a new person after I ate. We put our dishes in the dish bin. The chef was gone before I could thank him again.

We punched out, and I walked to my car and took my bill folder out of the trunk, then headed back into the club for some privacy. I sat in the back of the banquet room to go over my finances. I took out my checkbook and my phone. I called my bank to find out what the balance was in my checking account with the check I received today and the extra hundred dollars.

I was able to make all the important payments. It didn't leave me much room to grocery shop. I had to keep what was left for gas until my next paycheck. I could get a few things, but just essentials. This is what it's going to have to be. I can't take this kind of time off. It's not practical.

I put my bills back in my folder. I felt better knowing that the bills were paid. I went to my locker and took my purse. I was halfway to the car when I realized I forgot the flowers and the puppy at the front desk. I called the club. Mandy answered the phone.

"It's Amilia! I left the building, but I'm in the parking lot. I want to drive up to the front entrance and get the flowers, would it be possible you can meet me at the front door? I will make it quick."

Mandy told me not to worry and that she would be out front.

"I will be right there. Thank you." I drove the car to the entrance and Mandy was waiting there for me. She opened the back door and put the box and puppy in the back seat.

"Thank you Mandy, I will see you tomorrow."

"Have a good night."

Driving home I realized that I had no idea what Luke was up to, which wasn't unusual. Were the kids going to be there? Was he going to be there? He loved the perks of living together, but lacked the courtesy to share his plans. Kind of nervy when he was so worried about me calling him when I got to work. I'd been getting there just fine for years, without having to alert anyone. I guessed he was just protective. But it didn't seem sweet so much as…well, maybe possessive.

CHAPTER SIXTEEN

I was home alone and it felt relaxing and wonderful. I fed Feathers, tended to a few things, showered and prettied myself up a bit for when Luke got home. Doing that was always so important to me now. I felt less comfortable in my natural skin. Then to my great delight I received a text from Matthew.

Matthew: Mom, hi, how are you?

Me: I'm all right. I hope you and Rachel are doing well. Send her my regards.

Matthew: Mom, are you sure everything is all right?

Me: Yes, I'm fine, really. How about I call tomorrow?

Matthew: That'd be great. Love you too.

His call got me thinking. I hadn't spoken to my friends since Luke came into my life. I hadn't seen them or spent any time with them in over two weeks and I missed them greatly—the camaraderie and laughter when we were together. I needed to call them, too. Maybe it would reignite the spark that was clearly missing.

I looked up at the time, seven thirty already, and still no message from Luke. There was a half of bottle of red wine on the counter and I decided to have a small glass, retire to the living room, and kick back with some TV and wait until he showed up...whenever that would be.

My chilling time barely started when I jumped, startled by the front door swinging open and all the voices coming through. It was Luke, and the kids. I turned around and smiled.

"Hi." I got up and went to give him a kiss on the lips and he turned his head so I got his cheek. No hello was offered, just the declaration that the kids would be staying over.

"Okay, great. Did you want me to order some pizza for the girls? Did you have dinner?" He informed me that they'd eaten and still refused to look at me.

I was uncomfortable and chose the girls for a reason to escape. "I'm going to take the girls upstairs to change and brush their teeth," I said.

His fangs came out, accusing me of being drunk and declaring that I should keep my drunk ass self away from them. I was heartbroken and shocked. I'd had a few sips of wine, nothing more. I was fine. Plus, who was he to talk about being drunk? That was his pattern, not mine.

Then he stormed upstairs, leaving my swirling thoughts trying to justify him—again. It must have been something else with the ex-wife. I kept my distance, but couldn't calm down. And he didn't either. After an hour he stormed back downstairs, and said that if he wanted a drunk, he'd be with a drunk.

"What's the matter with you?" I asked, shocked and hurt.

"I worked all day, anticipated seeing you. You are acting crazy," Luke said.

His ability to easily cast cruel words reared its ugly head. I was told to leave him alone, that I disgusted him. Then he went to the kitchen to pour a glass of wine and sat down right next to me, pulling out his phone again to go through it.

My body ached from the intense emotions I was feeling. I needed someone to sound off about this with. I was desperate. I left and went to my room and changed into my nightclothes, brushed my teeth, turned off the light, and propped my pillows up so I could text my friend Bianca.

It wasn't easy, but I explained what was going on. It was tamer sounding than my emotions, but as close as I'd come to confessing my confused state of mind and heart.

Me: He treats me so poorly. I feel like I'm trapped, and have no way out. I'm always walking on eggshells. There is no decent conversation, everything's cursing and yelling about his ex...

I kept going until I froze, hearing Luke walking around. Was he coming to the bedroom? My stomach was in knots.

I quickly shoved my phone under the covers and sat there silent, breathing as lightly as I could. Then I heard a wine cork pop, and him walking again, but not up the stairs. It was safe, so I continued to text.

Bianca responded not with immediate words of comfort, but with the suggestion that we needed to talk. It was too hard to share what she had to say over a text. Hard for her, but it had been so much easier for me. I didn't know if I could bear to hear my voice repeat the things I'd texted.

It was time for sleep. I set my alarm, removed the pillow that had me propped up, and set my phone on the nightstand. I heard Luke doing something. I couldn't make out the sound. My eyes were getting heavy, then I drifted off to sleep.

I awoke to a raging monster, his finger tapping my forehead and his other hand nudging my arm aggressively. At first it felt like a bad dream...hard to process. His voice getting louder and louder. Then the tirade of angry insults flowed, starting with a command to get the fuck up. When I opened my eyes Luke was staring at me and yelling, holding my cellphone.

"What's going on, why are you yelling?" I asked. I had a suspicion, but I needed to buy time. My head was foggy from sleep, and my fear was skyrocketing. He demanded to know why I was texting people about us.

"It's not everyone. I needed someone to talk with and express what I was feeling. She's my best friend," I told him. My confession added fuel to the fire. Suddenly I became the fucking bitch slut who was talking shit behind his back. I brought up that he'd been drinking. I shouldn't have, but I did, and as unreasonable as he was, he latched on to those words. He threw the phone at me with all his might; it hit me right in the middle of my forehead.

"Stop!" I begged. I reached up and put my hand on my head to protect me.

He told me he was sleeping with the kids and that I should stay the fuck away from him. Then he slammed the door and the pain set in. Physical and emotional pain that wouldn't allow me to maintain control of myself. I began crying, and I cried hard. I just stared up to the good Lord and begged through my sobs.

"Please, help me, I do not deserve this treatment. I do the best I can. Please help me, give me strength."

I began crying harder and snuck to the bathroom so I could muffle the sound from Luke. I didn't want to give him the satisfaction of knowing how badly he'd hurt me. It took so long to calm down and I clenched my fists and pounded on my legs, begging the Lord for some sort of comfort in that time. I was breaking down, and there were no signs of rebounding that I could sense.

"Lord please, are you listening to me?" I got up and splashed some cold water on my face, went to the hall closet, and took out two Tylenol to relieve me from the pain I endured. Fearful to leave my room, but in need of a glass, I snuck to the kitchen for some water. I tried not to make any noise to trigger another fight. On the counter were two large empty bottles of wine. This was the source of all the midnight madness. It wasn't worth the fight. Back in my room I looked at my phone, fearful it might be broken. It wasn't, and the alarm was on.

It was hard to sleep. My head was in pain, my nerves were frayed, and I was so confused. At four thirty in the morning, Luke sent a text; it was a simple "good night." I didn't reply. It didn't seem like a good idea. Plus, I suspected he might not even remember what he'd done to me in the morning.

***

My alarm felt harsh that morning. I felt I slept a minute, and the job I loved was suddenly one I didn't want to go to, but I had to. I made my way to the kitchen and put a pot of coffee on. I noticed the kitchen was clean and saw that Luke's car was gone, too. I didn't even care where he went. I was alone, which was a relief in a way, but the emotional scarring of feeling alone when I was in a relationship weighed heavily on me.

I hoped a shower would help my mind, as much as it would be a relief for my bruised head. The phone left a knot with a black and blue mark in the center of my forehead. There was no easy explanation for that.

"This isn't right," I whispered. *But what are you going to do about it?*

I sighed and gently wrapped my towel on my head and put my bathrobe on. Then I walked out into the bedroom and screamed. There was Luke sitting on my bed, looking at me, his eyes wide. He got up and walked toward me and I flinched. He grabbed me and held me so tightly, repeating, "I'm sorry, I'm sorry Amilia." His voice was a whisper. The tears began again and I didn't know how to respond. I cried so hard, as if I turned on the faucet. Should I be cautious for my own safety, or bold even if it put me at risk?

"Why do you treat me this way?" That's what I got out.

He hushed me and apologized again, not letting go and whispering every word he said. His last words were that he had to go to work and he'd call later. He separated from me and said he loved me, and then left. I was so pained I didn't know how to respond, but an "okay" was the only thing I could get out.

I went back to the bathroom, splashed more cool water on my face, and wiped my tears. I took a deep breath and began to get ready for work. I started to feel very lightheaded. I sat down on the bed for a minute. I needed to stay calm, and shake off this feeling.

I'm so tired.

CHAPTER SEVENTEEN

I did the best I could to cover up the bruises, but looking into the mirror was painful. I could hardly look at myself. All I could do was hope that I'd be able to shake it off and forget what happened as my day grew busier. A tall order, but a dream I had nonetheless.

Once in the car and on my way to work, the question I had going through my mind offered no logical answer. Why was he spying on me? I wasn't his ex-wife, whom he didn't trust. That must have been the problem. Perhaps, if I were more careful with him, he'd realize that he didn't have to worry about me like he had her. If only I'd known more about their relationship, I could have helped him overcome those insecurities. Now that I knew, I'd try. The sun was shining so bright I put down the visor, and I couldn't believe how bad I looked. *I definitely need to put more makeup on when I get to work.*

That thought of last night washed over me all the way to the parking lot of the club. I saw Chef pull in right behind me. I got out of the car.

"Good morning," I called out and waved.

He walked right toward me and I suddenly felt awkward. There was no morning greeting back.

He said, "What happened to you?"

"Oh, I tripped and fell face first into the edge of my open bedroom door." (I lied of course) My heart rate quickened, hoping I was believable and he wouldn't ask anything else. He nodded his head and paused and only then did he answer in a cautious, quiet tone.

"Okay, really what happened?" he softly asked. "You know you can always speak to me."

I wouldn't admit anything else. I just couldn't do that out loud, and I'd just spent an entire ride to work trying to justify it all.

As soon as we were inside the restaurant I punched in and we each went our own way. Not another word said for now. When I heard Pierre speaking, I noticed that he sounded very anxious. His voice was loud and he kept repeating, "Let's go. Let's go. We have a very busy day."

I walked into the dining room and he immediately paused and looked at me and said good morning, assigned me to the patio, and then immediately asked, "What happened to you?"

I gave him the lie and said I'd be fine. However, if the bruise was that noticeable I'd better pay closer attention to my makeup. I quickly went into the restroom and applied some more foundation and powder over my bruised and swollen forehead, praying it would be good enough to get me through the lunch period. *It already looks better*, I thought. I had to believe that, really.

On my way back through the dining room, Pierre came up to me and this time his voice was very quiet. He asked me if I was okay and I replied, "Yes, really!" And strangely, the only thing I could think about was how I was hungrier than usual. My mind was desperate for any thought other than one of my forehead, or even Luke.

Then the day began and with all its madness. I had no time to eat. And Chef kept asking me if he could do anything for me. I kept saying that there was nothing I needed at that moment.

Another waiter, Jason, asked me what happened to my forehead. I had to do something so people didn't keep bringing it up.

I loudly said, "I don't want to talk about it." Everyone else heard, and it worked. No one else asked me anything. But I wasn't naïve enough to believe that they weren't curious.

Finally, the busy morning was off and running and I was in a good flow, all things considered. But it was going to be a hot day, and that meant disaster. Heat meant perspiration, which meant my makeup plan was a real struggle to maintain. I did the best I could just to pat my face down but the makeup stuck to the cloth like glue and came right off.

I had a chance to sneak away into the air conditioned bar for a glass of cold water. It felt so good going down my throat, and I felt some desperately needed temporary relief. I couldn't believe people would choose outside over the bar area. Then I placed an order and heard my name. My eyes hadn't adjusted from being inside yet, but when I turned around I saw who was calling to me. It was Luke.

He waved me over and was acting casual. I honestly didn't think he got that I could not just relax and chat with him. I was busy, and I had to say that I had to get back to work, which instantly annoyed him. I could see it in his eyes and his mannerisms. I didn't want Luke upset, but I sure didn't want my boss or the patrons upset, either.

I walked away and quickly realized how far behind those few minutes put me. I began to double up orders and try to catch up. The heat made it a challenge, just as much as Luke's presence, which rattled my nerves. I wanted him to leave. Why couldn't he just understand I was working and go?

On my next trip back into the bar he was gone. I don't know what he'd expected me to do, but now my head was starting to ache badly. I was still hungry, and I was at the point of being overheated.

I had to get some Tylenol or something. I went to the kitchen and asked Chef if he had any, but he couldn't look right away so back I went into the heat of the patio and tried to focus on work. It was growing tough and I was so grateful when Jasper came out and handed me some pills. They were Advil, but I was so grateful. I thought my head was going to explode.

Finally, at half past three, I was thrilled to hear the announcement that Chef had lunch waiting for us in the kitchen. He'd made us roasted sliced chicken with rosemary potatoes and asparagus and a big bowl of mixed green salad. I took a plate and put a little bit of everything on my dish, grabbed an iced tea, and went into the banquet room, which was the coolest room in the restaurant. And I enjoyed every bite. The food made a world of difference and brought a little clarity to my muddled mind.

There was nothing I could do about how Luke felt that I'd been working and couldn't just talk. But his actions last night had made my day challenging, just as much as his showing up at the club had. I couldn't really enjoy my lunch because I had to leave enough time to reapply my makeup after I ate, and start preparing for the dinner crowd.

When I looked at myself in the mirror this next time, with a few minutes to spare, I assessed how awful I looked. I could barely manage to look at my own self in the mirror. Two thoughts came to mind. First, Luke didn't even seem fazed by it when he'd seen me. Second, I couldn't believe that no customers had said anything. I was horrified, and grateful to both.

Such relief swept over me when I found that the rest of my day would be easier. The heat had settled down. My headache was gone. It was a bit slower during the dinner crowd, and I was actually able to leave work by half past nine that night, along with a wonderful meal from Chef that I'd have the next day for lunch. I packed up my dinner; he made penne pasta with broccoli garlic and oil. I packed some salad also. I was very thankful for all of this. It kept me strong and moving forward.

I had a day off, and it was a much needed day. And best yet, no more questions for a while. I punched out, went to my locker to get my things, and walked to my car. Mandy came rushing over to me in the parking lot and asked if I was all right.

"Thanks for caring, Mandy. You're really kind, and I have faith that I'll get through this."

She smiled and reminded me that I had her number and should use it. I gave her a hug, and then got into my car to go home. I knew I had many wonderful people I could turn to, which felt great, but I just couldn't make myself vulnerable to Chef, or Pierre. I just couldn't. I'm grateful to the good Lord answering my prayers to give me strength.

My drive home went quickly and all I hoped was that no one else would be there when I got there. And my wish came true. The driveway was empty, the house still. I took my food, grabbed my purse, and unlocked the door. It was very warm in the house. I switched the lights on. I heard Feathers making noise in the kitchen. I placed my purse on the table and put my food away in the fridge, turned on the air conditioners to cool down the house. I gave Feathers fresh water. He finally calmed down.

I went to my room to take my sweaty dry clothes off and take a shower, so gross. I got in and lathered up my entire body. It felt great to get that caked on makeup off. I had to apply it all day to cover my bruise, I was so uncomfortable. I brushed my teeth, put my hair up in a bun, and I rubbed lotion all over. I was so dehydrated. I even put some across my lips. I didn't have to set the alarm. I put my cell on the nightstand, pulled back the covers, but before I got in bed, I wanted to check the door and turn off the air in the kitchen.

I shut the light off in my room and closed the blinds. *I do not feel like getting up early tomorrow.* The heat really knocked the wind out of me, amongst other things. I went right under the covers and fell asleep.

CHAPTER EIGHTEEN

My eyes barely opened up as I took in the morning light in my room It was only seven. I smiled, rolled over, and went back to sleep. My body and mind still exhausted…Then I drifted back off.

Tap. Tap. Tap. Was I dreaming? My eyes flickered open again and I saw a figure standing by my doorframe, tapping on it softly.

"Good morning Luke," I murmured, still only half awake.

He walked over to me and knelt down at the edge of the bed, and then put his elbows on top of my blanket and pressed his hands together. I just looked at him, waiting to see what he was going to do next. He finally spoke, sharing with me how sorry he was. I sat up a bit and propped a pillow under my head so I could see him better, and he began to confess.

Through his words of apology it was strange how distracted the scent of his cologne made me. Something that smells so good can be so bad for you. Poison in a bottle.

Finally I asked, "How did you get a drink at the club? You're not a member."

He explained that he told the bartender he was waiting to see me and he offered it up. Luke could charm anyone, which was just as much a part of his appeal as it was what I feared most.

Then he commented on the bump and bruise on my forehead, almost like he was trying to piece together that it was a result of him. I brushed it off, making light of it and commented it was already getting better. He continued to explain his problems, and how he got wrapped up into his own matters, and didn't always understand what he was doing.

"Amilia, can you please forgive me?" he finally asked.

"I guess," I said. My voice was trembling and I could literally hear the tears dripping off my cheeks and hitting the blanket one at a time. I was hyper alert to everything. It might have been best to be quiet, but I had to say something.

"You put me on this rollercoaster ride. I don't know how to feel any more. It needs to stop please," I begged.

He said he understood. He said he'd try to make it better. He shared how life wasn't easy for him with the divorce and the kids.

"Are the girls moving in with us?" I asked. Before he could answer, I continued pouring all the thoughts that had cluttered my mind and been weighing so heavily on me. "We do not talk anymore. I never know what is happening next."

I held my breath slightly, uncertain of how he'd respond. His voice stayed calm and he said the girls would be moving in at the end of the month. He offered nothing else.

"Don't you think you need to let me in on their schedule so we can plan every day? We both work. You brought all their things here and that was it."

He promised that we'd do all of that in time. But at that moment he wanted to take me out for breakfast so we could spend some time together.

When I told him he was in luck, that it was my day off, he seemed a bit surprised so I added, "You don't communicate with me to know what I'm doing."

His response was just to wipe my tears and get ready. He'd put coffee on for us. Then he stood up and walked over to me and extended a hand to help me out of bed. Afterward he kissed my cheek, but I didn't kiss him back.

This love-hate relationship I'm in is tearing my life apart. I know in my heart this isn't what love feels like. The love I was shown in my life was gentle and kind. I can't even explain why I was happy he'd come over. So uneasy.

I couldn't relax. The next deep, calming breath I took was when he was out of my room and I was getting ready for the day.

After I showered, I took out my turquoise dress and white wedge sandals. I decided to wear my hair down that day and put on a light coat of makeup, heavier over the bruise—the bruise I wished would go away.

When I walked into the kitchen I had this pit in my stomach. Luke stopped and complimented me, then poured me a cup of coffee and asked me to sit down so he could talk to me.

I instantly became nervous and uncertain. What now? He started to lay out the plans for our day, which included a breakfast café near the beach that I loved. And he was right, I couldn't help but smile. The beach honestly was the most special place I knew, the only place other than my home that I could relax. I ignored that I could no longer really relax at home. That had changed.

"That sounds wonderful, Luke," I said. Then I was quiet, as was he. The hurtful feelings were thick in the air despite the apologies. Some things don't just fade away quickly.

Then we left and my hopes were high for a special day with Luke, a day in which we could really talk.

I had to laugh when he said that we were going to be using his work truck that day; that the SUV was getting serviced. I looked at it, and it was huge. A white four-door cab Ford with an extended bed. It had chrome wheels and mirrors, it was so shiny. It sparkled like diamonds when the sun hit it. *I can't believe he calls this a work truck!*

He opened the door for me and I started to get in, only to be stopped by him. He kissed me and held me gently. I stop breathing for a minute, unable to speak. I was wrapped up in the moment, eager to forget the past and excited to feel wanted by someone like him.

Once he pulled away from the house, Luke reached over for my hand and gave it a soft squeeze, saying that he couldn't wait to be with me today. That he'd thought of me all night.

"This is a nice surprise. I wasn't expecting to see you since we haven't really spoken in a while." He ignored those words and responded with a question about what I was hungry for.

That was easy to answer, because I was still so hungry. Whether it was stress or just not eating enough, I don't know. But crispy bacon, eggs over easy, breakfast potatoes, and juice sounded amazing. He said he likes his scrambled, and we both laughed.

Luke put the music on and turned it up, and we just listened to the music. I was happy to do so, not wanting anything to ruin the day. I suspected Luke felt that same way.

We arrived at the café and there was a big sign that said it was closed for renovations. I saw Luke's anger starting to flair and he began cursing the place. It wasn't necessary.

I took his hand. "Luke, there's a place right around the corner that makes everything. Let's try it," I said cautiously.

He asked if I was sure. Strange question, but I had to show evidence, I guess, so I commented on how some of the club guests have mentioned it.

Once we got to the new place Luke asked what I wanted, and he went to place the order. He brought two coffees, then sat down until it was ready. I felt hopeful after he calmed down so quickly about the other café, and began to relax. It was nice.

A young man from behind the counter brought our food over and I thanked him. The second he left, Luke turned to me and confessed that he didn't know if I'd ever talk to him again after what had happened.

I said that I didn't want to talk about it. That we should just enjoy the day. And what else could be said, really, if truth be told.

Then I added, "I know it can get overwhelming when you're dealing with personal matters."

It felt strange to explain who I was and what I was like to a man who was now living with me. I shared how I wasn't a selfish person, or somebody who would bother him or chase him down. That wasn't me. He asked me a question that did throw me off. Luke wanted to know if he'd done that to my forehead. I couldn't forget, and he couldn't remember. When I told him that he did, indeed, do that, he just promised to never do it again.

However, I was paranoid again and excused myself to go to the ladies room so I could make sure it was covered up as much as could be. When I got back, our table was cleared up and it was time to go to the beach. The thought made me so happy.

CHAPTER NINETEEN

The day was turning out beautiful and we had to park a bit away from the beach because of the size of Luke's truck. I didn't mind though, and the fresh air was so rejuvenating. Everything just felt better, and I was desperate to accept that type of feeling. We'd gotten some coffee to go and got out of the truck with our coffee in hand, making our way to the entrance of the beach. We kicked off our shoes and began to walk. Luke asked if I remembered that this was the place where we'd had our first date. Of course I remembered. It wasn't that long ago and it was such a special day for me.

He reached down and grabbed my hand, weaving his fingers into mine, and we began to walk. We didn't say much, but I think Luke was enjoying the peacefulness of the ocean, the waves lapping up onto shore and rushing over our feet. Above, the seagulls were circling about and calling out. I was transported to another dimension. The way Luke kept holding my hand tighter and brushing against my arm let me know that he felt my energy. He understood the importance of the beach to me. Maybe it would be just what we needed to break through our rough spot.

When the comfortable silence between us was broken, Luke mentioned how wonderful it was to be at the beach with me, that he loved it. And seeing his contentment brought me real joy.

He quickly ran over to a garbage can to throw our coffee cups away and I stared out at the water as I waited for him to come back. He came up behind me and held me so tight, reminding me of how dreamy he'd been all day. He'd been perfect, which was amazing. I couldn't think of a single thing that I'd change in my day thus far.

His strong hands wrapped around my waistline and he turned me around and kissed me, softly and passionately.

"You're so beautiful," he murmured.

I turned away, embarrassed by the compliment and softly said, "Thank you."

Then we walked again until we found dry sand so we could sit down and not get wet. I smiled at him, and asked if he was staying over tonight. He said he couldn't, because he had to get the girls and then go to work. I didn't want to ask too many questions to keep things light, but I really didn't understand all the long hours.

Instead I said, "I'm really happy we've had this time to catch up."

Luke told me that he'd missed me and needed me. I felt so special, and the flips my stomach was doing confirmed that I was really connected to his words. Then he reached in and kissed me again. It was so wildly romantic in that moment, and…perfect.

He grabbed my chin and started to kiss me passionately. We fell back on the sand and laid there for a few minutes. We both needed to get air, but when we did, reality returned. Luke said he had to get going. He stood up and gave me his hand to pull me up. We brushed off the sand and wrapped up our beautiful day at the beach.

In the truck on the way home, it was calm and wonderful, and when we arrived at the house Luke said he'd call me later. I liked the thought of that and he added that I had a habit of not picking up, though. I just ignored that and smiled. I was on cloud nine and didn't want to be knocked off of it. The day had been too ideal.

When he hopped out and went to the front door, he began to kiss me aggressively and wildly, like he wanted to make love to me. I told him he better get going. Luke replied that he'd call me later. He walked to his truck, blew me a kiss, then drove off.

I realized I left my purse and keys in his truck. I stood there for a minute, and Luke began to back up. He must have seen it in the passenger seat, thank goodness. I walked over to the truck, he was smiling with my purse in his hands, and asked gently if this was what I was looking for. We both laughed. I thanked him. He waited until I got into the house and left.

CHAPTER TWENTY

I wanted to keep my mind on kind thoughts until Luke called, which I was anticipating. I took a shower, got all the stray bits of sand off me, and put some lotion on. Changed into some comfy clothes.

Then it was time to clean. Feathers' cage needed some cleaning; there were dead roses to throw away and laundry to do. As I kept busy, I smiled and enjoyed the music I'd put on. Before I knew it, it was six thirty when I glanced at the clock, and I was getting hungry.

Lucky for me, I had one of Chef's great meals to eat. I ate the entire dinner, not even heating it up. Chef's food was good hot or cold. I laughed to myself. I had two pieces of Italian bread, dipping them in his sauce. It was delicious, and I couldn't help but notice that I'd gained a few pounds. *I'd better watch it*, I thought. I don't know if I'm hungry at times or just nervous about what is happening in my life.

My mind was so free and happy. All the people who'd been so kind to me lately were so appreciated. I really felt blessed by have them in my life. I was so thankful to the good Lord.

Finally, I was done eating and it was time to sit down. I turned on the TV and fell asleep watching. I jerked awake and quickly ran to my phone, which was in my room, to see if Luke had called. He hadn't. And he hadn't called my home line either. I was so relieved.

I turned everything off for the night, aside from a light over the stovetop, and made my way to the bedroom. Since the night was so nice I opened up the window and looked forward to sleeping with the gentle breeze of the fresh air washing over me. I didn't even need to set my alarm because I didn't have to work until two the next day.

I fell asleep, and like a dream, I felt the covers slipping off of me. I turned to my side to pull them back up but down they went again. I opened my eyes and tried to focus them. It was Luke. I could see his silhouette.

"Luke," I murmured.

He said, "Sssh."

He was naked and so physically fit, and very sexy. He started to slowly take off my panties, and then reached behind my back and held me up with his strong hands as he slowly peeled off my nightshirt.

His hands were so warm. He began kissing me, and I accepted. As we caressed each other I felt the bond of our closeness, and I was so drawn in. The fire between us was intense and as he made love to me he proclaimed how he needed me in his life, now and forever.

"I love you too, Luke!"

The passion we were experiencing was right out of a romance novel, and I could barely believe it was me. I became so hot, and I screamed with pleasure. Luke picked me up and sat me down on top of him. I bent in and bit his shoulder, which he liked; it made him crazy. He was in deep pleasure at this moment and we were enjoying each other so much.

I laid my head down on his shoulder, we were both breathing heavy. He kissed my face and neck. I loved everything I had with him at that moment and I was both scared and excited that I'd fallen for him. I couldn't deny it, and despite how hard I tried, I couldn't think of anything else. Nothing else mattered.

I couldn't stand the feeling of separation that took over me when Luke said quietly he had to go to the bathroom and get cleaned up so we could get to bed. I moved to the side so he could get up, and then I went to wash up in the other bathroom.

I noticed the light on in the living room. I went to shut it off and there was an empty bottle of wine and a glass. I turned off the light and headed to the kitchen. Another empty bottle was on the counter. Then I finally took note of the time: 3:30 a.m.

At that moment, I decided not to move anything. I didn't want Luke to know that I'd seen this, or that he was obviously home hours earlier. I hadn't heard a thing. But saying something might be bad. As great as the passion was, if he'd drunk all of that my words would likely start a fight, and I didn't want that.

I went to back to the room and found Luke in bed. I slid in and he gave me a kiss good night, and I kissed him back. Whatever had upset him wasn't something he took out on me, which was good. Maybe things really were different now.

✳✳✳

Morning came along, and I reached over with my eyes closed to wrap my arm around Luke, but he wasn't there. I looked and saw a note on his pillow: I will call you later, have a good day. Miss you. Then he drew a bunch of smiley faces. I got up, picked up my nightshirt and panties off the floor and put them back on. I went to the bathroom and brushed my teeth and took note that the bump on my forehead was almost gone. Thank goodness!

I went into the kitchen, and the empty bottle of wine was gone. So was the one in the living room. Luke obviously didn't want me to know he'd been drinking. And what could I say…I just thought it was wonderful that we shared our love with each other early that morning. I loved the way he made me feel. There was no need to say anything that might pull us apart.

I was down to my last essentials; I needed to get to the grocery store. I put a pot of coffee on, and went into the living room to watch some news to wait until it was done. I thanked God for this glorious day. I poured a cup of coffee, made a quick egg sandwich, and went to my room to get my phone. Darn! There were three missed calls, all from Luke. That's right, I'd forgotten to take the phone off silent, so I quickly called him back.

I was greeted with anger, him wondering what the fuck was wrong with me that I didn't answer my fuckin' phone, or call back right away.

"I'm sorry," I said.

He didn't give me a chance to say anything. He hung up, and there I was, back to the older feeling of chaos. My joy had been stomped out by his meanness. What had I done to have him not trust me exactly?

The way he acted toward me just bound me up inside. It really hurt my feelings when he unleashed on me for nothing more than a phone. His words made me lose my appetite, and I didn't even want a cup of coffee. I threw my sandwich away. I sighed, and decided to get ready for work.

Luke made me so batty. Why does he take his frustrations out on me? It's hard to take this rollercoaster of emotions that he gives me, and I'm not equipped to keep going along for the ride.

He was consuming my mind, too much of it, and it was my fault. Why was I allowing this behavior? There was definitely an underlying issue here. He had deep anger from last night eating away at him.

Finally, I was ready to go. My phone was on vibrate and in my apron. I did not want another call with Luke like the one I'd just had. It was so upsetting to me. With all this energy I built up, I was hungry, and now wished I never threw away my breakfast.

As I drove to work I turned the radio on loud to drown out any thoughts. It worked; I could barely hear myself think. It was a reprieve I desperately needed for when I got to work and started to prepare for the day. I found my thoughts going toward *him*, as always. Was he okay? Why hadn't he called or texted?

Then I thought of a constant source of sunshine in my life—Matthew. *I should call him during break.* He has so many amazing things happening in his life, and I am so proud of him. I could also imagine his father looking down from heaven so proud as well. It made me feel good.

I looked for the assignment sheet, hoping I wasn't working on the patio today. Pierre hadn't posted it yet. He came into the kitchen out of breath, behind schedule and handed me the floor plan according to the reservations. He didn't even say good morning, and I didn't want to ask. I had so much of my own stuff going on. I can't seem to get away from working in the heat.

It was another warm day on the patio in store for me. Eighty-five degrees and zero breeze, ugh. I could only laugh, though. Honestly, it amazed me that people wanted to sit outside and eat in that kind of heat, but they did. Very busy, I was running on empty, I felt so tired. I couldn't wait for lunch. Chef came in late, I was hoping for a little something this morning. Boy, I appreciate him when he is here in the morning!

Finally, I got a break and called Matthew. It went to his voicemail, and as fate would have it, as I was trying to leave a message, Luke was calling in. I wasn't going to cut my message short, but I called Luke back as soon as I finished the message. There was no answer. I left him a message and apologized, hoping it would suffice.

Chef made a wonderful lunch as always. I finished my entire plate and went back for seconds. Everything in my life felt so messy. One moment of happiness to hours of despair.

Luke never called back, and I figured he'd gotten busy. I'd see him that night, explain all of this better, and make it right. It was time to get back to work. There wasn't too much business outside, but Pierre wanted us to stay.

Around eight o'clock, he finally told the busboys to bring all the setups inside, without interrupting the guests sitting in the dining room. I looked up at the clock, and was grateful to get eight hours on the clock. I kinda chuckled, I didn't have to work too hard today. I closed the umbrellas, wiped down the rest of the tables, then proceeded to punch out.

CHAPTER TWENTY-ONE

I was on my way home and thinking about—who else?—Luke. Before we'd met, I was always on top of my game. My cupboards were never empty and Feathers always had a stash of food, but now I was always playing catch up and adjusting my plans to suit Luke's whims. I had to get a grip and develop a better backbone—and quick. He had no right to walk all over me, and I was stupid to let him.

One thing was clear. I needed to take responsibility. How would I explain the way Luke acted if Matthew came home to visit me? I couldn't keep making excuses for Luke, even if I found that to be the only acceptable way to reconcile his actions. And honestly, I did not owe him anything.

By the time I got home, I felt determined and strong. I pulled in my parking space and noticed the living room light was on, as well as my bedroom light. I opened the door and my eyes went right to the empty wine bottle and glass in the living room. I called out to Luke.

There was no answer and I went into the kitchen and put my purse and the bird food down on the table. There was a half empty bottle of wine on the table. I could only sigh, and then I heard Luke call out. He was in the bedroom.

I walked over to the room, and stared at my bed. Pictures of my past life were scattered everywhere, and Luke instantly began to curse at me from the top of his lungs. As I struggled to process everything, I could only stare in shock as he accused me of horrible things, all through slurred words. You whore. You piece of shit.

"Why are you doing this?" I screamed, "Stop touching my things! My husband was a loving and good man who died from cancer. This is very personal to me. You have a past, an ex-wife, and girlfriends. You created two children with your wife. I don't do that to you. I could date who I wanted to. You were not in my life then. You're here now. So what's the problem?"

He spewed more angry, hurtful words. "Your pictures show what kind of lowlife person you are, look at how you are acting in these photos."

"Like a person having fun and enjoying her life raising her son alone, like someone who doesn't want any outside interference. I do not regret having fun. I'm happy I didn't involve any one in my life. My son left four months ago, and if he hadn't you would not be here right now. Trust me on that one. So, stop calling me names because you had a bad day or have something else that is bothering you. You cannot take it out on me, and on that note, stop snooping around and trying to find something bad about me, you are not going to win."

And with that liberating declaration, I started to collect all my photos from my bed one at a time. The pictures of my belated husband put tears in my eyes. I held his picture close to my heart. All I could say is that I wished he was here.

Luke was stating something about me being a no good, lowlife person. I could barely hear him, but I replied like a robot.

"Thank you for all your compliments and kind words. There will come a time you will eat what you say. Karma is a bitch, my friend."

I was told to go fuck myself. He started to leave the room and then pushed me so hard that I lost my balance and fell against the wall. Only after that did he storm out of the house. I heard the door slam loudly. I regained my balance and began to put my private, precious memories back into their box, and into the corner of my closet.

My reaction to Luke had thrown him off. I could tell, and I was glad. He didn't know how to handle it. What really rattled me at that moment were my conflicting thoughts. Part of me was so glad he'd left and then there was that part of me that thought we could be on top of the world if he'd just gain some control, stop drinking, and maybe his emotions wouldn't get the best of him. He'd be nicer.

Luke had underlying issues, and I needed to point them out if we were going to go anywhere together.

At that moment, all I knew was that I needed to clean up his mess, take a shower, and then slide into my crisp, clean sheets for a good night's rest. Tomorrow was going to be busy, and I wanted to have a night uninterrupted. My reflections demanded attention, though.

What if that argument had taken a bad turn? I couldn't even fathom what might have happened. I'd taken a risk with a drunk man. I'd wanted to use my backbone, but it was a huge chance to try it at that moment. But when I'd seen my husband's pictures I felt this strength inside of me swell up. I wasn't scared to take a stand.

Morning came, and I got ready for the day. When I opened my bedroom door, I was greeted with the wonderful aroma of coffee. It wasn't my original blend. I walked cautiously, and Luke turned and smiled, offering me a carefree, "Good morning." I wasn't expecting him to be here.

There was my preferred version of Luke. I was taken aback that he was there and said so. He only commented that he left last night and didn't like how I treated him, but it wasn't smart to go there. I had to finish getting ready for work and that day I had a party to work from 11:00 a.m. to 6:00 p.m. I was going to be very busy.

I poured two cups of coffee, fixing mine just the way I liked it, and then went to sit down. I handed one to Luke as well. When I took my first sip I thought it was delicious, and Luke said that it was a Mediterranean blend, and then he offered an apology—again. How many times had he had to apologize to me in the amount of time we'd been together? Endless, and honestly, I was probably due a few more. My conversation with him was very cold.

My thoughts were elsewhere and I really wasn't absorbing his words, or buying the few that stood out. He could tell, I think, because he kept rambling.

"Luke, I'm sorry to interrupt you. I don't have time to sit and talk. I have to get ready for work. If you want to speak more about everything, we can talk later."

He said he'd be there and then I said I had shopping to do after work as well, so I wouldn't be home right away. It felt strange to have to explain it, but I knew it was necessary. He said he'd grocery shop, and I could just handle the pet store. He wanted to be of help.

"Are you sure?" I asked. It maybe wasn't nice to sound so doubtful, but I was. He was saying he was quite capable so I left that task to him.

I went to my room and got ready, not even putting makeup on because now I was running late. He told me I was beautiful, even without it, and I smiled. What woman doesn't love to hear that? Luke kissed me and told me to be careful and stood on the porch waving as I walked to my car.

"Call me when you get there," he called out. I smiled and nodded. What was I supposed to make of all this? He seemed so humble and I wanted to believe that he recognized that he'd stepped way over the line. Why was I putting up with this uncertainty and chaos, exactly? He had to change, because I didn't deserve it, or need it.

The drive to work was smooth, and I got there fifteen minutes early, sent a quick text to Luke, and still had enough time to walk down to the beach and charge myself up for the day. I slid off my socks and shoes and walked on the chilly sand, loving that feeling between my toes. The mist of the water gently landed on my face, and I released my hair from the bun it was in.

I loved the way the ocean breeze felt against my body. In the corner of my eye I saw Chef walking toward me and turned to say good morning. He asked why I was out there and I said, "The ocean helps me stay calm and strong through difficult times."

Then he repeated what he'd been saying to me so often. That he was there for me. And I knew he was, and I was grateful for it.

We began walking toward the club. He bent down so I could use his shoulder for balance as I put my shoes and socks back on. He was so kind and sweet, and I genuinely appreciated it.

When I walked into the club and punched in, I was instantly thrilled. Two of my favorite people were working with me that day—Momma Monica and Cindy. I hugged them both tightly and couldn't hide my delight. Cindy was beautiful and so kind. Momma Monica was just as her nickname indicated, wise and motherly. Her famous saying was: "This shall pass, and life gets better. Things that happen are supposed to. We need to embrace them and accept them, and then, thank the Lord." I love Monica.

Pierre came into the kitchen and handed us the assignment sheet for the party. He was very short with words and it was obvious he was having an off day. We were all entitled to one.

Once he left, we all began to talk as we prepared for the day. I asked Cindy about her son and she beamed with pride in her responses, and then showed some recent photos that she'd had in her apron.

Monica talked about how she was going back to Jamaica for her daughter's wedding, and then we all talked about that. Those special moments are so important to us moms and it felt great to talk about our children. We are very proud of them.

I talked about Matthew, how he moved to Texas to work in a high profile investment firm, and then added, "I met a man."

Cindy gave an, "Aww, someone's in love."

"Well, he is a bit tough, has a lot of anger. I believe it stems from his ex-wife. We're so happy one day, and then he drinks and something happens that destroys the joy. He becomes aggressive, and then apologizes. It's kind of crazy." As I said the words I was surprised to hear my own voice admitting these things.

Monica cautioned me to be careful, as that was not a good sign for a man to treat you that way right from the start. Cindy added that it was a warning sign and things would likely get worse, not better.

Overall, they thought I should start to end that relationship. I'd barely told them a fraction of what had been happening, and they thought that. What if they knew everything?

I was fairly certain that no one would understand the story about the bump on my forehead last week either. Knowing that people knew I was lying to them felt horrible, but what could I do? I didn't want them to hate Luke. After all, he was going to change things around. It would all be better after his divorce was finalized. Things would become stable and wonderful. Still, I held out hope that when his divorce came, Luke would be more settled.

Momma Monica kept telling me to put my foot down. What I allow will eventually become destructive. Someone will get hurt. She didn't want this to happen to me. *She is so right. I need to get into my hard skin.*

Pierre came in the room and looked around; he approached me and asked if everything is all right. I told him we served the first course, we will be clearing shortly. He replied, "Thank you Amilia," and he walked away.

Jasper came out of the kitchen. I asked him if he could help us start clearing the finished tables. He jumped right in. We had the dining room clear very fast.

Monica went into the kitchen to let Chef know we are ready for the next course when he is. We are serving prime rib, roasted potato, and string beans.

Chef called his kitchen staff. He looked at me coming through the kitchen door.

"You ready?"

I replied, "Yes Chef," and he smiled.

Monica looked at me and said, "What is going on between you two, you have this man blushing."

Chef said, "Pick up!" We each picked up three plates. We went to the host table first and worked our way around the dining room. We followed Cindy. I went to the kitchen to put the coffee on for service. It was done.

I turned around and Chef said, "I got you, no worries." I thanked Chef. He told me he's always here to help. "Please Amilia you can come to me, you never have to feel afraid."

The host went out to the front desk and told Pierre to take the cake after pictures, and have it cut up and served along with coffee service; there would be no singing. We served coffee, and cake. I wanted to thank the Chef, but he seemed to have left. At the end of the party the host gave us each a fifty dollar bill. I was so thankful. In the back of my mind I had bills to pay, which reminded me to make sure I got to them tomorrow. This was a blessing.

We finally got the room cleaned up. It didn't take much. I was happy I was able to work with such wonderful women. When we finished I gave Momma and Cindy a great big hug. We punched out and walked together to our cars. They told me again to be careful, and call them if I needed anything.

Momma said out loud, "He is not a good man."

I looked at my phone to see if Luke had called or texted. He'd sent a text, apologizing for not texting me back. I smiled and was on my way. Traffic was heavy.

I didn't need to stop at the pet store. I bought Feathers food yesterday on the way home, but I will stop and pick up some treats for him. I love him. Having him live longer than his timeframe is wonderful. He is a special gift from my belated husband indeed.

After I got the seed and some treats, I pulled into the parking lot. I saw Luke's SUV there, and all the lights on in the house. I instantly felt a bit nervous and forced myself to remember to be positive. This was all new to both of us, but I wished I knew who I'd get when I walked through the door ahead of time. Just to prepare.

Luke was in the kitchen with his apron on. He looked so cute and began to share that he'd gone shopping and was preparing dinner for us. I set the treats down and smiled and he asked me to come give him a hug, and that he hoped I was hungry. I was glad to give the hug, and I was indeed hungry.

"What's the occasion? This is really special." I was grinning, and grateful. Then I saw the table, which looked beautiful. It had cloth napkins and candles on it, and I noticed my favorite rolls from the Italian bakery on there, too. "I'll go change and I'll be right back," I said.

Luke just smiled and I went to my room. I looked on the bed and saw a box of chocolates and a long-stemmed rose. I picked up the rose to smell the scent and Luke came right behind me. He put his arms around my waist and kissed my neck. He whispered promises of encouragement that things would get better and I'd see.

I went to take a shower and he went back to fixing dinner. *I will put the rose in a vase when I get out of the shower.* A short while later I was in the kitchen in a summer top and a pair of white shorts, eager to have dinner with Luke. He seemed so happy and ready to make a change with us as well. It was ideal.

He asked me to pour some wine while he plated the Caesar salads for us, and I did. When I handed him the wine he smiled and said he was cooking homemade stuffed ravioli with Portobello mushrooms and that he'd sauteéd fresh mushroom and onions on the side with a parmesan cheese sauce.

That was a lot of work, and so thoughtful.

"I can't wait to have some, it makes my mouth water."

Luke nodded and finished his wine, asking me to refill it. I did, and then we sat down to eat.

Once we were settled in I wanted to take advantage of the good mood between us to clarify what I felt when things went so crazy between us.

"Luke, I don't like it when we have an argument to the extent of what's been going on. It leaves a big hole in my stomach, that no matter what I do throughout the day, I can never fill it. It's a terrible feeling," I said.

Luke replied that he understood and we continued to eat our salad. Finally he talked about how he didn't know what came over him at times, and he knew he had to get his head on straight. And that was all I wanted.

After that the conversation flowed more freely, and I asked about the girls. He seldom brought them up on his own, unless it was to use them against me in some way. He mentioned that they were getting better, but it was still hard. He stood up to remove the plates and I stood to help, but he asked me to sit back down. He was treating me so special, and I'll admit, I loved it.

He poured another glass of wine. I couldn't help but be mindful that I was still on my first glass.

Then it was time for the ravioli, and it was out of this world. Just about anything could have happened at that moment, and it wouldn't have been as bad because that ravioli was that good!

Luke mentioned that Monday was around the corner and the girls would be with us then, and if I was ready for it.

"We'll work together and schedule our hours accordingly. You have to let me know what the daily routine is," I requested.

He said he would and then we finished eating. Afterward, he told me to leave all the dishes there for the time being. He wanted to go to the living room and relax together. Two wine refills later, and we were in the living room.

Luke lay back on the couch and extended his legs. I turned on the television, and then covered us up with a blanket as I nestled in his arms. Within minutes he was passed out, and snoring.

I snuck away and went into the kitchen to clean it, scraping the rest of our dishes quietly in the garbage. I put the rolls back in the bag, and put the dishes in the dishwasher.

When I was done I crept back over and whispered in his ear, "Luke, come to bed." Then I ran my fingers through his hair and repeated myself.

He opened his eyes, stood up, and stumbled right to the bedroom. I thought for a moment he was going to fall right over. I turned off the TV, checked the front door to make sure it was locked, folded the blanket, and put it away. I went to the bedroom to go to sleep. I noticed the rose bent in half and thrown on the floor, and the box of chocolate stepped on with a footprint going across it. I didn't pick it up.

After I brushed my teeth, Luke spoke. "When I buy something for you, and you don't respect it, this is the reaction you will get. Do you get it?"

I didn't respond and just pulled the covers over my shoulder and went to sleep. *I can't believe I forgot to put the rose in the water and he got really offended by that.* Out of all things, an overreaction to a small scenario. I couldn't play into it.

There was no need for an alarm. I didn't have to work this morning, and I was glad about that. My thoughts drifted to Matthew, and I hoped he was okay. It's not like him not to call. I had to call him, though. He hadn't called or texted me back. Finally, I fell asleep, but I was wide awake by three o'clock with all the thoughts I had.

I do not rest well when I don't hear from Matthew as often as I expect. Knowing that I would only toss and turn in bed I went to the kitchen, poured a glass of water, and sat down to watch some TV—but with no sound.

Luke got up around five to go to the bathroom and asked why I wasn't sleeping. I just said I woke up and couldn't fall back asleep. He walked over to the remote control, picked it up, and turned off the TV. Then he extended his hand to me to help me off the couch.

"Come to bed, you need to get some rest."

I didn't want to tell him I was worried about my son, he seemed to be very jealous of me having any kind of relationship with anyone else but him without argument. I went back to bed and Luke covered me up, and I finally drifted back off to sleep. When I awoke it was eleven thirty. I hadn't heard Luke go to work and slept longer than I could recall sleeping in a long while.

I picked up my cellphone to see if I missed any calls or texts. There was a text from Matthew:

Hi Mom, I left you a message the other night, and I never heard back from you. Is everything all right? Please call me!

I'd never received a message from Matthew. The only other person who had access to my phone was Luke. He wouldn't check my messages and then erase them, would he? Being jealous of my son—surely not, right?

Now I was bothered, very bothered. I got up, went to the bathroom, splashed cold water on my face, brushed my teeth, and went to the kitchen. Luke had thrown away the rose and chocolates. His train of thought was baffling to me, but I couldn't even think about it at that moment.

Once in the kitchen, I poured some OJ and sat down to call Matthew. I dialed and Matthew picked up. His voice relieved me so much and as he spoke and shared how he'd tried to get a hold of me, I truly didn't know what to say, exactly, but the words were still true.

"Matthew, darling, good morning. I didn't receive a text from you. I was so worried about you, too. Last night I woke up at 3:00 a.m. and couldn't fall back asleep."

He told me the text stated "received," and I didn't know what to say. I couldn't confess that it probably was, just not by me.

Then he gave me exciting news that sent me into orbit. He had a week's vacation coming up soon, and he wanted to come see me, and bring Rachel. It would be close to the end of the year, maybe the first week of December. I told Matthew I was very excited to see both of them.

"That would be great! Gives me something special to look forward to."

Then our call was cut short. Matthew had to get back to work. We told each other we loved one another then Matthew had to go. Why would Luke keep Matthew's messages from me?

I needed to ask Luke why he was erasing my messages, and how he thought that would even be acceptable behavior. He'd crossed the line with my son, someone I love endlessly. There was no better time to find out than the present, while I had the courage. So, I called Luke, and he answered, going into an explanation of me being so sound asleep when he left.

"Thank you, Luke, for everything last night! I need to ask you an important question. Do you have a minute?" He did, so I breathed in, and began.

"I received a message from my son, and it was deliberately erased. I need to know why you did that!" My voice didn't remain as calm as I'd hoped it would.

His tone changed and he feigned shock at my accusation.

"Don't think I'm ignorant because I do not say much. I'm very well-tuned in on what's going on. Please do not do that again," I stated.

He didn't know what I was talking about. I couldn't let it go.

"I don't get involved with your private conversations about your girls; don't interfere with my messages with my son. I love my son and you will never take that away, regardless how many texts you erase!"

Apparently his time for my "shit" had run out. He hung up.

It was hard to even imagine what was going through Luke's brain, and I knew that I was more daring behind the phone than I might have been face-to-face. The only thing I knew for certain was that it was not going to be a pleasant night. He would not take this dispute lightly.

CHAPTER TWENTY-TWO

I showered and started my day, ready to pay bills and organize things, to get some sense of order. I felt desperate for it actually. I opened the front door to get the morning paper, but there were several on the lawn. It'd been days since I picked one up. I gathered all the old papers and went to the dumpster to throw them out. On my way back I stopped at my car to get my bill folder.

I'd left my bill folder in my trunk, and then made my way to the kitchen, ready to take on the task. It was a perfect day to do this. No one here and I could concentrate. I locked the door behind me. Only I wasn't alone.

Luke was charging at me. I froze and didn't know what was going on, and couldn't quite process it. All I could do was scream as loud as I could. Fearful noise erupted from me—I dropped my folder, and my bills scattered all over the floor. He put my robe belt around my neck and hissed at me.

"Don't you ever call me on my cellphone and talk to me that way. Don't tell me what to do and what not to do. Who do you think you are now?" he raged.

I closed my eyes and prayed for the good Lord to get him out of my life. I couldn't hear him yelling anymore, I was praying so hard. Then

I felt the constriction around my neck being released, and Luke bolted out of the house.

I fell to my knees in the kitchen and cried and prayed. I asked the Lord to give me the strength to save myself. It couldn't stay this way, and all I could focus on was that December was four months away, and how could I let my son come into all this mess. Matthew never witnessed anything like this, and although he was a man now, it was still traumatic.

Thoughts of his father flooded me. He'd been such a gentle soul, and I began to cry. The tears came more frantically and I couldn't stop for a great while. But finally they subsided and I looked around at all the bills on the floor and began to pick them up, and then I picked myself up.

I went to the bathroom and looked in the mirror. The bump on my head had been replaced with a red rash mark that went all the way around my neck. How close did I come to dying in that moment? That mark wasn't going to go away, and it couldn't be covered up. I went right into explanation mode. What would I say at work tomorrow? It was the weekend and it was a busy one. I had to work. My heart told me to call the police.

I wanted Matthew there to help me, although he shouldn't even have to be exposed to what was happening. Then the girls… they were coming that day. All their things were upstairs. How could I call the police on their father? There was only one choice for me. I needed to collect myself. Until I knew the right thing to do for everyone, I'd just manage.

Monica's words from the day before crept into my mind, and I thanked the good Lord for all He does for me. Then the tears came again harder than before. I wanted to run a bath and soak in the tub. I drew the blinds, shut the lights, took off my clothes, and stepped in. I cried until I became silent. I closed my eyes and prayed to the Lord. I stayed until the water became cold.

I started to feel better, and did my best to try and ignore the redness around my neck when I caught my reflection in the mirror. I got out and began to dry myself off. As I was coming out of the bathroom I heard a noise, and I froze, fear overcoming me. Was he back?

I listened, and then I heard the front door shut very loud, and I went to the living room and peeked out. It had been Luke. He was pulling away, and I quickly went to make sure the door was locked again. What did he want?

I was nervous again and walked back into the kitchen. I found checks on the counter, written out to pay my bills. Money in exchange for forgiveness... I wasn't so sure I could accept it, or if I wanted to use his checks to pay my bills. If I didn't use his checks there would be another fight.

Everything was confusing, and I couldn't focus. All I did was grab my cellphone to check it and then go to lie down on my bed. Again, Matthew was on my mind. My phone had been in the kitchen, and if Luke checked what I'd been doing, he'd know that I had spoken with Matthew. These concerns lingered in my mind until I drifted off to sleep.

I woke up around three and looked at my phone. Luke had sent a message that he wanted to send me some lunch, and what did I want. That was at one. No contact from him since.

There was nothing that I wanted from him, but I did need to eat so I went to the kitchen to make a sandwich. I took two slices of Italian bread, put on some sliced ham, provolone, tomato, lettuce, sprinkled some balsamic vinegar, and cut my sandwich in half. With my sandwich on a plate and tea in my hand, I sat at the kitchen table. My eyes couldn't avoid the checks. They carried no value in my heart, and certainly didn't fix what had happened to me.

The day was so confusing, and I walked around in a trancelike state. What was happening was not acceptable, and I needed help, but how? So many people had offered, but I was so embarrassed. How could I admit what I'd allowed into my home?

I forgot all about Feathers today. I changed his water, and gave him a treat. He was very excited to have it. I didn't feel like bringing out the vacuum. Instead, I took the dustpan and small brush, then swept up what I could to keep the area clean around the birdcage.

I made another cup of tea; I added a little honey to it and mixed it very well. I sipped it slowly. It felt so soothing on my throat. I went to my room, fixed my bed, picked up my towel, and emptied out the trash in the kitchen wastebasket. I took my tea and sat down on the couch to watch TV, and relax my nerves.

I can't believe this is happening. I want to phone my friends, but if he finds out, I don't know what he is capable of doing to me. I need help; Luke makes it clear anything goes.

I went into the living room and turned to a romantic movie, captivated by its story, and the extents a man went through to see his "love at first sight" again. It was ideal and dreamy, it was not unlike what I thought Luke and I had at first. That was the way it was supposed to be, right?

It was a movie about a young couple who met on a train. They were having a delightful conversation; the young man looked down and reached in his briefcase to get a pen to write down his number. Before he had a chance, she got out at her stop and all he could do is extend his voice for her to wait, and the doors closed. He was left staring through the glass.

He only had her first name, but was determined to find her. He went everywhere holding up signs with her name on it. He put up fliers all over Manhattan.

The news station got a hold of the story and called him in to do a broadcast to find this girl. He had help from all walks of life, holding up signs with her name on it. She finally turned on the TV, and saw her name all over New York City. She called the TV station and told them her name was Samantha.

"It's me, I know who he is! I'm the girl you are looking for!" They asked her for her address, saying the station would send a car to her apartment and pick her up. When she got to the TV station she ran to him, and he got down on one knee and proposed to her. This was the most amazing love story I have ever seen.

I thought Luke was my love at first sight. *I wish our love could be like this. I feel I can never do anything right in his eyes. Luke always takes out on me what is not going right in his life. When I met him at the club I thought he was my prince charming.* I began to cry.

I looked at the time on the TV. It was eight o'clock. The time went by fast. I was so engulfed in the movie. It was nice to get my mind off of things and smile in faith. There is so much love in the world. And this gave me peace. MAYBE NOT FOR ME!

CHAPTER TWENTY-THREE

My throat hurt and my body was so exhausted. I just longed to go to sleep for the night and wake up again to all of this being a bad nightmare. I happened to notice a message on my phone when I went to bed, from Luke. His words spoke of sincere sorrow that his actions never quite lived up to…at least for long. Did he really think paying my bills made up for the harm he'd done to me? It wasn't just physical, it was also emotional. And he certainly didn't get it that I couldn't just take off work. I had an obligation.

I set my alarm for seven and then slid into bed. Waves of exhaustion set over me again and I went into a deep sleep, not waking up until four thirty when I had to go to the bathroom.

When I got up I noticed a light beaming through the living room. I didn't go out there to see. I wanted to peek, but didn't. I went to the bathroom then looked out my bedroom window to see if I could see Luke's truck. His SUV stood out. You couldn't miss it. I turned around to go back to bed.

Luke was there and he grabbed me. I was so panicked I couldn't even breathe, much less scream for help. He kept telling me that everything would be all right. I smelled the alcohol on his breath. He just needed to leave.

"Luke, I have to get a little more sleep. I work a double tomorrow," I said. My goal was to sound calm and assured, to not reveal my terror. He opened his mouth and I added, "I don't want to talk about what happened right now." He released me from his arms and said he was going to go sleep on the couch. I just wanted him away from me.

* * *

I woke up to my alarm, which I was grateful for, and began to prepare for my day. My immediate thought was about my neck, and when I went into the bathroom to look in the mirror I could see the marks of the terror Luke had put me through still there. I was going to have to cover it up, but how? After looking through my closet I went with a small white scarf. It was the only option that would work. Hopefully! Thank goodness I loved scarves and had a big collection of them to choose from.

As I got ready, I grew more upset with myself. I should have called the police. That way I never would have had to endure what had happened again. It was fine to worry about everyone else, but what about me? I needed to worry about me more in this situation. My failure to do it was a source of agony within me.

On my way out the door, I glanced in the living room, and Luke wasn't there. He wasn't in the kitchen, either, but I noticed that the bills were gone from the table. He must have taken them with him. I picked up my folder and went back to my room to put it away in my dresser drawer. It was perhaps a silly gesture, as he'd seen them now. It was startling to think of how much everything I thought of as private had been violated in the past days, weeks really.

I'd have another ride to work to think about it all and I was running late, I had to get going. As I stepped out into the fresh air I detected another stifling day on the horizon. Not ideal, but hardly the worst thing I'd dealt with lately. I would get through my day. I had no other choice.

As I was driving my phone started to ring. As I reached for it, it slipped out of my hands onto the passenger side floor. I frowned, but wasn't about to reach for it. Whoever it was would have to wait until I was at the club.

Another day with lighter traffic was a blessing, and I got to work early, which would give me time to make sure my makeup and scarf were organized. But my extra time was taken away in an instant when I saw Luke there in the parking lot. I sighed, because what I wanted and needed was to be left alone that day.

He walked toward me and I said hi, then he bombarded me with what he needed. To talk. To give him a signal that we'd be okay. To move on. I could barely look at him and he demanded that I did, and made sure I was looking right at him.

His face was red and growing angrier as he was apologizing, but it wasn't sweet. It was intense and angry, not sincere.

"Luke, I can't handle your anger, or how you treat me anymore. I don't want my life to be like this. I would like you to leave me alone today. I have to work a double shift. I slept some, but am still exhausted, mentally and physically, by your actions."

He seemed to concede to my demands, then reminded me I was his girl. Then an "I love you" was added in, and he walked to his SUV and drove off. Was it really that easy? And would it remain so? I prayed so. Then I made my way into work to make sure I covered the evidence of *his* crimes. Then I called Matthew, who'd been the person who had called when I was driving.

"Good morning Matthew," I said.

He sounded frantic and my heart jumped. He said that he was calling because he was worried about me, and that he'd received a call from someone who works at the club.

"Who?" I asked, feeling quite unsettled. He wouldn't tell me, but said they were very concerned about me.

Then he asked the bold question, was I dating someone that was not treating me nicely? I couldn't speak. But he did. He told me about the bruise on my forehead, acting distant from my friends. It made me sick, and sad.

I begged him to tell me who told him, and how they got his number, but he wouldn't. He just added that he was my emergency contact, which was true. He reminded me how lucky I was to have people who cared enough about me to reach out to him. The only thing I could do was put my hand on my neck, and pray for the good Lord to help me.

"Matthew darling, I'm at work right now. Can I call you on my break, or tonight when I get home?" I asked.

"Mom, are you dating someone who is not treating you well?" Matthew asked. I didn't answer.

He told me to call anytime, that he'd be there. And I knew he would be. What a dilemma the call had created though. Do I lie to my son, whom I cherished more than anything, to cover for Luke? Or equally bad, to hide the fact that I was embarrassed about being in a situation in which I apparently lacked control. There was no time to decide anything. I had to go out to the dining room, and I knew that someone (or a few some-ones) had called me out on my coverup.

Pierre was the first person I saw. After exchanging hellos he asked about the scarf, and I said I had a bad sore throat. It wasn't a lie, really. He said he liked it. This was good, because that scarf had to stay on.

I hid behind the ice machine and had to rewrap my scarf in privacy—away from invading eyes. But Chef was there and commented on the sore throat, and then asked what the hell was going on. That he wanted to help me.

It was hard to even look at him. "Please, don't say what you saw, I promise, I'll explain later." I was fully aware of the desperation and panic in my voice as I begged for his discretion. And being the wonderful man Chef was, he agreed. But I knew he would not let me off the hook. I'd have to tell him something…but could I be honest?

The day began and work was crazy busy, making it challenging to make sure my scarf was in place and I was being efficient. And every small break I got was spent checking my neck and trying to connect with Matthew, but I didn't catch him. I knew he was worried, and it made my heart ache. Every once in a while I thought about who might have called Matthew, too. Pierre, his assistant Mandy, and Chef all had access to the files.

For the night's banquet I had to wear a tuxedo, which was good because the shirt covered up my neck, which meant I didn't have to deal with the scarf. A small, much needed break.

Chef asked if I was hungry, and he didn't have to ask me twice. My stomach was growling. I needed to get some nutrition in me. Chef made vegetable lasagna and Caesar salad. I wanted to sit in the main dining room to eat my lunch in privacy, but the decorators were there, so I went to the back of the kitchen and sat at Chef's table. I wanted peace. To be honest I couldn't think of anything except eating at that moment.

Chef peeked in on me; the corner of my eye caught him in a glance. He came back and brought me a cold glass of iced tea. I thanked him for being so good to me. Chef wanted me to know I could always turn to him. He'd been very supportive.

Break time moved rather quickly. Could be my thoughts racing. I had to change my uniform and get ready.

After I was dressed I tried Matthew one more time. This time he answered.

"Matthew, darling, are you busy?"

He was, but he didn't care. I didn't have time to do anything but reassure him that I was okay, and that I'd tell him more tomorrow because I was getting out of work late. He begged me to do it, and I promised I would. I told him I love him, and to have a blessed night.

I hung up and looked at my call list. At least Luke was abiding by my wishes. That was a relief. But now it was time to get back to work. I checked the assignment sheet that was posted, and I was disappointed to see that Monica and Cindy weren't working tonight. I love talking to them. I was looking forward to Momma Monica's words of wisdom. I could use that encouragement right now.

It was a simple buffet party thank goodness. The decorations for the Fiftieth Birthday Party made this event spectacular. They definitely emphasized on the drinks. Big martini glasses, and large goblets for wine, and mixed drinks with different decorations in every glass. Much fun, but I have to say the centerpieces of black and silver with top hats, and cigars with shooting stars and sparkles stood about four feet tall. I'd never seen anything like it.

Pierre came into the room, expressed that table maintenance was very important. He doesn't want us standing around doing nothing; there are plenty of us on duty.

"Keep your tables free of clutter. The party ends at eleven o'clock. Let's have a good night."

I went back into the kitchen to get a glass of water. Chef came over, and asked how I was holding up. I thanked him, and assured him that I was fine, and I would find a way out of this mess. Goodness I caught what I said!

He looked at me with a puzzled face. Chef began to get worried; I heard it in his voice. He asked if I would like to go out for some coffee and talk. I let him know that now wasn't the time. All I could think about was; *I could never go out in public looking the way I do, not even to talk.* It would also be unfair to bring Chef into this unkindness. *Knowing Luke's ways, can you imagine what would happen if I met Chef out for coffee? Luke seems to know every move I make.*

I turned to Chef and made the conversation very light. I thanked him again. I went back into the banquet room, erasing any thought of that conversation.

Toward the end of the night, the DJ announced to the party to approach the dance floor. Pierre rolled out the birthday cake. I looked up at the clock; I couldn't believe it was nine thirty. After coffee service, Pierre walked over to me and said that I could change and go home since I was working another double the next day. He asked me to bring the tuxedo into his office after I changed. I was grateful, and thanked him. I needed rest.

I went to my locker, changed into a shirt and linen pants I had, and put my morning uniform in a bag. I took the tuxedo to his office so he could send it to the dry cleaners. This was a great perk, for the club to take care of our uniforms. I walked in and Pierre's face dropped.

"What?" I asked, genuinely confused. He asked about my neck. I cringed, as I recalled forgetting to put a scarf back on. "It's nothing, really," I said.

Pierre didn't buy it and I didn't blame him. He asked me immediately who was doing that to me, and how he could help.

"This is something I have to do myself. I have faith, I will find a way. Thank you so much, Pierre, for your kindness. Can I still come to work tomorrow? I will wear my scarf."

He said that I could definitely come to work and he didn't understand what he was seeing. His concern and shock made me feel bad. I wanted to tell him everything but I was embarrassed. And what about Matthew? This would probably get back to him now, I imagined. As I left the room, Pierre spoke loudly to be careful.

"I said good night." I punched out.

I walked to my car and sat for a minute and shook my head with disbelief. Why did I allow this to get this far? I was never hurt this way in my life. I started my car and began to drive home. It should be nonnegotiable on how I'm treated.

What would I say to Luke when I got home? If I was fortunate, he would not be there so I could get a good night's sleep, and go to work refreshed, and hopefully with less of a mark on my neck. *I have to remember to get gas tomorrow.*

When I got home, I saw Luke's SUV and that the light was on in the living room. He was up waiting for me. It gave me chills up and down my spine. I got out of the car, took my bag of clothes, and then walked up to the door, unlocked it, and called out.

"Hello, Luke."

He didn't say anything and was sitting on the couch looking through his phone and watching TV, having a glass of wine. He finally acknowledged me and mentioned he thought I had to work tonight.

"I did work; I just finished and drove home." Then he asked about my clothes and I explained, then asked why he wanted to know.

Luke reminded me that I never had done that before, which wasn't true. I knew what he was getting at.

"Do you actually think I'm going to go out the way I look? Have you seen my neck? It is embarrassing. How would I explain this to anyone?" I said.

His response: I shouldn't have gotten him mad.

I knew I had to watch what I said at that moment. There was no chance that was his first glass of wine, and I had no idea how much he had already drank. Still, something needed to be said.

"Luke, this pain you caused me, I will not let happen to me again. This I guarantee."

He took it as a threat and I told him to take it as he heard it. Then I walked away to my room to take a shower, and then get ready for bed.

I had my purse, car keys, and clothes all in the bathroom with me, because I didn't know what to expect, and history had shown there might be something. Being on guard was important. There was no doubt about it, I was scared. He could not see that, though. I had to make him believe that my feet touched concrete and I was serious.

By the time I got out of the bathroom and set my alarm and slid into bed, Luke was already there. I'd taken my purse and tucked it next to my nightstand—just in case. But seeing Luke there had instantly taken away my tiredness and the adrenaline was surging through me. I was on high alert, and fearful of the thought of falling asleep with him right there. Luke murmured "good night" to me, and I softly replied the same.

I said a short prayer to ask the good Lord for strength. I knew I was going to need it, and I did know he had surrounded me with people who wanted to help—if I let them. Then I beat myself up a bit. What was my problem? What I was in the middle of wasn't love or happiness. I had to explain it—the real story—to Matthew tomorrow. Where would I begin?

My thoughts must have allowed me to drift off to sleep and I woke up at six to Luke getting up from bed, and I glanced to the side of the bed. My purse was still there. I laid there still and didn't want him to know I was awake. When he came back out from the bathroom, he must have sensed I was awake.

Luke said, "I will never take your purse or keys away from you ever again and should stop being that way towards you. I can't take back what I've done, but I can make it better." He leaned over on the bed and kissed me on the forehead and said he was leaving for work, and would see me later. I hadn't said a word.

Pain Behind Broken Vases

When he left I remained in the room, the scent of his cologne lingering. It smelled so good, and that made me angry. I wanted to grab his shirt and scream until I lost my voice. I wanted to say directly, not with kid gloves, what he'd done to me and make him feel a fraction of the pain he'd caused me. Why is he doing this to me?

CHAPTER TWENTY-FOUR

My body ached and I wasn't eager for work. I poured a cup of coffee and grabbed a banana, hoping to recharge and feel just a fraction like my old self. Anything would be welcome. I gave fresh water and food to Feathers. I changed his mat. I opened the windows in the kitchen to get some air. There was a wonderful breeze coming through. I swept around the cage. I went to the bathroom and took a shower, brushed my teeth; the time moved faster than other days. I got dressed quickly. I took another sip of coffee, it was delicious.

But alas, it was time to go. I slipped my shoes on and reached into my pocketbook for my keys. I felt a piece of paper there and I pulled it out. It was a note. How had he done that? Did my exhausted state of mind cause me to sleep so deeply that I was oblivious?

I looked at the note: *GOTCHA! Just kidding, I love you Amilia! I don't know what I can do to make you forgive me.*

The note was decorated with a heart and a smile in it. It was meant to make me feel better, but it gave me the creeps instead. He slithered around like a snake in the night, which meant I never knew when he was going to strike.

I shivered and went to get my phone from the bedroom, and then left. On my way to the car, I realized I forgot my scarf. I needed to go back and get it. We were going to have to talk, sometime. His girls were supposed to be coming tomorrow, and I had no idea what was happening.

My car was in need of gas and I drove to a full service station so they could put it on for me, and while they pumped the gas I tried Matthew again, as I promised I would. I got his voicemail and had to leave a message.

"Matthew, it's Mom. I know it's early, but I'll try you on my break. I'm thinking about you and love you very much. Have a wonderful start this morning. God bless you."

I was relieved he hadn't answered his phone, as I was still struggling with myself, much less any logical explanation about my situation to him. There would be so much to say. Luke is living with me... somehow that had happened. His kids were coming to live with me... somehow that had happened.

I realized that my "somehow that had happened" thoughts were legitimate. I had not extended any of these invitations. Luke had simply done as he pleased and I allowed it. I had allowed it. What have I done!

Creating reasonable explanations took me all the way to work and I pulled in just a minute before I had to punch in. I was ready for the day, said my hellos, and went to the locker room to put my purse away.

Pierre came in the kitchen and asked me if I could work with Jasper and set up a party of twelve in the blue room. Anything special? Pierre began to explain that it was regular lunch.

"How are you feeling by the way?" he asked.

"I'm getting better every day, thank you for asking." Jasper was in the blue room putting the tables together in a square. I walked in and said good morning to Jasper.

"Good morning Amilia!"

"While you put the tables together, I will go to the kitchen and get the things we need for setup." I took a small cart from the back. I began gathering all the things I needed for setup.

I was so deep in thought with what I was doing I didn't hear the Chef come in the kitchen. He came up behind me and said good morning. I jumped up and screamed! I dropped the ceramic sugar bowl on the floor and broke it, making a loud noise.

Chef put his hand on his heart and said, "Are you trying to kill me?"

Pierre ran into the kitchen and asked if everything was all right. I told him a sugar bowl fell.

"Was that it?"

"Yes sir, sorry about that," I said.

Pierre left the kitchen. I chased Chef around the kitchen hitting him with my towel, as he was laughing as hard as he could.

"I will get you for that," I said.

"The funny thing about that was I didn't mean to scare you," Chef affirmed.

"Stop laughing at me and get over here and help me pick up this mess."

Chef said, "Don't cut your fingers. I will get the dustpan and broom. Forget about the sugar packets, everything is going in the garbage." I needed that laugh. It's been a long time.

Thank you! I forgot what it is like to be human. Chef thanked me for starting off his day in a cheerful way.

I have to get out there. Pierre is going to have a fit. I pulled the cart to the blue room, and began to set up. Jasper and I put the room together rather quickly. I put a pot of coffee on for the staff.

The restaurant began to fill up quickly, but our party was late. Pierre asked us to stay in the room to greet the guests; he didn't have time to get over there. Time was moving along and the party of twelve never showed up. The other waiters were working extra hard to keep up.

I believe in my heart that there wasn't a party coming. Pierre wanted to give me a break from all of this. I know he felt so bad for me, seeing me in this position. Jasper and I jumped in to help clear and get drinks until things calmed down.

When lunch finally came to a close, I looked at the board to check start time for the children's party. It was five o'clock to eight. I was happy about that. Jasper and I quickly cleared the room up with the cart, emptied it in the kitchen. I punched out.

I decided to take a drive in the car so I could crank up the air conditioner and take my scarf off. There was a park nearby and hopefully I'd be able to talk with Matthew too.

What I loved about this park was how near it was to the ocean. There was a cool breeze and the view was amazing, the ocean sparkling in the sunlight in the distance. There was a small boulder under a palm tree that offered lots of shade and I decided to make it my destination. I made my way there and took off my socks and shoes, and climbed on the rock to have a seat.

I closed my eyes and dreamt about happier days coming. I saw myself smiling and laughing. I asked the good Lord for this, as it was all I wanted from life. Then I took a deep breath and my dream felt so real I opened my eyes. I looked at my phone; it was time to get back to the club. I walked up to the car, put my socks and shoes on, and began to head back.

There had been no call from Matthew, but I was so thankful to the Lord above for bringing me that moment of joy and reprieve. Unfortunately, it was time to get back to work. I hurried back to my car and to the club, and began to hustle in, realizing I'd forgotten my scarf in the car and I ran back.

My phone started to vibrate. *Oh, no, Matthew,* I thought. But it was Luke.

"Hello," I said. I probably shouldn't have answered, because I didn't have time.

He was calling to see how I was doing, as we hadn't spoken that day. He hated it, I didn't mind. Then the apologies started again and he asked for forgiveness. I didn't have time to talk though. I said we'd talk later, and I hung up. It was short, which was unnatural, but the only choice. He told me to call him when I got out tonight. I parked my car and punched in.

There really wasn't much setup. Chef made us French toast and bacon. I hadn't had that in a long time. I didn't see Chef to thank him, there was another cook there. His name was Don. I asked him, where was Chef? He told me he cooked for us and took off the rest of the evening. It's a party for children; he didn't have to be here for small bites.

"I don't blame Chef. He should take a break any chance he can."

Pierre came into the kitchen, gave us the assignment sheet, and began to explain to us that this was a swimming award dinner. He told us there would be four chafing dishes: chicken fingers, fries, mozzarella sticks, mini hotdogs. We needed to bring out cocktail napkins and appetizer plates along with the condiments. Pierre suggested the platters of cookies be placed on a separate table. This is all they are getting. He asked us to set up a lemonade and soda station together with plastic cups. This will be very simple and quick; they will show a short video, and give awards, and go home.

Working a children's party will be easy, I thought. The children were starting to arrive. Their coach was here already. I introduced myself. He was very laid back, and nice.

I couldn't believe my eyes, I froze. Victoria was there—Luke's child. I couldn't see her, and I didn't want her to see me. Thankfully, her mother wasn't there. I told Jasper that I couldn't see her and he was confused, for obvious reasons, saying I looked like I'd seen a ghost.

"She just can't see me," I said to Jasper. I was so anxious and he finally told me to calm down and we'd do the best we could do. And he told me he was there for me to talk whenever I needed it.

From there, I ran back and forth into the kitchen, remaining out of sight as much as possible. Jasper worked extra hard, covering me cleaning the children's dishes, and I felt bad for doing that to him, but I just couldn't imagine anything else. Luke was also impacting my job now, on an even greater level than the marks of abuse he left on me. I owed Jasper big time.

I finally caught a break when the lights were dimmed for a presentation. That way I could go in and out of the banquet room without worrying about Victoria seeing me. Thank goodness.

The kids were screaming and laughing every time they saw their pictures on the screen. It was such a fun time for them. It felt good to hear genuine laughter—the type of laughter that wasn't tainted by harsh realities.

By the end of the night I knew one thing—that I needed to tell Luke about this when I got home…just in case she'd seen me. I had no idea how much his ex-wife knew about me through the kids, or through him.

Finally we were all cleaned up and I expressed my profound gratitude to Jasper once more, before preparing to leave. Pierre walked into the room and thanked us for a job well done. I wanted to ask Don for a salad, to put chicken fingers on it, but he already left. I packed some to go, along with fries. I looked for the French toast and bacon, but I guess the kitchen staff ate it. We punched out, and Jasper told me that I can talk to him any time I need to. I thanked him.

My conversation with Luke was all that was on my mind on my drive home. I didn't even call Matthew. When I got home every light was on and I knew Luke wasn't doing something in every room. I breathed in, pulled my hair up in a ponytail, and walked in.

"Luke, you here?" I called out, already feeling tense. He came out of the bathroom right away, and he was yelling.

He wondered where I'd been. Seriously?

"Working!" I proclaimed.

"No, you weren't, Victoria was at the club tonight and said she didn't see you there," Luke said.

"I did my best to avoid her," I admitted. "I didn't know if your ex-wife was picking her up or how much she knows. That was a very uncomfortable feeling. I was coming home to tell you this."

Luke slammed me to the wall, and I dropped my purse and keys.

"Stop it! You're hurting me!" I screamed. He was seething, calling me a sack of shit, and accusing me of being with someone else.

My thoughts went to my cellphone, which was in my pocket, and I thought I should call 911. But he wouldn't give me any space. He put his face into mine and screamed at me that I was a whore and probably with those guys that are in the photos, carrying on like a slut.

He grabbed my arm and flung me across the room and I managed to look around when I was struggling. No wine was out, that I could tell, and I wanted to figure out his erratic behavior.

Finally, I was able to wriggle myself out of his grasp and I ran into the bedroom and closed the door. He threatened me to stay in there…"or else."

My purse was in the living room and I was glad that there was only makeup in there. I looked toward my bedroom closet and the door was open wide. When I looked in, I saw my clothes and shoes strewn about and my scarves were all shaved and sliced with a razor. Ruined.

I looked through my things that were still on hangers and saw he'd ruined just about all of my clothes, destroying them. It was devastating and made me angry and sick, but it wasn't my largest problem. I was trapped in my bedroom for the most part, and wished I had thought to run back out of the house instead of locking myself away where I couldn't flee.

I managed to find a t-shirt and shorts, and then started debating what to do. Luke barged into the room and pushed the door so hard that it slammed against the wall. When I turned my eyes and met his, he said that I'd just gotten exactly what I deserved.

The tears I'd been fighting began to fall. "What you sow you shall reap," I said.

He left the room and walked out of the house. This is the kind of thing he does when he hurts me. I began to cry harder when I was alone and felt safer. I held my clothes close to my chest and sat on the floor. It was as low as I could go. I wanted to call Matthew.

Finally, I left the room because I wanted to go get the food I'd left in the car and figure out what I could do. I saw the contents of my purse scattered all over the couch.

I needed help. I didn't want Luke. I actually hated him. I looked around before running to my car, not liking to be paranoid about everything in my life, and when I got back into the house, I locked the door and went to the kitchen.

The fridge was empty. I looked in the garbage and all the food was thrown away. I tied the bag and went to the dumpster and threw it out. He'd gone completely mad.

I looked on the couch and hoped to find my keys. I hadn't seen them. They'd fallen into a shoe and he missed them, thankfully. I picked them up and knew I had to keep them near me—like a second person. I had to be better prepared.

My tears turned to anger and I felt fed up. My emotions were changing so rapidly. I went back up to my bedroom and picked up my phone to call Matthew. Luke's latest bizarre behavior had been the last straw and I needed help. Matthew was who I needed to speak with first. As I dialed his number the tears came back. He answered.

"Matthew!" My voice was a giveaway and he asked what was wrong. "I'm in a place in my heart that I'm not supposed to be," I cried.

He could barely understand me because I started crying so hard.

"I met a man who treats me so terribly. I'm scared and alone I need to get out of this situation. I hate him, Matthew, I hate him!"

He said he'd heard about my neck and it seemed strange, but I don't think he knew how to respond. The mother he'd left not so long ago was not someone who would have been in the situation I found myself in. He went on to say that he'd be there in three months and we could figure things out.

"What do I do in the meantime?" I asked.

His logical and processed response took hold. I knew he was trying to understand, the problem was I couldn't even understand what was happening to me myself.

"Mom," he said, "why haven't you called the cops on him?"

"They're all his friends. They wouldn't do anything for me. Luke told me that more than once. I couldn't risk not being taken seriously by the police. If they are his friends they will turn on me. That would be too much for me to handle alone amongst everything else," I replied. Then I began to share everything, big and small, that had been happening.

Matthew kept saying I had to call the police, to get help. Finally he said, "I will see if I can come earlier, I'll talk to my boss tomorrow."

I had to tell him that Luke was also living with me and he told me to call the police, that he believed he was just trying to scare me. I told Matthew I loved him and then I began to cry hard again. I was breaking down fast and everything I'd kept hidden and pent up inside of me was rushing out of me at an alarming rate. I couldn't stop it. Maybe I wasn't meant to.

Matthew reminded me of his father so much in that moment.

"You are so big and strong like your daddy, if you were around this wouldn't happen. I know you can't be with me every second of every day. You have your dreams, Rachel, and everything else. I'm just so proud of you, Matthew. You're a good man."

Finally, the call had to end and Matthew said that he'd call every day until he could get home and reminded me to be cautious and alert, and to call if anything happened—ever. I promised that I would and when we hung up, I felt better, but didn't feel calm. The only thing I hadn't mentioned was Luke's daughters. Still… I knew my problems weren't over, but I had no way to predict what might happen, either. What remained on my mind was intense.

Either Pierre or Chef had been calling Matthew, as they were the only two who knew about my neck. I wasn't mad, but I wished they wouldn't have. I worried him enough that night on my own.

My clothes were basically destroyed and I had little money to replace them. It made me sad because my clothes made me feel good, as they were a reflection of me when I was at my best. Now they were shredded, just like my heart. Why didn't he tell me Victoria was coming to the club? Did Luke really pay my bills? I didn't know that, either. Because if he didn't, some would be late. I had to find that out, too.

It was time to get out of my bathroom and begin to get dressed. I opened my drawer, and I took a new bra out, and it was cut in half. I put the old one back on, and a shirt. I crept out my door like I was a thief in my own house. It was silent and I went to the kitchen to figure out a plan and make sure there was nothing else that was missing.

That's when I noticed Feathers. His cage was extra messy and he was edgy and nervous, like he was trying to warn me about something. I wished I could read his mind and I grew worried that he was being abused. Luke was just sick enough to do that.

I spoke to Feathers in a soft, gentle voice and he didn't seem to feel better. I knew the feeling. But, I had to get to bed because tomorrow I had a life to begin organizing.

CHAPTER TWENTY-FIVE

I didn't get up as early as I should have, but my body hurt so bad, and I just didn't have the energy. At some point I'd need to exert a great deal of it to have a necessary talk with Luke. His girls are supposed to be moving in. I need to know what he is planning to do and he needs to be made clear on how I feel.

As I laid there drifting in and out of sleep I heard the front door open and I held my breath for a second, and then remembered my phone and keys that were tucked under my side of the mattress.

Luke was in the kitchen; it sounded like he was rifling through papers and throwing things away. He didn't come in the bedroom. Then twenty-five minutes later he was gone and I crept over to the window to see his SUV drive away.

I was grateful Luke hadn't come to see me and also that I'd told Matthew what was going on. He did need to know, considering I had no idea when things might get out of control.

It was time to get up and I went to the bathroom to clean up my face and brush my teeth. The mark on my neck was almost gone, thankfully. After that, I made my way to the kitchen and found fresh muffins and croissants on the counter. I opened the refrigerator and it was packed with food, more than I ever had a need to have at a single time.

He was doing something nice—again. The problem was that I didn't want to eat any of the food he brought, because I didn't want to risk him saying what he did for me.

So, I put a pot of coffee on and took a quick shower, then went to try and figure out what I was going to wear. My options were very limited now. I took out a blue tank top and a beige skirt and hoped they'd still fit. They did, and I was happy about that. Then I went back to the kitchen and Feathers was squawking up a storm. He was flying around like he was scared and I opened the cage's door to try and comfort him.

He jumped on me right away and gripped tightly, then began rubbing his face against my hand. *Maybe all the fighting and commotion was upsetting him,* I thought. I talked to him lovingly and tried to calm him down enough so that he'd at least release me, and then I set him back in the cage.

I grabbed a mug from the cupboard and poured some coffee, but didn't want to use the half-and-half that Luke had brought. All I could do was try and organize my thoughts. I had to throw away my ruined clothes and figure out what I could afford to buy to start rebuilding what he'd taken away.

Finally, I made my way to my room and checked the cellphone. Matthew had texted to check in on me. I responded that I was doing better and would call him in a bit.

As soon as I put my phone down Luke started to call me. I didn't answer it; I let it go to voicemail. I played the message after, which said that he'd be home later that night with the kids. He'd brought food for the house and could I make dinner that evening. If there was anything missing I should just let him know.

I texted a response to Luke: *Sorry, I will not start supper for the kids tonight, just so you can throw what I make in the garbage, and call me names, absolutely not!*

He responded with his usual stream of nastiness: *You are a selfish bitch. Go fuck yourself.*

My reply: *Thank you for the compliments, coming from you they don't mean shit!*

He responded one last time with a "fuck off." I let him have that last word. Then I began taking care of all I had to do.

After my ruined clothes were bagged up I put them into the living room, made my bed, and then grabbed my keys from the spot under the mattress and headed out the door, locking it behind me.

Who knows what is going to happen tonight? Luke was clearly angry about my response, but I could not act as if everything was all right, and overlook his horrible behavior. What he'd done was completely unacceptable, from destroying my clothes right down to calling me up and assuming I'd feed his kids. Was he nuts? The answer, yes he was. Now that Matthew knew what was happening I felt less afraid than I did before.

The first thing I did was go to eat lunch somewhere. I was so hungry and I would have rather starved than eat the food Luke had bought. Everything he did came with a price, and I wasn't going to keep paying it. So the quiet, relaxing lunch at the diner was just what I needed.

I ordered a Rueben deluxe with fries, and salad. I asked one of the waiters if I could read the paper on the counter; he graciously gave it to me. My lunch was perfect. Great food in a nice environment, no negative energy or hassles. I felt better for it, and I just had to think of how to help Feathers get better too.

I asked for the check, I paid for my lunch, and headed to the mall. I was kind of excited. I didn't have much money on me, but I could check out the new styles and maybe get something on Thursday when I got paid, worst case scenario. I'd really loved the jeans he'd cut up— they'd been my favorites, which was probably why he'd chosen them.

When I glanced into my rearview mirror I noticed the grays in my hair, and then saw the bad condition of my nails. I'd really slipped in taking care of myself. No wonder everyone had begun to notice something was wrong. He'd had me so unorganized that I'd let myself go.

All of this made me feel the need to start reclaiming myself, and I was so excited by the time I walked into the mall. As fate would have it, the first store was Express, which was where I'd purchased my favorite (now destroyed) jeans.

I walked in and it was like heaven in there. The blouses were amazing, and they had my jeans. They were a little different but perfect. I looked at the price tag: $85.00. I remember buying mine two years ago for $60.00 and I had to pinch myself when I bought those for that price. I would have to work an entire double shift to get them. I reminded myself that this was just the first store…there would be other great things that were maybe more affordable for me.

Luke had torn my bras and blouses so I headed toward JC Penney's. They had great dresses, and I saw a large sign that everything was on sale. I could get a few things, instead of a single pair of jeans.

I kept shopping and browsing, enjoying my day off. I was anticipating my next check so I could get these things. It was exciting and I finally relaxed. Luke must have had radar about that because I felt my phone buzz and it was him calling.

"Hello?" his questions began. He wondered where I was, and when I replied the mall, he asked why.

"Are you serious, why would you ask that after you tore all my clothes with a razor blade?" I said. He replied that I was delusional and that he never did that.

"You're nuts, that's all I know," I told him. Everything is starting to make sense now. Then he said the kids were at the house and there was no dinner made.

"Make it yourself, I'm not your slave, I don't eat your food. We already spoke about that earlier today." He began to say I should be reasonable and do what I am supposed to do.

I continued, "The only thing I have to do is take care of myself like I always have. Try that shit again and you will have no clothes of yours left in the house."

He was ready for battle and it was back to the, "listen bitch" and "fuck you."

"I'm not your wife, I don't have to take your crap, this is the way you speak to me, you are getting it right back. It seems like this is the only language you know," I challenged.

Luke hung up. Right away I had to think about what might happen that night, but honestly, I didn't care anymore. If I did everything to please him things went wrong, if I didn't, things went wrong. Why? Because he was wrong. Wrong for me, and wrong in the way he treated me.

I had to find a way out. I prayed to the good Lord every day for help. Whatever needed to happen to get him away from me, I welcomed. He could go find someone else to be with, because it wasn't going to be me.

My shopping trip was over now and I began to make my way home. I took my time because I wasn't in a big hurry to go home to the nonsense. I wished tomorrow was Wednesday so I could start my work week and not have to deal with seeing him the rest of the week, only in the evenings when it was time for bed.

I went home and prepared for any possible trouble. I hid the car keys under a rock at the bottom of the stairs outside, and put the house key into my pocket. After that, I cautiously opened the door. The sounds of giggles came from the kitchen and I breathed a sigh of relief at that.

I walked in, avoiding Luke and looking at the girls.

"Hi, girls, how are you today?" I asked.

They gave a brief answer, then I turned to go to the bedroom so I could put my purse on the dresser and change into my nightclothes. I looked on my bed and noticed some clothes. When I walked over I found two brand new pairs of jeans and blouses similar to the ones he cut. The tags were still on the jeans. These were the pants I had seen at Express for eighty-five dollars. Was it a coincidence, or something more?

I didn't know if I should thank him, although he really should pay for the damage he did. He just replaced what he ripped up. It's not like he went out of his way to do anything nice.

There was also a bag on the floor from Victoria's Secret. I picked it up and opened it. There were three bras and three sets of panties. It should have made me feel better, all of it, but I felt numb for him and what he'd done. I don't like this man as a person. That's all I could say to myself.

After changing I sat on the floor and looked up. *Good Lord, how do I approach this situation? I don't have feelings for this man anymore; he's very cruel and unkind. I have started to inherit the same attributes.* Luke walked into the bedroom and startled me. My eyes had been closed. He asked if I was hungry.

"No thanks," I said.

He asked if the clothes were the right size and I mentioned they were. Then he left, removing my debate of whether to say thank you or not. I closed my eyes and thanked the good Lord once again for keeping me quiet, and the conversation gentle. I didn't want those clothes and when I got up I kept the tags on them and hung them in my closet. I would never wear them, never. I didn't want to hear, "look what I have done for you," forget that.

After that I remained in my room, feeling like it was the only safe place in my home. Again, that nagging question of how this all happened pressed my emotions. There was no way I could pull off small talk and act like nothing was wrong when everything was wrong with the situation.

I heard the girls going upstairs and remembered that I'd never put the sheets back on the bed after Adrianna had her accident. Since Luke didn't ask me anything he must have taken care of it. It was hard not to say good night to the kids, as they hadn't done anything wrong, but if I would have, it wouldn't have been genuine.

After he tucked the girls in, I heard Luke in the kitchen and I slid into bed, putting my cellphone near me, and then I closed my eyes. I felt safer because of it, although I really was not protected. Luke came in the room, changed, and slid into bed, saying good night.

"Good night," I said. Then I lay there all night, not moving a muscle and stiff as could be. When I woke up in the morning and began to stretch Luke was gone, the bedroom door was shut, and it was quiet in the house.

When I glanced at the time I saw it was eight thirty. I'd slept a long time, but still felt wiped out. I was sore sleeping in one position. Was I ever going to feel right again?

CHAPTER TWENTY-SIX

I got out of bed and opened the blinds to let the sun come in fully. The warmth felt so good on my body. It was going to be a beautiful morning.

When I went into the bathroom, I brushed my teeth and took a shower before I went to the kitchen to make some coffee. I was anxious and felt like I had to do something different. Who was I kidding? I felt the need to be prepared for the unexpected, and running out of the house in my nightclothes wasn't going to happen.

Once in the shower I felt its warm water wash over me and it felt so good. It began to calm me and that allowed me to collect my thoughts. I wasn't sure if I could treat Luke's daughters kindly, not that they'd done anything wrong, but I was so busy, and I couldn't sacrifice my life to take care of them. I needed to work, and I loved to work.

In fact, before Luke, I'd never realized how work was probably ninety percent of my life. That wasn't necessarily healthy and it did make me realize that there were things that needed to change in my life, but what they were eluded me. Aside from getting Luke out of my life, that is.

Strengthening my inner self was still a work in process, and without doing that nothing else would be possible. However, it was worth all my energy because I had to get off the rollercoaster ride before I derailed.

Finally I got out of the shower, and as soon as I began to get dressed I thought I heard something. I listened closer and heard a gentle tap on the door. For a second I froze, but then I opened the door. There was Victoria.

"Good morning, what's going on, I thought you left with your daddy?"

She said that she hadn't wanted to go to the babysitter's that day and wanted to stay here, and that Adrianna didn't want to go without her, either. So, they were both there.

There was this innocent child who Luke had just used to trap me at home, not even considering what I might have going on.

"That's fine, come with me, I'll make you some breakfast. What would you like?" She wanted pancakes. "Follow me to the kitchen."

I looked to see what I had to make pancakes. I didn't, but in the freezer were some waffles and breakfast sausage. She nodded her head, and then I asked her to go tell her sister to come down.

As soon as I had privacy I grew more irritated at Luke's nerve. He'd known I had off that day and took advantage of giving me a jab without even having to talk to me. But it would have to wait until later. Victoria and Adrianna were down in the kitchen now, very excited for waffles and sausage. They were really happy to be involved.

"I'll call you when they are ready," I said.

Victoria wanted to help. I smiled at her sweet and thoughtful gesture. These girls didn't deserve less than good attention, despite who their father was. We decided to eat outside since it was a nice day, and Victoria began to clean off the patio table while I cooked. Then she began to set the table. When I walked out, I smiled.

"This is going to be a breakfast made for princesses," I said. She giggled and her giggles actually made me feel good. I'm sure Luke hadn't hoped for that.

By the time we began eating, it was a really nice time. I was happy that they were animated and chatty and comfortable with me. However, this could not be their home for much longer. It just couldn't be.

Then Luke pulled up and parked, and the girls grew so excited, calling his name.

"Daddy, Daddy!" they screeched.

He learned that we were having a princess breakfast with plenty of syrup, and sausages, and two glasses of milk. Luke said he wanted to have one too, and that he'd be a princess.

"Daddy is acting silly isn't he?" Oh how they giggled, captivated by their daddy.

I told him he could go into the kitchen and help himself and he smiled. Then he leaned in and gave me a kiss, saying I smelled good. I followed him into the kitchen, hoping for an explanation for his latest action. All he did was compliment me on being able to handle the girls okay. It was hard not to say something, but one glance toward Victoria, who was very alert, made me choose silence.

He said he had to get back to work, that he would see all of us beautiful girls later. He kissed the girls, and gave me a kiss on my forehead. Then he left and I was faced with dealing with a lot of intense emotions, while also watching the children of my abuser. I needed to be on top of my game.

Trying to relax and just do the best I could in the moment, I drank my coffee and watched the fountain. I was so focused on it and then my tranquility was snapped when I recalled that I hadn't checked my mail in some time. I'd been out of my head and so off kilter.

I got up and told the girls I was going to check the mail. When I got there, no mail was in the box, which was strange. I usually had magazines, junk mail, bills, and everything in between. But after all those days it was empty, it was puzzling.

Wondering if Luke had done something was the natural conclusion. Maybe he'd brought it into the house. After I got the girls back inside, I'd try to call him.

We cleaned everything up and made our way into the house. I started a bath for Adrianna, and a shower for Victoria. I was running around and making sure the girls were okay, helping them wash their hair and clean up. Then they got dressed in their sweet and adorable little girl clothes, and I put their hair into ponytails. Admittedly,

Adrianna fussed more than she was excited about the entire process, but it had to be done.

The girls started to play and I began picking up. I heard them yelling at each other loudly and went upstairs to see what the fuss was about.

"Girls," I called out. They both jumped from not hearing me come up the stairs and wanted to play hide-and-seek. They ran to hide and I began to count.

"Ready or not, here I come!" I crept downstairs and it was so quiet.

I looked everywhere and on the last step I said, "I'm here." I walked into my bedroom and there was nothing. Then I looked in the closet. No one was there.

I couldn't find them. I went into the second closet behind the clothes and the pile of folded blankets. I checked under the bed. I went into my bathroom and looked behind the door and in the tub. So far no sign of the girls.

Then I went to Matthew's old room and called, "I'm coming to get you." It was still so quiet. Those giggly girls were certainly good hide-and-seek players. *They must be in the living room*, I thought.

I checked behind the sofa and recliner. I looked in back of the TV. Still no girls. I went into the guest bathroom and looked behind the door and in the tub. I checked the hallway closet. I lifted the tablecloth in the kitchen to look underneath—the kids weren't there. Panic wanted to erupt and I struggled to remain calm. Now my playful game was more of an intensive search. Where were they?

"Girls, this isn't funny, where are you?"

I was met with silence. After this went on for a while I knew what I had to do. I called Luke to ask him if he knew where they were, or if they'd contacted him. He did not answer the phone. I needed to stay calm. What I prayed was that this was another one of his practical jokes. Definitely cruel and insensitive, but better than the thought of the girls running off. I couldn't grasp my mind around the notion that they'd do such a thing.

Fifteen minutes later I called again. Still no answer. I put on my shoes and took my door key and phone and went walking around the condo complex. Maybe they'd decided to go to the play area. That wasn't the case. They were gone and the uncertainty was terrifying. An hour had already passed by.

The girls hadn't been found anywhere and I headed back home feeling defeated and angry. It only grew worse when I saw Luke pulling up with them in the car. I was grateful that I hadn't called the police and embarrassed myself. What a cruel man, it was just like him.

But my patience was spent. "Why did you do that?" I asked. He said he was free to take his daughters out for ice cream. "I knew it was a stupid joke of yours. It's just like you not to care about anyone. Take care of the girls yourself next time. That's why I didn't call the cops. You probably thought I would. I'm not crazy enough to give you that kind of satisfaction, the person who is nuts is you!" I exclaimed.

He thrust the car door open, and it smashed into my chest.

"Don't think for a minute I'm scared of you." He told me to get away from him, and I couldn't resist.

"With pleasure," I said. "You don't have to ask me twice." I walked quickly toward the house, and glanced toward the rock where my car keys were. I'd keep them there until I went to work tomorrow…just in case.

Victoria came over to me and said she was sorry.

"I'm not disappointed or upset with you girls," I said softly. "The way your dad handled it wasn't right. He should have told me he was taking you for ice cream, but he didn't. This is between your father and I."

We were back in the house and the girls headed upstairs. I went to my room. And Luke did what he did best—got a bottle of wine and began drinking. Nothing else seemed to make him happy.

After some time, I heard the girls go into the living room to talk to Luke. He had the nerve to tell them I was just being a bitch. He said it loud enough so that I would hear, but if he thought I was going to come out of my room and start something, he was wrong. I remained at peace with myself and didn't say a word. I was not going to fuel his ego.

Then he yelled out that the kids were hungry for lunch and I should feed them. I didn't respond. Then I heard them run up the stairs quickly and my stomach sank. Was this the type of activity they were used to between adults? Luke came to the bedroom door and was holding a glass of wine, asking if I'd heard him.

"I heard you what you said, I'm not your servant." He commented that was what I did best at work. "And drinking is what you do best," I retaliated.

He walked in the room and took the glass of wine and poured it out onto the bed, and then demanded that I clean it up. That I was ungrateful, and he'd bought me all those clothes. He'd already played his card with them, not even twenty-four hours after getting them.

"You act as if this was a gift. You destroyed my clothes and replaced them. This is not a present by any means. I will not wear them, anyway, because of what you do. Bring it up like you're doing me a favor. Like right now, they can stay on hangers as long as I'm alive. I'm fine with it. I don't have much and it's still okay."

Luke left the room and shut the door real hard, calling me a bitch under his breath. I got up from the bed and took the sheets off. The best thing I ever did was buy a top cover for my mattress. It would be a mess. I went out to the linen closet and took fresh sheets and I began to redress the bed.

The sheets wouldn't get washed right away because I heard Luke in there making dinner for the girls. I just could not see him. Not only had he made me lose my appetite, but he was pouring glass after glass of wine as he made dinner for the girls. My thoughts were so muddled they were almost indescribable.

I never thought I would be thinking that I couldn't wait to get back to work on my day off. I used to look forward to these days, especially the times I had at peace at the beach, my favorite spot, but now they were torture. It occurred to me that I hadn't called Matthew and I hoped he knew I was all right, that I wasn't in any distress.

After a bit I heard Luke tell the girls that dinner was ready. Victoria asked where is Amilia? He told her that I wouldn't be joining them because I didn't feel well. They were too young to know what was really happening, at least I hoped. *I never hear a peep out of the girls when he cooks for them. They sit in silence, I don't know if that is a good or bad thing.*

I decided to pull out a book that I liked to read at the beach and sat down on the floor and rested my back on the bed. I opened it up, eager for a distraction. How ironic is this title, *Can I Smile Today*. It actually put a smile on my face, silly isn't it? It was wonderful until... Luke came into the room and snatched it from my hands and threw it. He said I didn't know how to read so why bother trying.

"You're right," I said. I wasn't going to challenge anything he had to say through his slurring words.

Then he left to attend to the girls and his voice was so loud that I hoped they were okay. I wanted to help, but I couldn't risk what might happen by doing so. The best I could do was hope that he wouldn't be cruel to them. He hadn't been yet. I feel he found his release through me.

After the girls were tucked in, Luke went back to the living room. I sat still for a while when all this was going on. I picked up my book, and went back to reading it. I wasn't sure how much time passed by. I heard him go into the living room, but I didn't hear the TV; guess he was on his phone. He suddenly came into the room and proclaimed he wanted to go to bed. It scared me!

I wasn't tired so I just got up and moved so he could. I took my phone and I went out to the living room to sit in peace. I found an escape from the noise through my book. I didn't want to put it down.

He shouted from the room that while I was out there I should clean up. I didn't pay him any mind. He needed to go to bed and leave everyone in the house alone. Eventually, I fell asleep reading and woke up to Luke and the girls leaving. I told the girls to have a great day! They didn't say a word to me, but I breathed a sigh of relief.

I went into the kitchen and threw the leftover food in the garbage, and put the dishes in the dishwasher. I didn't want to spend too much time on this; I had to start getting ready for work. I gave Feathers some clean water and more food. I wiped down the counters, threw the empty bottle of wine out, and put the clothes in the washing machine. I didn't have enough time to make coffee this morning. I went to the bedroom, made the bed, and got right into the shower. *Thank goodness for work. I'm starving, and I can eat in peace there.*

I didn't go upstairs to tidy up the kid's area. *I will get dressed real quick, and see what's going on up there.* I dried off, brushed my teeth, fixed my hair, and I wrapped the towel around me and went upstairs. I couldn't believe what I saw. It was like a war zone. I fixed their beds, picked up the clothes, and put them in the hamper. I cleaned off the bathroom sink. I couldn't really do anything else.

I went back to my room, got dressed, put my shoes on, took my purse and cell, and left, locking the door behind me. I walked to the car and I remembered I put the car keys under the rock. I walked back quickly and took the keys, ran to the car, and drove off.

I need to put makeup on when I get to work. I only clean up because I feel bad for the kids. Luke is a mess. I can't wait to get to work and eat, and have some fresh hot coffee.

CHAPTER TWENTY-SEVEN

On my way to work I was trying to deal with all the thoughts I had. When I got to work I'd need to put my makeup on. To Luke, I was really just a maid, nothing more. There had to be a way to take care of myself, and not risk having to fight. He obviously didn't want me to have any time to myself. He wanted to control my life.

I was a mess. It would be good to get paid so I could get my nails done and touch up my roots. I desperately needed to look into the mirror and see a reflection of my missing self.

By the time I got to work I was just in time and when I walked in, something was awry. Don was working Chef's station. I asked where he was. Don told me he was home sick with the flu. *Maybe I could bring him some soup on a break,* I thought. He was always so considerate to me, and I wanted to return him some kindness. Don already started the coffee. I thanked him.

I grabbed a roll from the bakery bag—they were still warm—and I put some butter on it. I poured a cup of coffee. It was so good, I was so hungry. I had to eat before preparing the dining room. I couldn't think anymore, my stomach was doing all the talking.

I put my apron on, and I realized I'd forgotten my phone and ran to my locker to get it. There were two missed calls from Luke and I called him back. He began by telling me he was at the house. He was cordial and casual, thanking me for cleaning up the house and that he'd see me later. I told him I only thought of the girls, how unfair it would be to them to go to their room and see it in such disarray. Then we hung up, no other words said. Everything was *normal* to Luke.

I opened my makeup case, put on some coverup, powder, and mascara. I put some lip gloss on. I started to feel better. I looked at my hair. Oh goodness! I took out my mascara again, tried to touch up my grays the best I could. I put everything away.

I went to look at where I'd be working, and I was outside on the patio with Jasper again. When I went out there he asked how I was doing and gave me a hug. He was so kind, and I truly did appreciate it. Then we hustled to set everything up and it looked like it was going to be a slower day, which had its benefits, although I really needed the money now.

There wasn't much to do in terms of set up out here. We kept busy until break. I wanted Pierre to see that we were working. We wiped down table and chairs. Cleaned our waiters' station.

Don came out and told us lunch was in the chef's window. Jasper and I went in. Don made cold sandwiches and salad. I was very grateful. I took my plate and a glass of lemonade, and went to the back to eat. *I really miss Chef today. He makes me smile, and laugh.* Pierre came back to tell us guests were coming into the dining room. We stood up, took our plates to the dish bin, and went to our stations.

My phone was buzzing. I looked down and it was a text from Matthew that read: Hi Mom! Checking in on you. I hope things are all right. Please text back.

I responded: Good morning, darling! Yes, everything is fine for now. I'm at work and I will call you later. I love you.

Matthew wrote back: I love you too, Mom!

Then the day proceeded and it was so slow, and I hoped we didn't get a last minute rush. We didn't. Jasper and I put everything away, and I found myself with some free time until five, when Pierre said we had to be back.

I went to the kitchen and asked Don for a container of chicken noodle soup to go for Chef. Don put it in a bag for me. I wrapped a fresh roll. I thanked him. He asked me to say hello to Chef from him.

I punched out, took my purse out of the locker, and headed to Chef's house. Knowing how surprised he'd be made me smile, even if he might not answer the door. But I could leave a message and the soup on his stoop.

With the great fortune of little traffic, I arrived in his neighborhood in less than twenty minutes. I couldn't remember his house number, but I did recall what it looked like from the summer barbecues he has for the staff. He is a great person. I pulled up on the street and saw his Jeep and knew I'd made it. There I was, and suddenly I felt a bit strange, like an invader. It wasn't like me to just show up at someone's house, even if it was with good intentions.

I parked in front of his house, walked up the stairs, and rang the bell. Chef opened the door right away and I greeted him with a smile.

"Chef, I brought you some soup. I heard you weren't feeling well."

He told me that was sweet and invited me in. I walked in and heard laughter in the next room. It was from a woman and I went red.

"I'm so sorry I intruded. I should have called first."

He told me not to be silly and I responded about having to get back to work. I told him to feel better and then I quickly left, with him thanking me as I left. Only once I was in the car did I let it sink in. Of course Chef would have a girlfriend. He's a tall handsome guy, Light brown hair, green eyes, and so nice. He has a gentle voice and a kind heart.

I had feelings that came over me for Chef. It sparked a sense of jealousy. *This is nonsense. I have so many problems going on in my life. I feel my emotions are just getting the best of me.* I needed to focus and redirect. My issues needed my attention and fixating on Chef doesn't help.

I proceeded to the club. I went back on the main road and the traffic had grown thicker. I glanced at the car's clock and knew I'd be okay.

Just breathe, I thought. My phone started to ring and I instantly prayed it wouldn't be Luke. When I took out my cell I saw it was Matthew, and I was glad to answer.

He was checking in on me and I had to assure him that I was fine, just out doing some errands and catching some fresh air between shifts. His concern was met with mixed emotions. I didn't like having him worry, but hearing his voice was so calming to me. What was happening to me? I was changing rapidly, and how could I explain it to others when I couldn't understand it myself? I tried to stay on happy subjects, like his job, and Rachel. I didn't want to speak about Luke. I sent him my blessings, told him I love him, and I would talk to him tomorrow.

He replied, "I love you Mom."

I drove into the parking lot, and in the parking lot stood Luke. I parked near him and got out. Before I could say a word he asked me where I'd gone.

"I went for a drive to clear my thoughts."

He immediately challenged me, telling me he'd asked Don the cook where I'd gone, and he said to see Chef because he was sick. I ignored the boyfriend reference Luke made. That's what I did, and I shouldn't have had to lie about it, but he was so irrational.

"Yes, I stopped at his house. He was there with his girlfriend," I said.

Luke demanded to know why I'd go when his girlfriend could bring him soup. Didn't he get being nice just to be nice? Not to make up for something you did wrong? I found myself explaining what shouldn't have to be said.

"I thought it would be nice. He is always cooking for us and kind to everyone. I figured it would be a nice surprise. What's the problem?" I said.

The problem was that I wouldn't cook for the kids last night.

"Look, Luke, you treat me terribly, you're a very angry man."

He threw a dozen roses at me and they hit me in the face and fell to the ground. I'd been so tense about him that I hadn't even noticed he was holding the flowers. Then he got into his SUV and drove out at a crazy speed. I didn't pick the flowers up. Instead, I walked right on top of them, crushing the rosebuds.

I walked inside, numb to it all. Time to get back to work. Don, who had mentioned I'd gone to see "Chef," was there and asked if I was okay.

"Yeah, why do you ask?" He told me he'd seen what happened in the parking lot. He was sitting in his car on break. "Yes, I'm really fine with it, whatever it is," I replied.

I didn't know this guy that well that I was comfortable to share anything I was thinking at that moment. So, I moved on, learned I was on the patio that night, and I was thankful. The more I could not talk to people the better. I just wasn't in the mood.

Jasper was with me and I was glad to have him there, as we did work so well together. He told me he looked at the reservations and it looked very slow. I told Jasper that there have been so many mistakes over time that he'd have to see it to believe it. Then he began to tell me that Mandy said hi.

I realized something, and I was quite ashamed of myself at that moment. I'd been so wrapped up in the turmoil of my life, I'd really forgotten about all the friends I did have. It had happened so craftily that I hadn't even realized it. I needed to catch up with her.

CHAPTER TWENTY-EIGHT

The night had been slow, no mistakes with reservations tonight, and that had been a good thing. Jasper was kind, not pressing me to talk about what I didn't want to disclose. He made sure that I knew he was there for me. Don made pasta and chicken for dinner, but I wasn't hungry. I packed mine to go. My nights have been unpredictable since Luke's been in my life.

We cleaned up, closed the umbrellas. I punched out, took my container of food, and left. The roses were gone as well. The groundskeeper must have cleaned them up. No presence of Luke in the parking lot, but in my mind, he was occupying all my space, suffocating my perspective.

He'd said to call him on my way home, and I debated whether to do it or not. I decided to, hoping it would allow me to just go home and get ready for bed with fewer hassles. When was the last time I was able to do that since he'd moved in? I couldn't remember.

"Luke, I'm on my way home now."

He asked what I was calling him for, and then hung up. Indeed, another one of *those* nights was likely on the horizon.

So many thoughts stirred through my mind, none new, and all reminders of what I hadn't been doing. I had to check on paying my bills.

I hadn't been getting my mail, and I was completely out of control in all aspects of my life…at least it seemed that way.

I pulled up to the house and parked my car and when I opened the door I heard blaring music coming from the house. Every light was on…again. I walked up and rolled my eyes, that common sigh escaping my lips. When I tried to unlock the door I found it unlocked.

As soon as I was in, I walked to the living room, and found the remote to turn the music down. There was no sound of human activity.

"Luke…kids." There was no answer, but there was a bottle of wine opened up in the kitchen. I called out again and this time Luke came stumbling down the stairs. I immediately tensed as he began to yell at me for turning down the music.

"It's late. Someone's going to call the cops with it that loud," I said. A logical answer. He made me out to be the inconsiderate one, the one that never liked to have fun.

"Where are the kids?" I asked. The thought of them seeing Luke so drunk broke my heart. He said they were in bed and I said I was going to head there, and he should too. I remembered leaving my food that I got every night after work in the car—again. I forgot to bring it in more often than I remembered. Luke declared that he was staying up.

I didn't want to look at him directly and chose to look around. The place was a mess. Feathers looked stressed and anxious, and feathers were actually shedding from him. I just didn't get what was going on, but cleaning would have to wait. I needed to get to sleep.

I walked toward the bedroom and thought about Feathers on the way. He was very old and I really didn't know if he was sick or just fading away. Maybe Chef or Jasper would take him for a bit…just until I sorted things out. When I turned into the bedroom a new thought came to my mind. What was going on?

There were rose petals all over the bed. I couldn't believe it. Luke had come back to the parking lot and picked them up. It was just too much and the uncertainty of every minute made me tense. I went in to take a quick shower, got dressed, and went to the hallway to get the vacuum. Luke began to scream, asking me what I was doing.

"I'm going to clean up the mess you made in our room."

What I called a mess, he called romantic.

"It would have been romantic if you were nice to me, but you are not. This is just your craziness acting out."

It was all because he was "sorry." The same old story, and no matter how he tried to show it, I turned him down continuously. I was the one who was cruel, not him.

"Let's just go to bed, tomorrow's a new day," I said. I forced as gentle a tone as my exhausted mind and body could muster.

Too much had happened by that point for me to think of anything else. I had to be out the door by eight thirty in the morning tomorrow, as well.

Then I added, "When you're not drinking, we can talk."

I left the living room and went to my room to go to bed. I picked up as many rose petals as I could and threw them out. I shut the bedroom door, turned off the light, set my alarm for six thirty the next morning, and crawled into bed. He stayed on the couch—who cares?

I woke up at seven thirty. Garbage was all over my bed and I had fifteen minutes to get out of the house. My alarm had been shut off. I went into speed mode. I got ready quickly, grabbed my makeup to put on at work, gave Feathers water, and then grabbed my purse and keys so I could bolt out the door and get to work.

Thank goodness I woke up. I couldn't believe him. He'd shut my alarm off. Who did things like that? *Luke, that's who,* I realized. And the garbage on the bed, what the hell? I didn't even know what to do or how to process such erratic, stupid behavior. Luke had gone mad.

As I neared work my phone rang. I pulled it out of my bag and it was Luke.

"Hello."

He responded with a question about me getting to work on time.

"Of course I did," I said, playing dumb to his sabotage. Wouldn't he be surprised to find the garbage still on the bed when he got home?

I said I had to go, and as I parked my car at the club and began to walk in my phone buzzed with a one-word, precise message from Luke: *Bitch.* There were a few smiley faces for his perverse pleasure, whatever that was. I erased it, punched in, put my makeup on, and walked into the kitchen. Chef was back.

He gave me a friendly and sincere good morning. Then thanked me for thinking about him. I smiled, and then offered an apology for showing up unannounced. He said that his sister had come to visit, that she was home from school and that he would have loved for her to meet me.

Now I felt a bit silly, and confessed that I thought I was intruding. We both laughed, and then he gave me a hug. It felt good to get a hug from a tall, kind person, a nice guy. We parted ways with a reminder from Chef that I owed him a coffee date.

"I won't forget," I said. I really wished Luke was more like Chef. Stable and certainty, not a constant unknown…like what I'd receive that night when I got home. Well, either way it was time for work. Make some money, have a good day, and hopefully find a temporary home for Feathers.

I was working with Jasper, which meant I'd get a chance. But nothing surprised me more than when we were talking and he referenced that Chef and I were growing rather close as of late. Jasper believed he liked me. I think I blushed.

"I like him too, but I believe our feelings are those of good friends. We joke and have fun."

Chef had the coffee ready, which I was thankful for. I needed a cup. Jasper mentioned that's what people do when they begin to have feelings for someone.

"What makes him an expert on love?"

He told me that was how he met his wife and everything had gone from there.

I'd had enough of this subject. I smiled and suggested that we get back to work. I was in a disaster and hardly equipped to even entertain such a notion, as wonderful as the thought of a genuine, loving relationship was.

And the day moved on, and by lunch time we were all hungry. Jason, another waiter, sat by Jasper and me, casually inquiring if everything was okay with me.

"Yeah, I just have some things I need to take care of," I said. He asked if Chef and I were fighting. I was shocked, and he explained that we seemed like an item.

What was going on? But then it was back to work, and only after things slowed down again did I recall one of my tasks for that day.

"Jasper, I have a favor to ask." I think he was shocked that I actually asked for one. "I have a bird and I need to put him somewhere for a little while until I can figure out my personal situation. Do you think you can take him?"

His eyes were sympathetic, but he nodded his head and apologized. He couldn't, his wife didn't like animals.

"Thanks, I just thought I'd ask," I said. Then some of my customers caught my attention and I made my way over to them.

Then I ran into the kitchen, getting some fresh water pitchers, and also to ask Chef. Hopefully he'd be okay with watching Feathers for a bit. He smiled at me.

"Chef, I have a favor to ask," I said.

Before I could tell him, Pierre dragged him away. I was getting nowhere fast. Chef apologized and said he'd catch me later.

I had time before my dinner shift to go over my finances and get a grasp of how much I owed. I'd never been clueless about them before, but I sure was now. I prepared to take on the task, and saw a text from Matthew. That's right…I'd forgotten to call him this morning. I sent a quick text and then got to the task of handing my bills.

I began looking up the numbers to my bills and started to call. I began with JC Penney's to verify they'd received my payment. Thankfully, I was up to date and I asked them to put me on paperless billing, as that was the best way to assure that my bill didn't disappear again. I'd have to do that with as many accounts as possible…just to be sure.

Next was Power Surge, my electrical company. Sadly, they hadn't received a payment and when I asked how much was owed they told me $345.34. My stomach plunged, as I could not pay that entire balance at once. Thankfully I could make a payment that week and then go on a plan to make up the difference.

The rest of the bill verifications offered some relief, and some concern. All it really cemented was that I could not trust Luke. He'd written checks for those, took them, and then never sent the payments. I couldn't get paperless for my water bill; I needed to keep an eye on that.

In the end, it was another reminder of me having to regain control of my priorities, which reminded me of Chef. I put everything away and was going to find him, but my phone buzzed again. It was Luke. I was so grateful I know where I stood now. This was an uneasy feeling amongst everything else that was going on.

I answered and he began to rant about me leaving the house in such a mess.

"You shut off my phone and tried to make me late," I said. I didn't feel bad about the mess, although a mess like that irritated me greatly.

He told me I deserved what happened to me, and I wasn't going to get into that argument, as there was something more pressing.

"You clean the house, and also stay away from my bills. You're a liar saying you paid them. I called everyone today and no one has received payment," I said.

He ignored that and threatened that I would be cleaning the house when I got home.

He repeated, "So what about your bills, that's your problem, you better clean up this shit, you got it!" he said in his rage. "You deserve everything you get, fuck off bitch!" he said.

My voice was so calm. "Thank you for everything you do." I shut off his noise, and hung up.

I'd had enough. I had to take care of Feathers and I made my way to the kitchen to ask where Chef was. I learnt he'd taken the night off, he had something to do. There would be no resolving Feathers' problems that day.

Don asked if I'd heard they had hired a new assistant banquet manager. That was news! I wondered who he was. It sure would make Pierre's job easier, as the old one hadn't been around in quite some time. I was happy for Pierre, but like all people in the industry, I hoped that I'd like him. The relationships with these people are everything to a server. Then what the chef on duty said next surprised me. He was sure that I would have been asked.

I'd never thought of that, and it must have shown, because he added that the club seemed to be run by men. When he noted that Chef had really been pulling for me, it made me feel good. Again, it was a reminder of Luke, and how he tried to drag me down. A good man, a caring man, wouldn't do that. And Chef was just a friend with good intentions. I told Don that I knew Pierre wouldn't have chosen me. There were always men in that position for as long as I worked here, and I felt he would continue with that process. So anyway I hoped that this person would be nice man and treat us fairly.

The kitchen door swung open but no one came in. I saw Pierre through the small window and was pretty sure he'd heard what we said. It wasn't bad, but it still made me feel strange. I sighed, because I still had an hour and a half left before I had to punch back into work. I went to the locker room to freshen up. I added more mascara, some powder, and lip gloss. I felt better and more alive.

I went to the banquet room for some peace and quiet, grabbing a buttered roll and cup of coffee along the way. Once again, I started to dread going home that night. The home I used to walk into and feel wonderful in had become a nightmare. Thinking about taking it back wasn't enough. I had to do something.

How many times had I vowed action so far and not taken it? Too many to count. I finally could sit in peace, feeling I had a grip on my life again on certain issues. I thank GOD every day for giving me the strength to get through this difficult time.

I wonder when the new manager will start. I will ask Don if he knows when I go to the kitchen.

I punched in and looked at my assignment. I have the same station with Jason and Jasper. These guys are terrific. I like working with them; we don't have any problems with each other. We work well together. *I hope they do not tease me about Chef tonight.* There wasn't much setup to be done. Some tables with missing silverware and water glasses; not a big deal to get done.

Jasper and Jason walked in the dining room.

Jasper said, "Hey Amilia!"

"Hi Jasper!"

Jason walked into the dining room. "What's up Jason? How come the long face?"

Jason replied, "I don't feel like working tonight. Do you ever have those days when you don't feel like doing anything at all?"

"Yes," I responded. "I have had a lot of those lately." I, on the other hand, wished for it to be busy so I could keep my mind busy.

Jason replied, "I guess you are right. What do we have to do for setup?"

I told him it was simple, just the side stations with water pitchers and butter dishes. Jason wished for it to rain so we could all go home. I on the other hand wished for it to be busy so I could keep my mind busy. I had to laugh at this.

"Come on fellas we have to get through the night, stop being so gloomy. Jasper, stop complaining and be more grateful things are fine for you." I understand he wanted to go home. I don't blame him; he has a loving wife and much happiness. Things I still dream of.

Pierre came into the dining room and said, "Good evening, everyone's stations are the same for tonight's dinner as usual. Nothing special going on, no big tables. You can ask Don if there are any specials. Work together, and have a good night."

We went into the kitchen, and Don had dinner ready for us. He made lasagna, and salad. The love of food that Chef carries in his heart, you could see it. Don seems to cook because he has to. You can taste the difference. Anyway, I'm grateful and thankful I have something to eat.

I asked him if there were any specials. Don only made wedding soup. He didn't do anything special since it was a very slow night.

I find myself eating alone lately. I still have to go home and deal with Luke. I don't know what is going on in his mind right now. I never thought I would feel this way. I really believed he was my prince charming. That Luke would love and care for me. I know he is not my everything. I pray day and night for something to happen so he can get out of my life. I know in my gut this is not the way love is. I had real love, with a person who was gentle, kind, and respectful. Luke doesn't come near that. He's hot and cold all the time.

I took out my phone and checked the time. Break time was over. I had to get to my station.

It's going to be another one of those boring nights. I didn't have time to get my nails done. I have to dye my hair. I haven't had any down time with everything that is going on at home to take care of myself. Tomorrow I will buy a box of hair color, and fix my hair on my break. I will get myself back together again. Luke has brought me down so much I forgot about me, how important I am.

Jasper walked over to me and asked if I was all right. I told him I was deep in thought with something going on in my life right now, and I couldn't help but to ask him if it showed that much. Jasper said he made an observation, because we know each other and he can tell. I thanked him for being a good friend. Members began to come in.

CHAPTER TWENTY-NINE

It was a slow night and by nine o'clock we cleaned up, and I was out of there, but so nervous. My stomach had butterflies in it as I weighed out all the uncertainties. I thought I might pass out. A cold sweat came on. I had to sit down before I could even leave, just to be sure.

I went into the banquet room to sit down in the air conditioning to pray. I prayed that I would be all right that evening and there wouldn't be any problems. But I couldn't stop sweating and was so warm. I stood up and wiped my forehead. I took a bottle of water from the waiters' pantry, punched out, and grabbed my things.

As I made my way toward my car someone ran up behind me and touched me. I began to scream and whipped around, hitting him with my purse. It was Jasper, and he was yelling my name over and over, and I could barely bring myself to stop. But when I did, he grabbed me and held me tightly. Then I began to cry. Now my fists were softly pounding on his chest and I couldn't stop the emotions from consuming me.

He asked, "Amilia what the hell is going on?"

"I'm sorry, Jasper. I didn't mean to hit you," I cried.

He asked if he should follow me home to make sure I was going to be okay, and I shook my head no. I might be okay if he was there, but afterwards, things would undoubtedly be worse.

He walked me to my car and I got in and left, not bothering to drive a minute over the speed limit. I'd grown so uncomfortable in my own skin that I hardly recognized myself. I used to be able to joke, and none of the silly things ever affected me. I didn't feel like *that* person any longer and it made me so sad.

Ultimately, I didn't want to go home. I'd had a smart mouth with Luke, and he wasn't likely to forget it. My phone started to buzz and I wasn't even thinking when I pulled it out of the apron and said hello.

Luke asked if I was on my way home, and I don't know if I really answered him or not. But I heard him say that he was sorry for his anger—again. He was making me dinner to show how sorry he was.

"Sounds good," I said, like a zombie. I couldn't even feign enthusiasm.

We hung up and I knew I had more time than what I'd suggested to Luke, so I decided to go to CVS and get some hair color. After that I drove home, and I witnessed that person who wanted to believe the best come out in me again. It was nice that Luke had apologized and was trying to make good for what he'd done. Maybe he'd be in control with the girls there.

✳✳✳

I parked my car and put the keys under the rock outside the house—their new home. I grabbed my house key and went inside. It was so silent. I called out to see if anyone was home. I looked around and there was no dinner on the table, and everything was dirty. Dishes piled in the sink. The garbage was still everywhere. He'd lied.

My eyes went toward Feathers to assess him, and he seemed quite relaxed. There was no one here to curse and make noise. It was strange how the calmness of the house superseded the messiness of it. I could relax and just clean up and go to sleep, hassle free. His lie didn't matter, and I wasn't going to call him and ask about it either. With everything else he'd done to me, this was actually okay. I get some alone time, I'm all right with that.

I went into my room, got undressed, put my dirty clothes in the hamper, and took a long warm shower. I didn't want to get out, but finally I did. Then I began to clean everything up, vacuumed the mess on my bed. It was mostly rose petals and Qtips. Then vacuuming around Feathers' cage, putting some laundry in the wash. I tried to create the home I was used to walking into. Just myself, in a lovely, clean environment.

By the time I was done with everything, Feathers was whistling. I knew he was happy and that made me happy. I put my hand in the cage and he sat on it and rubbed his beak on my fingers. I gave him one of the treats, and he was so happy that he opened his beautiful red wings up wide in appreciation. I laughed.

Luke walked in behind me and I hadn't even noticed at first. He asked what I was so happy about.

"Just cleaning and thought of something funny," I casually said. But I walked away from Feathers because he was finally relaxed.

Luke said the kids had eaten dinner already. I saw them and said hi, and asked how their day was. Victoria began to talk so fast that I couldn't understand her, but she sounded happy. Just the way a child should sound. Adrianna remained quiet, though. Shortly thereafter, Luke told them to get ready for bed, leaving the two of us in the kitchen together. Victoria asked if I was coming, and I said I would be soon. I was tired and had a long day and had to get up early. I walked the girls to the stairs and then went to the bedroom. Luke was silent.

I walked to my room, took my cellphone from my purse, set the alarm, and put it into the pocket of my shorts. The same thing wasn't going to happen to me again. It seemed that Luke was waiting for me to respond differently, but I wasn't going to give him the satisfaction. He'd lied again, and tried to trick me again. It was no surprise.

Really, I was happy he didn't make dinner so I wasn't forced to sit there and pretend. I began to pray for the day when he'd leave for good, and I could reclaim everything I'd lost—especially myself.

After reflecting on something positive, which felt great, I went to grab the laundry and do the last few things before I turned in. Luke was on the couch and I ignored him. It felt great to have taken care of business and I just turned off all the lights and retired to the bedroom, eager for a content night's sleep.

I actually laid in peace that night as I came to terms with all the unhealthy things in my life. How overthinking at work caused me more stress.

I said, "Good Lord, thank you for a calm night. Thank you for the strength to keep moving forward. I'm grateful for Matthew and my job full of nice people. In the Good Lord's name, Amen." I closed my eyes and went to sleep.

Then I heard Luke come in. He wasn't stealthy, and was going out of his way to make sure I woke up. I didn't move a muscle, and I had no idea what time it was because my phone was in my pocket.

After he finally changed clothes, he plopped into bed like he was jumping into a swimming pool. The entire bed shook, but I didn't say a word. I wasn't going to accommodate whatever need he had. In fact, I fell back asleep and awoke to my alarm. Luke and the kids were already gone.

CHAPTER THIRTY

The next day I woke up to peace, got ready for work, fixed my bed, gave Feathers water, and looked at my cell. I had enough time to make a pot of coffee, but I decided to treat myself to Dunkin Donuts. I put my shoes on and locked up the house. As I was driving out of the complex, I saw Luke driving in. Our cars stopped, and I rolled down my window.

"Hi," I said. He immediately explained that he'd forgotten something he needed for work. "Okay, then, have a good day," I said.

He rushed away quickly, not saying goodbye. It wasn't unusual, but I did wonder what he could have forgotten. Nothing that I'd taken note of, that's for sure.

I rolled up my window and drove, making my way to the highway and my next stop—Dunkin Donuts for a cup of coffee. With a deep clear perspective. *I need to get myself together and become strong enough to cut the ties with Luke. He always has me on guard.* I ordered my favorite latte, and turned around. There was Luke in line behind me.

"Luke! Why are you getting coffee so out of your way?"

He snapped at me, telling me to mind my own business in a loud angry voice. I was so embarrassed because it was really crowded in there, and everyone turned around and stared at me. I just quickly walked out and got back into my car. Once in the car I said a small prayer, thanking the good Lord for the beautiful day and the great cup of coffee.

Then I looked at my phone and saw a text from Matthew. He wrote: Good morning Mom. How are you today?

I sat for a moment before texting: Good morning, Matthew. I'm fine today, and thank you for checking in. I hope your morning begins wonderful. I love you! Say hello to Rachel.

The message gave me a big smile.

Luke tapped on my window, and I rolled it down just an inch. He is so unpredictable, and these were the only clothes I had for work. I didn't want him to get smart and pour coffee on me. He asked who I was texting, and I said Matthew, and asked why. He just said he wanted to know.

I rolled up my window and drove off to work. I couldn't wait to get away from him. I still had a great smile on my face. Hearing from Matthew makes the sun glow brighter every day. I turned the music on to KLove, the contemporary Christian music station that helps keep me connected to faith and prayer. My song, "Need You Now" came on, performed by Plumb. I sang it all the way to work, even after it was done.

Knowing that the good Lord would direct me encouraged me. Singing released the emotions and freed my mind and heart. It felt so good to sing at the top of my lungs. I knew I was heard, and I pulled into the parking lot and walked towards the club. I tossed my coffee cup in the garbage and went in to start my work day. I put my things in the locker and proceeded to punch in.

I looked at the assignment sheet and saw that I was working with Dawn and Cassie. I didn't work with them much, but they were nice. I went out to the patio and said good morning to everyone.

Dawn immediately answered abruptly, "What's so good about it?" Dawn was really bitter and negative and I did all I could do to stay clear of her. I pretended I didn't hear her comment. I needed to have a positive attitude, and even though the sky looked like it might pour down rain, I had much needed sunshine in my heart.

Cassie said, "Good morning."

Pierre came out to the patio and, greeted us with a good morning. He wanted us to know if it started to rain to bring everything in and close the umbrellas. He wasn't sure what the day was going to bring.

As Pierre walked away Dawn mumbled under her breath, "I hope it rains so I can get out of this place, I've seen enough of it all week."

I didn't respond to her comment. She was trying her hardest to get something out of me. Little did she know I had already received training from Luke how to handle someone like her. All I could do was shake my head. I can't seem to get away from people like this, good grief.

Chef came out to the patio; we looked at each other, and I smiled. He said good morning everyone.

I replied, "Good morning Chef!"

"I have lunch ready for everyone." Chef walked back into the kitchen.

Dawn said, "Wow that's a first. He never comes out here to say anything." She glanced over at me and smirked.

I quickly commented, "Come on let's go get lunch before the kitchen staff eats everything."

Dawn with her smart mouth went, "I don't think you have anything to worry about, he would probably save you a plate."

"Stop," I cautioned. "We're friends. I don't need any rumors." So I grabbed my plate and decided to eat in the banquet room so I could just enjoy a positive lunch without any chatter that didn't fit the mood I wanted to be in.

When I opened the door Pierre was sitting with Chef and someone that I assumed was the new assistant banquet manager. I turned around quickly and left the room and decided to eat in the locker room. Not the best place, but a quiet place.

After break, I went out to the patio. Dawn and Cassie were standing out there. Pierre came right behind me. Pierre wanted all of us to work together out here as a team. Dawn told him she'd rather have her own station and if either one of us got busy, the other could jump in. Pierre agreed.

"Very well then. Amilia, you take the left side, and Dawn take the right."

People were starting to come in and sat at my tables. It was fine, I stayed busy. Dawn didn't even ask me if I needed help and Cassie didn't want to do more for me than he had to, because he was scared that Dawn would get mad at him. They work together all the time; it would be hard on him. I stayed quiet and worked very hard, my station nearly full.

Pierre was at the patio opening watching what was going on. I didn't complain about anything. Dawn had one table sit in her station.

Service finally ended. I was so happy that the members I had today were not high maintenance. I didn't have a cooperating busboy and Dawn—forget it! She was waiting on the sidelines to make nasty comments. We were cleaning up and putting everything away as it started to sprinkle a little bit.

Work proved to have strange challenges that day with the other wait staff. I missed Jasper and Jason, who were so easy to work with. But I kept smiling to myself, and didn't care how hard I had to work. If I didn't have backup, I didn't.

I was grateful Pierre had been taking note of the dynamic duo of Cassie and Dawn, because he came to the patio during cleanup and called them out on their behavior. He asked how it went out here today. I told him everyone was great, no problems. Pierre began to explain that's not what he had heard.

Dawn immediately responded, "What do you mean?"

Pierre asked who had the Mantels today.

Dawn said, "I did!"

"They told me you were very rude. You only had one table. Amilia had the others, and from what I was observing you wouldn't even help her with anything, not even pouring a glass of water. Cassie, what's going on with you? Do you not like working with Amilia? Did she do anything to you?"

"No sir, I will do better next time."

In the end, they were told to go home for the day and given an ultimatum to contribute or quit. Everyone in earshot was left silent, unsure how to respond. Pierre was so kind, but he was definitely irate about what he'd seen. Dawn left. Cassie asked for a word with me. He explained how sorry he was about how he acted.

"It's okay. You were under a lot of pressure. My advice, next time you should just do your job completely, because you never know who may be watching. You need to get the focus off of you now and work extra hard so you don't lose your job."

Then Pierre was back with what I also needed—a paycheck! I thanked him, punched out, and went right to the bank. I needed to pay bills.

My bank was only one exit from the club and I was glad to have the time to put the check into my account and have it register for that day still. *I need to get direct deposit,* I thought, that way Luke couldn't do anything that I didn't know about. The best way to do that was with a clean slate—a new account.

I took off my apron, went into the bank, told the teller I needed to close this account and open up a new one. She asked me why. I told her I had guests at my house and they went through my things, I didn't know how much information they had. She referred me to a supervisor and then excused herself to help someone else.

I reached in my bag to get my cellphone and I remembered I left it in the car. The supervisor walked over to me and asked me to follow her to her office and reassured me it wouldn't take long. I told her I had to get back to work fairly soon. She did everything I needed quickly, ordering me a new card and having it sent to the bank instead of the house. She set me up for e-statements, and deposited my check. I made sure all my accounts were updated, which gave me a clear mind. I held off on ordering new checks until I could think of where to send them.

I breathed a sigh of relief, feeling happy to take this big step toward solving my problems.

✳✳✳

A few minutes later, on my drive back to work, Luke called. He said he'd written a check from my account and it hadn't cleared.

"Why would you do that? Those were old checks, (I obviously lied), and you have no idea how much I have in my account." He didn't need to know about the new one.

He kept on repeating, "I would have paid you back!"

He hung up on me. My gut instinct was right. It felt incredible finally taking steps to take control of my life. I need to do what I can to protect myself in all areas of my life.

Something was strange. I speculated that it was for that checkbook that Luke went back to the house today. He wasn't sharing something, but what?

I pulled into the club lot with forty-five minutes left before I had to punch in. I went into the locker room and began to make phone payments on my accounts that were behind, which felt so good. When I was done I had only $130.00 left. Not much, but it was mine.

I was not going to risk taking any of this information home and I decided that I'd keep it in my work locker. It was a lot safer there. I freshened up with some powder and lip gloss, and locked my locker.

Then it was time to work and Jasper was there, who was a breath of fresh air. But having a skeleton crew wasn't. Even a slower night would likely be a chaotic one. Thankfully it was Thursday. Pierre asked us to wipe down the patio since it rained, get it ready out there for service.

Jasper asked me what happened today. I told him I didn't get any help; Pierre wanted us to work as a team. Dawn received a complaint, and Pierre was very upset. He sent them home. Jasper explained to me that Dawn is like that to everyone, not to take it personal.

"Jasper, being unkind to people obviously doesn't pay off in the long run," I said.

Members were starting to come in. We were very busy. I had Pierre jump in and open bottles of wine and get the glasses. I wouldn't have gotten through this without Jasper.

We finally cleared the last table; I couldn't believe it was so late. The time flew. Pierre thanked us for a job well done. He expressed what a great team we are. I thanked him. We said good night. Jasper and I gave each other a high five!

I looked around the kitchen to see if I could find Chef, I hadn't spoken one word to him all night. He also leaves food out for us at the end of the night. This time there weren't any leftovers.

It was eleven o'clock, long day, and I was happy it was over. Hopefully it would be an easy drive home. I already started to feel uneasy about going home, all my thoughts racing ahead of me.

Luke started to consume my mind again, and not knowing what he was up to was so stressful because he was always shocking and angry about the most unexpected things. But when I got home everything was dark. It was almost eerie.

I opened the door, turned on the living room light, and locked the door behind me. I seemed to be alone. I went to the kitchen and Feathers was good. Then I took off my shoes and went to the bedroom to see if Luke had left a note. He hadn't, but he'd been going through my things.

My closet was wide open with my bill folder on the floor, along with my old checkbook. Something was strange, but I could not be sure of what. I picked everything up, organized my papers, and put them in the right file. I changed and went to the kitchen to grab my purse so I could hide it.

I hid my keys in a drawer, but then I decided that this wasn't a good idea, and I put them under the rock at the bottom of the stairs. I took my purse in the bathroom with me so I could take a shower. Having everything close to me was what made me feel best.

After all the small tasks I had to do were done, I was so tired. My second wind: gone. It was time for bed. I was tempted to call Luke, but resisted. I put my phone into my pocket again and went to bed, my eyes heavy and ready for sleep.

I woke to the sounds of Feathers chirping madly from the kitchen. I looked at my cell. It was only five in the morning. I got up to see what was going on, surprised to find Luke making coffee. He must have flipped the lights on and startled Feathers, who was not a fan of abrupt bursts of light. When Feathers saw me he calmed down and I smiled at the bird and said good morning to Luke. He wondered what was so good about it.

"We're alive and well," I said. "What happened to you and the girls last night?" I asked.

Luke told me that I obviously didn't care, because I hadn't called.

"You're right, I didn't, but I wanted to. I don't know what is going on with you lately. I left you alone last night. I knew you would be all right or you would have reached out to me," I stated.

He said he went to sleep at his mother's with the kids. When I asked why, he said due to the tension we have at the house. He was still battling it out with his ex-wife on a daily basis, and he just wanted a break from everything.

"We are on the same team. You have to realize what happens here with us was created by nonsense. It doesn't have to be this way, you know. You take all your anger out on me and I'd rather not be around you when you do," I said.

He said that was why he went to his mother's, so he could think in peace and with a clear head.

"Maybe it's too early for all of us to be together Luke," I said. He didn't get what I was saying. "We should take it slow. This is so over-whelming. I don't know how to process anything and make sense of what is going on. Too much confusion has been created. I don't even go to bed unless I have my phone in my front pocket."

I clamped my lips. I shouldn't have said that. Luke said he didn't know what to say. I sighed and said I had to go get another hour of sleep. He asked if he could come lay down too, and I said he could. We shut off the lights and went to the bedroom, and I fell asleep again. When I woke up it was to my alarm, and Luke snoring. My eyes were so heavy, and I was dreading going to work. I was exhausted in every way I could be, which always made for a tough work day.

But I got up, got ready, and then snuck back into the bedroom to get my keys from behind the dresser. What a lot of unnecessary work to go through just to feel comfortable—and realized I put them under the rock. I need to make it easy for me to get out of my own home quickly if I had to. I hide everything, I get tired, I forget myself. Goodness, what a way to live.

When I turned around, Luke's eyes were open. He asked if I was leaving for work and I nodded my head. I asked him if he had to get up for work and he said no. This was another strange thing. Then he spilled his heart with all these additional apologies about how he treated me and how lousy he had been. He wanted things back to the way they were.

They *were* more filled with new romance feel than anything. It had turned volatile quickly.

"Luke, I don't know if it will ever be the same," I shared.

He confessed that he was willing to try and this time it would be different. He got that I didn't believe him, but he'd prove me wrong.

"I have to get going right now. It's not the time to address all of these issues we're having," I said.

He nodded, his head committed to me, but I could not commit to him. I left. I went into the kitchen and blew Feathers a kiss, gave him a treat, and when I turned around, Luke was there. He told me to have a good day again and took my arm and kissed me. Then he repeated his commitment to us again. His words were ideal, his touch tender, but I knew they were deceiving. I was touched about it, but I still felt the overwhelming sense of foreboding.

"I will see you later Luke." I slipped into my shoes and left for work.

Once outside I breathed in deeply, took the keys from under the rock, and walked over to my car. There was a long-stemmed rose on the door handle with a note that read: *I will make us better... I promise.*

I looked back at the house and Luke was at the door staring at me. I waved goodbye and got into my car and drove off. Any weakness I may have had with him in front of me vanished once I was in my car and had gained distance from him. My gut instinct told me that everything would not be all right. After everything that happened I didn't love him anymore, and I didn't believe that I could recapture those feelings ever again.

My home was no longer mine, and I had no idea how I could get him out of it either. Why couldn't he go live with his mother? It would beat the two of us lying and trying to make something out of nothing. He was a tormentor.

But enough of that…I had to call Matthew. I took my phone out of my purse and dialed Matthew. I put him on loudspeaker because I was driving. He immediately asked if everything was all right.

"Yes, Matthew, I'm fine. I just wanted to check in with you before I got to work."

He asked if Luke had been nice to me.

"I haven't seen him, really. I've been working a lot during the week."

I could hear my son's relief and he didn't hold back on telling me that he feels better being in touch every day. I agreed; it made me feel good. I can't believe I was going to fight this battle alone. I needed someone to know. Matthew is right by my side, even though we are a distance apart.

Matthew grounded me so well, and just that small conversation, which was basically the same every time we spoke, was enough to keep me optimistic. I told him I love him, and to say hello to Rachel.

Then we hung up, I just drove, and felt great. I'd left the house early and was at work about forty minutes before punch in. A perfect opportunity to take a cup of coffee and head down to the beach. I went to my locker to put my purse away, and headed to the kitchen to make coffee. Happily, it was already made. I poured a cup and went out back to the beach. This was the best tasting coffee I have ever had. The aroma immediately took me to a different place.

***

It was a little cloudy, but perfect by the shore. I sat on my apron to the lovely sounds of seagulls, and a fresh breeze from the ocean. Just what I needed.

I ask myself every day what does someone do when they are out of love with the person they are living with? The problem that I have is that he is violent and drinks a lot. I have to be very careful how I handle him. I have already seen his nasty side. That is instilled in my thoughts, and in my heart. I know what I'm up against. It is a scary feeling.

I heard a whistle come from behind me. When I turned around a big smile formed on my face.

"Good morning Chef." He walked over. I smiled again and thought about how I would love to stay in this spot all day, with Chef there to talk with, and just forget my troubles.

"You're here early, a busy day must be in store," I said.

He said that it was actually a quiet day, but he had to meet with Pierre and the new banquet manager. I asked when he was starting. Chef was telling me that he was on staff already, and he would begin the next banquet event. I wanted to know if he was a nice person, because that was most important to me. Chef didn't really know how to answer that question; he doesn't know him. I thought to myself, *I hope and pray he treats everyone with kindness.*

Chef looked at me, and said, "Amilia don't worry, you are fine. I know Pierre spoke very highly of you, and so did I." I thanked Chef for all of his kind words.

We talked about work a bit and it was casual and hassle free, nice and relaxing. Then it was time for me to get in to begin my day. I stood up and dusted off all the sand. We walked into the club. I had to punch in, the time went fast.

After punching in, I heard my phone buzz. I pulled it out of my apron and saw that it was Luke. I ran into the kitchen and answered. He just wanted me to know he was thinking about me, and repeated the same words again. He was trying, but I really wasn't buying this. It wasn't easy to remain pessimistic because I wanted him to be a good man, but history had proven differently. He was hot and cold in the nice department. My inner peace lost a place in my heart for anything he says. I shook my head. No words came out at that moment.

I'm scheduled to work inside today with Dawn and Jasper. Thank goodness for Jasper. *Maybe it will be different with Dawn today, with a clearer understanding about how to work together.* I went into the dining room and began putting the tables in order.

Pierre walked into the dining room, and said, "Good Morning Amilia!"

"Good Morning!" I mirrored back.

Pierre asked Jasper to gather the waiters for a quick meeting. He wanted us to know that Dawn would not be back with us. The complaint she had from Mr. and Mrs. Mantel reached the board. They wanted her dismissed effective immediately. Pierre emphasized the importance of working together as a team. He wants us in our stations, ready to go after break.

Chef came into the dining room and announced that staff lunch was in the kitchen. I was ready and hungry. Jasper and I raced in like two little kids, laughing so hard; we are silly. Wow, Chef's famous country fried chicken and garden salad! His food has so much flavor.

Jasper sat with me during lunch and asked how I was doing. I am sure that night of smacking him with my purse and crying had impacted him, and who could blame him.

"I'm all right. I take one day at a time to see where it takes me. I hope and pray things get better."

He told me that while he didn't know what was going on, exactly, he hoped good things for me too. His words touched me and I asked about his family, wanting to change the subject so I maintained my happier mood. He talked about his days off and having fun with his family, and then asked me what I did on my days off.

"Well, my situation is a bit more complicated than a simple answer. I will explain it to you one day," I said.

He nodded and then our lunch time was over. Time to get back to work. I asked Jasper if he didn't mind putting away the bin he left in the dining room. I just remembered it; we don't need any trouble. Pierre made it clear to be on top of our stations. I needed a minute to freshen up. He didn't mind. I took out my lip gloss, put a swipe on, added a little more powder, and prepared for the rest of the day.

Very slow today, members wanted to sit outside. I kept busy in the dining room folding napkins, and polishing silverware. Pierre had Jasper work in the kitchen to help the staff clean, and organize the items on the shelves. The bar became a little busy. I helped with servings, and taking orders. Pierre walked through and thanked me for jumping in.

Lunch came to a close, and I decided to color my hair, right there at work. There was plenty of time to do it. The box of hair dye was still there, I was ready to get this done. I wanted me back! I punched out, and got to work.

Chef told us that tonight was more of the same; there are no reservations, and he doesn't know what Pierre was thinking of doing. If he was going to send anyone home or not. I thanked him for telling me. I really didn't want to go home. That was the last thing on my mind.

I know it sounds crazy. I feel safe here, at peace. I can laugh, and smile, be silly with the important parts of myself I love.

CHAPTER THIRTY-ONE

I walked quickly to the locker room, mixed the color, and began to dye my hair, eager to be forty-five minutes away from a new person. It wasn't the typical action you'd find at the club, but I needed it, and it seemed others did too.

The staff was coming in and making jokes, and we'd banter back and forth. While my color was processing I decided to make a nails appointment for the next day. A manicure would also make me feel great, and that's what I needed to do. It was time to take care of myself again and let nothing stop me. It was time to rinse, and I forgot that I wasn't prepared to dry my hair! I didn't have a towel, so I used a bunch of paper towels from the wall holder—what a mess!

Once I was done I freshened up my makeup. I felt so good, recharged and ready. The slow day had turned into the day I needed. And as a bonus, I hadn't heard from Luke. This fact created a very peaceful day.

The real weights of my world were still there, but manageable. I thought about how nice it would be to get caught up on my bills with my next paycheck and return to a sense of normalcy in that area of my life.

Before I knew it, it was time to punch in and begin work again. I ran into Chef first, who said I looked beautiful. It was a wonderful thing to hear, and I smiled. All I'd done was put my hair back in a bun, since I didn't have a blow dryer or anything else. But if it worked, I'd take it.

As the day went on, hearing so many wonderful compliments about how happy and refreshed I looked made me realize how much my struggles must have shown externally also. Jasper, who worked with me daily, mentioned to me that he was happy I was coming back from whatever brought me down. I thanked him for his support, and I knew I had a way to go yet. But I didn't want to think about that. I just wanted to get done with work and go home, and hopefully do the one other thing I needed—catch up on sleep.

Jasper and I were working in the same area; not much for him and I to do in terms of setup. I went to the back and picked up an empty bin and a couple stacks of cloth napkins to give myself something to do after break was over.

I wasn't really hungry, but Chef put food out. It was the same as today's lunch, it was so good, but I was still full. Jasper grabbed a plate and stayed in the kitchen to finish what he was doing this afternoon.

I had this burst of energy; just getting back to the way I was, is a big deal. I felt lost. Getting a grip on my life was a much-needed deal that I should never break again.

Pierre came into the dining room and made a comment on how rested I looked. I thanked him, but was not sure of that one. I laughed to myself, knowing I looked run down. Well, I have the bounce back in my step. I feel great!

But what a slow night it was…even kitchen staff were going home early. Chef had gone home to allow another worker to stay so I didn't get to say goodbye—or ask about Feathers yet. He was so nice. However, it was getting into dangerous territory for me to keep comparing him to Luke, as there was nothing similar about the two, aside from being male.

I remembered that amazing cup of coffee I had this morning, the aroma stuck with me all day. I went to the kitchen and asked Scott the line cook if he knew who made the coffee this morning. Scott told me that he did. I asked him, what was his secret? Scott didn't like the club's coffee, and he brought his own from home. He had enough left to make another pot. I was so happy. It was delicious. I thanked him and walked back into the dining room.

I ended up not having any guests sit in my station. But the bar was packed. I went over to the bartender to ask if there was something I could do. Chip is a nice man, but when the bar gets busy, Chip gets very nervous. He's much older than the rest of us around here. I saw him take a cloth napkin out of his pocket and wipe his forehead. He was behind.

Members waved me over to take their dinner orders. I cleaned, picked up dirty dishes; I was doing the best I could. It was getting overwhelming.

Chip yelled out my name.

"Yes Chip!"

He leaned close to my ear with his flushed red face and coffee breath and said, "Thank you for jumping in to help me my dear lady. It's very kind of you to do this."

"No problem, I'm here if you need anything," I said.

Chip looked at me with those grateful eyes, and said, "God Bless You Amilia."

Chip has a very deep Irish accent, the members love it. He speaks very gently to me, but comes off rough under the collar to the staff. No one likes to work with him. I believe he held his job thusfar because of the members.

People kept flocking in to the bar. I felt we would never catch up. I walked over to the waiters' station quickly to ask Jasper if he wouldn't mind coming over to help out.

Jasper said, "No, I'm sorry Amilia, but that man is so nasty to me, he's not a nice person."

I tried pleading with him to help me get my orders out of the kitchen. Jasper refused to help. He'd rather not deal with Chip. I began to walk away when he told me he would help, only for me. I thanked Jasper. He told me that he doesn't like trouble, and he'd rather stay away. Jasper was a big help.

Chip yelled out to Jasper. He responded with a loud, "What?!" and hesitantly walked over to Chip. My heart fell to my stomach.

Chip said, "Please Jasper come here, I just want to thank you for helping me today. You're a kind lad!"

"Oh, you're welcome," Jasper said, relieved. Chip put out his hand, and Jasper and he shook hands. The issue seemed to dissolve in that instant. I was so happy to see it. Jasper asked Chip if he needed ice from the back. He noticed the bar was running low.

"Yes please, if you don't mind," and he handed Jasper the ice bucket. Chip looked up at me, winked, and I smiled back. There was such a big sigh of relief, and no more tension.

We finally caught up. I looked up at the clock I couldn't believe it was already seven thirty. *Where did the time go* I thought. People were leaving, and most of the cleanup from the rush was done.

Pierre walked into the bar, approached me, and said, "Amilia you and Jasper can punch out at eight. Thank you both for helping out Chip. I love the teamwork. I would like to speak to you for a minute before you leave."

"Yes Pierre, ok."

Jasper came out of the kitchen and poured the ice behind the bar for Chip. I told him that we could leave at eight, he was very happy about that.

I went to Pierre's office before I punched out. Pierre wanted to tell me that he was behind the waiters' station when I was speaking to Jasper, and he was very pleased how I handled the problem. Pierre continued to say I had a way with words. I thanked him, and we said good night. I thought to myself, *I wish I could handle my personal business the same, my goodness.*

It was nice of Pierre to take notice, but he always says thank you to us and appreciates our hard work. He is a great boss to work for.

On my way out, I made a cup of iced coffee from that delicious coffee Scott made. I didn't have time to have a cup once we got busy. It was a great ending.

***

I left work and went to my car and started to drive. As most always, thoughts of Luke were on my mind, growing stronger with each mile I went that brought me closer to home. I really hoped Luke meant what he said that morning. It would make it less unbearable to have to go home and see him, and to maybe talk. My thoughts drifted to starting over. I was surprised to hear my thoughts reveal that I would love to start over, and try to make what we had work out. If only he would…

Maybe I should call, I thought. I grabbed my phone and dialed him, but he didn't answer. Maybe he was working late, or something. With light traffic, it was a quick ride home and I pulled up to my place and parked. Luke's SUV was there, and I thought he must have just gotten in. But it was strange about not answering the phone, that thing never leaves his side.

Eerie feelings began to seep into my mind. *Please be wrong, please be wrong*, I silently repeated.

I detached my car keys from my house keys and put them under the rock in front of the house. I walked up the stairs and entered my home. Lights were on the, the television was softly playing, and Luke was sitting at the kitchen table. There was no sound from Feathers. I took my shoes off at the door, put my keys in my purse, and called out "hello" to Luke a bit louder than normal.

He was texting like a mad man and had an angry look, his eyebrows close together.

I repeated, "Luke, hello."

He didn't yell, but his voice was tense and he told me to shut up, he was in the middle of something. What could I do? I turned away and headed toward the room. I'd only been home for a half a minute and my dream of starting over was brought to a halt for another day. Why did I keep daring to go there?

The kids weren't there, either, but I wasn't going to ask. That was not my problem. I decided to take my shower. I went into the bedroom to get undressed. Luke came charging into the room and grabbed my arm, demanding to know who I was with that day, where I'd gone, and what I'd done.

"Luke, are you crazy or something? I bought a box of hair color from CVS and dyed my hair on my break in the girls locker room. I was starting to feel old and I didn't like it. I did it for me, not for you. I still haven't had a chance to do my nails, but I'm doing them tomorrow."

I stopped. I owed him no explanation. Luke replied that I was going to listen to what he said.

"Excuse me, no I'm not. If I would have listened to what you said, I would be behind in all my bills. So, I will not!" I said.

He pushed me with a lot of force, and I fell against the bed. He called me a bitch—his eyes were wild with anger, and his jaw tense. He looked out of control.

"Thank you!" I shouted back. It hadn't been my plan, but it happened. Then he marched out of the room, pounding his feet like a child that didn't get his way.

I didn't get him and I realized that we'd only been together for two months, yet it felt like years. What had happened in this period of time floored me. We don't go anywhere together, or talk about anything important. I don't even like coming home from work. He always seems to find a way to fight. I really believe this is what he does best, besides drinking that is. It was even more drastic when I acknowledged the short time span. Eight weeks to a changed me, sadly not a better one.

When I got in the shower I looked forward to attempting to wash my tension away so I could go check out the house and see what I'd find next. I had no idea if Luke was there or not. I hadn't heard any doors slam.

The air conditioner was on high and the house was pretty cold. I shut the unit off in the bedroom before going to the kitchen. I heard Luke on the phone. I could tell he was talking with his ex-wife and he was screaming and yelling at her, calling her every nasty name you wouldn't find in a book. I felt bad for her, but I hoped he'd stay on with her, because I couldn't imagine what it was going to be like for me when he got off the phone. I seem to receive the repercussions of every nasty phone call to his ex-wife.

Maybe I should turn around and go back to my room to bed and cut my losses. I wasn't tired, but I didn't want to be yelled at because of their disputes either.

He hung up and shouted, "Amilia what's up?" and asked if I wanted a glass of wine.

I wasn't in the mood for a glass of wine, but I replied, "All right, that sounds nice."

He told me to go into the kitchen and he got another wine glass and filled it up for me—right to the top—and handed it over. I had to sip it so I didn't spill it.

Luke walked into the living room, sat on the couch, and turned the TV on. I followed and sat next to him. Neither of us spoke, but he occasionally laughed at the show we were watching. There was no mention of his day or mine, or the kids, finances, anything. Just two people there, existing but not really in the moment.

I had to commit to not getting wrapped up in his false promises. I did not want him in my life. If asked, I'd be able to say that from the bottom of my heart. May the good Lord be listening to me, because this was not who I envisioned the love of my life to be.

Luke stood up and asked if I wanted more wine, and I said no. I still had a lot in my glass. When he was in the kitchen I heard him uncork another bottle, which was another sign to tread lightly that evening. He came back and I wanted to go to the room, but didn't want to risk a fight. He also had his cellphone and was searching something and texting. I didn't ask what.

I took note of Luke looking at my wine glass from the corner of his eyes. It was almost empty, and the only reason it was came from my futile effort to calm my nerves. Without saying a word, he got up and went to the kitchen to refill it and came back into the living room. He didn't even ask, and I apparently had no choice. I sensed he was trying to get me to lose my cool like he so easily did when he was drunk. I had to remain vigilant, since I was likely going to be in the living room for longer than I cared to be.

I had to breathe in and just get through this. It was ten thirty at night and I was lightheaded from wine and emotion, and I wanted to go to sleep. I stood up and told Luke, and thankfully he didn't fight it. We didn't kiss or hug. The only offering made was me giving him the rest of my wine, which he gladly took.

After my alarm was set and everything was in its secret place, I turned off the lights and went to bed. The night had been so stressful that I could barely express it. There was no moment of relaxation, and now that there was a physical wall between us, I still wasn't more at ease. After everything I'd gone through with him, I still didn't know what to expect. How was I supposed to rest?

I finally did fall asleep and woke up at about three in the morning. Luke had never come to bed and I walked out into the living room. There he was, passed out with his phone in his hand. I crept to the kitchen and the second bottle of wine was emptied as well. I left everything as it was and went back into my room and went to bed.

Not so long ago I would have gently woken him up to come to bed. My heart wasn't in it anymore though. I had lost all semblance of love. My love at first sight had only lasted for a fleeting moment. Ever since that time, it had been downhill.

I love who I am as a person, and I've always felt beautiful inside and out. And, yes, I'll always hold the love I had with my beloved husband dearly, but at the same time, for the future, I know there is someone out there who will love and embrace what I had to offer dearly, and treat it like a gift of goodness, not something disgusting.

The bedroom door squeaked and I didn't move my body, but opened my eyes. I was scared because I couldn't hide. Luke sat on the bed hard enough that it would have woken me if I hadn't been awake when he came in. He said that he was going to be at the house that night, and he wanted to talk to me about something important.

I didn't turn my head, but replied, "All right, I only have to work lunch today."

He said it would be more like six, then he got up and left, not saying anything else.

CHAPTER THIRTY-TWO

Luke was gone and I had optimistic thoughts of him moving out and moving on in my head, and I was so excited. Somehow I managed to fall back asleep for a few more hours, but with pleasant thoughts in my mind.

By the time my alarm went off I felt relief. I opened the blinds and looked out the window; the sky was very gray and gloomy. I loved having the sun out, but I felt a ray of hope in my heart, and that was good enough for me.

"Thank you, Jesus, for this glorious day. Please keep Matthew and Rachel safe," I prayed.

It would have been great to get to the beach today with my schedule, but Luke seemed to have radar about when I had half days. Hopefully he really would be there for "the talk" and the talk would be what I prayed: That he realizes this relationship is not working out.

Just the hope that it brought me made for a great morning. Feathers was doing great, making cheerful sounds. I got to enjoy my coffee and did some cleaning around the house. These simple things helped my system feel it was getting back to normal, and the tension in my face and worry in my stomach left. Luke always stopped my mind from working.

Time was getting away from me. I took a quick shower, fixed my hair, put on some makeup. I had to get on the road. It's about that time for work. I blew Feathers a kiss and left, getting ready to call Matthew on the way. On my way to the car, I had to turn back to get my keys from under the rock. *I can't wait until I don't have to do this anymore.* I got into the car and was finally on my way.

I couldn't wait to call Matthew. He picked up on the first ring.

"Good morning, Matthew," I said. He said I sounded very happy this morning. I told him that I had big news to tell him. He sounded as excited as I felt.

I said, "Luke wants to speak to me tonight about something very important. We haven't really talked in a long time and we don't spend any time together, or really do anything social. It was nice only the first week of us being together, but the rest has been nothing but unkindness and torment. He slept on the couch last night and came into my room and sat on my bed and told me that we need to have an important conversation.

"I believe this is it. He is going to leave and I won't have to worry about any of this nonsense anymore." I didn't plan on saying as much as I did, but saying it released it from within me, and that felt wonderful.

Matthew was so happy as well, and then he turned into the parent, cautioning me about having a healthy relationship. I smiled. He was such a good son, and a good man too. I told him I love him. Matthew made me promise to keep him posted with everything going on. I promised that. Then we hung up.

By the time I got to work, everything was still good, including me getting into work just before the rain began to pour. My energy was high.

I know Luke is not the right man for me. I will have peace again in my life. I can't imagine taking that abuse any longer. I like it better this way; that he is leaving on his own, instead of me trying to get him out and having to fight with that tyrant.

I walked into the kitchen to punch in. I greeted everyone with good morning! No replies, I kept moving towards the dining room. Chef and

Pierre were talking. Jasper and a few other servers were setting up, but there was already talk of another slow day because of the rain. A few were a treat, but too many were not good.

Who would go home? That was what remained to be seen. Jasper sure wanted to go, because his wife had the day off and that meant they could go do something special together. He would not be in a good mood if he had to stay here.

His words were another reminder of what couples that were really in love did. Mandy came up to me with a smile. I hadn't talked to her in so long with everything going on and today was the perfect, slow time to play catch up. She said she missed me and asked how I was doing.

"Everything's getting better every day. I have such exciting news. We should get a drink so we can talk...soon," I said.

She made this funny, inquisitive expression and said she wanted to know now. I only laughed. I wasn't going to break the great news until I heard it right from the rooster called Luke's mouth.

Pierre entered the dining room and said, "Good morning ladies."

We both started giggling. We both replied simultaneously, "Good morning Pierre." He walked away quickly, blushing, with a grin on his face.

"He is so sweet," Mandy whispered. Pierre is really nice to all of us. Mandy told me how he relies on me, and she thought he would have chosen me for Banquet Supervisor. I didn't say anything to that comment. I was happy and grateful he appreciates my work. Mandy had to get back to the front desk. We gave each other a big hug.

Much of the staff was released right away, including Jasper, and they were relieved and hustled out the door, not even bothering to say goodbye. I couldn't believe it. Jasper came back in out of breath, running across the parking lot feeling bad he didn't say goodbye to me. He's a good person. I understand how it feels to want to be with the person you love. There was no harm done. I told him he was silly. We both laughed.

"Come on now get out of here," I demanded.

Then I turned around and saw Chef's eyes on me. "Good morning," I said.

"I was looking for you yesterday, but you left early. I wanted to see if you would have liked to have that cup of coffee with me."

Chef mentioned how Pierre had his head spinning. He wanted menu changes per members' requests, and everyone seemed to want something different. He'd even been given a date and time for the board members to come in and try all the potential new menu items. That had never been done before. I just listened and allowed him to vent, and it felt good to be able to do that for someone else. It had been awhile.

He wanted me to know that he was not trying to ignore me, which I hadn't thought he was. As for me…I just wanted lunch to be over so I could go home and prepare to have the conversation that gave me my life back.

Chef told me he had to go. That he had many things to do, that lunch was in the kitchen, if I was hungry. I think I was more nervous than hungry, but I grabbed a plate of food. It was the last sandwich in the kitchen, with a few onion rings. You have to be quick around here, or you won't get anything. I poured a fresh glass of lemonade. They make it homemade at the club, you can't resist it.

I went into the banquet room to sit. I didn't want to answer John's million and one questions. He is very nosey. All I keep hearing from my inner voice is that I don't want any more upset in my life. That is enough.

I took my cell out of my apron, and there was one missed call from Luke. He texted me to let me know he would be home at six. I texted back to let him know that was fine. I don't have any feelings for this man.

Break time was over; I had to get into the dining room. Pierre came in and asked if I'd seen John. I didn't answer. A few minutes later John walked in.

Pierre was upset. "When break time is over I want everyone at their stations."

He asked John if he had any problems. He told Pierre that working with Chip is very hard. That he is a very mean person. Pierre told him that he would address that. To do the best he can. He wanted all of us to work together as a team. Pierre walked away, and John went into the kitchen, slamming the swinging door against the wall. It made Chip jump from the noise.

***

The day was busy again, but only in the bar, and with so little staff working, I hustled around the entire time. I didn't mind because it was now three thirty and the time had gone quickly, and I'd be able to get home and get ready.

There was something strange happening at the club, though. Pierre was very odd, watching us closely in the dining room and in the bar area. Not helping or saying anything; he was just observing. I know he saw John standing around not lifting a finger to help. Cassie and I ran around like crazy throughout lunch—what a madhouse! I glanced over at John, and he was following Pierre to his office. We continued to clean up while everything settled down. Once lunch was over I didn't see John, but Pierre came over to us and thanked us for doing a good job.

We said good night. Cassie looked at me, and said, "Do you think John will get fired like Dawn did?"

I told Cassie that Dawn got fired because of complaints from guests. John, well, he didn't want to work like a team. He'd possibly get a warning.

I punched out, waved goodbye, and took my apron off. I went to my locker to get my things, and quickly got into my car, eager to get home.

I have to adjust my focus now to what is going on tonight. Personally I hope things go smoothly and there is no bitterness in this awful relationship.

Traffic was light. I turned on KLOVE and heard a great new song— "Air I Breathe" by Mat Kearney. It was so ironic that I was hearing that song as I headed home to end the upset and torment in my life.

Everything had me feeling relaxed inside and this sense of strength came over me which let me know I could overcome any obstacle I had.

I pulled up to the house and saw Luke's truck in visitor parking. I put my car keys under the rock and walked upstairs to unlock the front door. When I opened the door an entirely different home was revealed. I blinked in disbelief.

Rose petals were thrown all over, long-stemmed roses were in crystal vases, candles were lit and placed in every area of the house. I took off my shoes and walked to the kitchen. The table was set up fancy. Champagne in an ice bucket, a beautiful burgundy cloth that fell to the floor—my favorite color. There were big wine goblets, and an amazing centerpiece—so tall it almost hit the ceiling. It was breathtaking, and I felt as if I'd just walked into a private room at an elite club.

Soft music was playing in the background from Luke's cellphone. Food was simmering on the stove and smelled delicious. I was speechless and confused.

Luke came out of the bathroom and all I could say was, "This is magical, something out of a romance novel. What's going—?"

He put his fingers over my lip before I could finish the sentence and told me to go freshen up and then come back. He had a surprise for me.

The candles all over the apartment were glowing like little stars. I was confused and didn't understand what was happening. I thought he'd be packing, and yet he'd been preparing me for a romantic night. It was supposed to be our breakup night.

As beautiful as it was, I didn't know what he was up to. I refused to go through another one of those episodes with him after he's had a few drinks and could no longer contain his nasty comments.

Okay, what to do…I decided to put myself together so I could find out what was next. After a shower, I got ready and put on one of the few summer dresses I had that wasn't a casualty to the razor blade day. Then I went to the kitchen. Luke handed me a glass of wine, and I admitted my confusion.

This is a trap. Even though this is peaceful for the moment something always happens and I don't trust the way I'm feeling. Another way for him to stick around.

He guided me to sit down at the table and I saw an assortment of sushi laid out. He told me to try one and I said that I'd wait for him. I got up and looked at the stove and took in the wonderful aroma of shrimp scampi. Then he looked at me strangely and asked what type of talk I thought we were going to have today, that I didn't seem very excited when I'd gotten home.

"I have to be honest. We haven't been intimate with each other, we don't speak to one another. We don't do anything with each other. I never know what is going on with your life. I'm in the dark. There has been a lot of fighting. I really thought we were going to end this civilly and move on from here. I see I don't make you happy. It seemed this is what our relationship was leading up to. I felt I could never do anything right in your eyes," I said without hesitation.

I'd started the conversation. Luke replied that it was all his fault. and it hadn't been fair to me or the kids the way he'd been acting. He'd been a jerk and he knew it.

"My feelings toward you are not the same anymore. After the way you've been treating me...I really wish you would leave forever."

All he said was that he didn't blame me, and then he begged me to sit down with him and have some sushi.

I was at a loss. I sat down with Luke and tasted everything he'd made. It was all delicious, and I was aware of how Luke was watching every move I made. All I could do was make small talk and try to figure this all out. But I was already getting nervous. Luke had finished a glass of wine quickly.

"Thank you for all of this goodness. It is so romantic. I dreamt of nights like this with you every time you were unkind to me."

Luke shared how he knew I didn't want to hear any more "I'm sorry" statements, that he'd overused that. He added that he wanted me in his life forever, to be a part of me, and to not lose me.

"You have me on the edge, always. I hide all my things, I feel very uncomfortable. You lied about my personal wellbeing. I almost fell behind on all my bills. How do you take that back? I have to pay the rest of them on Thursday, my next paycheck."

Luke wanted them and said he'd take care of them. I would not allow that to happen, no matter how broke I was, until they were caught up.

"I won't do that. I will not allow myself to be in such a vulnerable position ever again. My bills. My clothes." Then he begged, and I began to weep.

He wanted me in his life. I took a sip of wine, unsure of how to process all this. It wasn't what I'd expected, or wanted. Then he said he loved me.

"I loved you and respected you. I never asked for anything, just your love," I said.

He dismissed my dismissal and told me to stop, he knew I was a good woman. Then he got up to begin preparing our dinner plates. When I got up to help he asked me to sit back down. I thanked him when he brought the plates over. He topped up our wine, and then he sat down. It was strange how we appeared to be having a conversation, but each of us had our own agenda.

The food was so good, and when I told Luke that he was happy to hear it, and then added in how he knew I loved flowers and candles.

I smiled. "I feel wonderful right now." And I did. Luke told me to just take it moment by moment, to not think ahead. That he wanted me to love him the way I used to. "I want to love you, I'd love for us to be magical together," I said.

Then he asked it, the big question, could we make this a start from this day forward? I didn't answer right away and continued eating. He said that he'd asked me a question and begged for an answer.

"I'm willing to give this relationship another try. I would love to be in love with you. I have to work on my heart, so many things have happened—" My, how the conversation had turned.

Luke was thrilled and we finished dinner, got up, and I looked around at all the flickering candles. They were so lovely, and aside from not being with someone I was in love with, everything was ideal. He opened up another bottle of wine and poured us more, and then came over to me at the table and set down the glass, and then slid a small velvet box in front of me.

Uncertain what to think of that, I finally managed to whisper, "Luke, what are you saying?"

He asked me to open the box. I lifted its lid slowly and the most incredible diamond ring I have ever seen was revealed. He reached over and took it out of the box and took my hand and put the ring on my finger and asked me to marry him. I froze. He asked if I heard him and repeated the question.

I was shaking now, unsure of what to do, and actually in shock. I looked Luke right in his eyes. He told me that he was serious about me being in his life forever.

I hugged him and cried, "Yes Luke, I will marry you, I love you."

We drank wine, kissed, and I looked at the beautiful silver band with a two carat square cut diamond on it. It was beautiful…a princess cut. He stood up and took my hand as we walked into the living room and sat down on the couch. I put my wine glass on the coffee table, while Luke gulped down his.

You know what's going on, I thought. I was stargazing at my ring. I didn't have thoughts of "ever after," but an assessment that I'd give it one more try. He kept attending to me, filling up my wine glass to the brim, smiling and cleaning up. The entire time I kept thinking about how he'd never ask me to marry him if he didn't love me.

I took a deep breath and looked at my ring. Luke took note and hoped I was all right.

"I'm good, Luke, this ring is so beautiful," I said.

He told me that it wasn't as beautiful as me and he sat down and I leaned into him, resting my body against his. He talked about the good life we were going to have, and I just listened. He added that my life would change before my eyes, and that I wouldn't have to work so hard anymore. We'd be a family of four, happy together.

"This sounds too good to be true." As I spoke, I realized that I was getting quite tipsy. Luke reached over and put his hand on my face and tilted me up gently to kiss me. It was so passionate I didn't want it to end. He held me so tightly. The sparkle of the room with candles made me feel as if I was floating in the sky surrounded by stars—what an amazing night! After our lips parted Luke stood up to get another glass of wine. He could barely stand up and walk straight.

"Are you sure you want another glass of wine?" I said casually, trying to make light of it. He instantly grew bothered and asked why I was trying to ruin the night by starting in with my "shit."

"I was just kidding. You were balancing while walking…it was funny." I started giggling, just being silly, not to hurt his feelings.

He seethed and told me that I wasn't kidding, and that I'd fucked up the entire night. I was a stupid bitch again and he'd gone through all this trouble and all I did was try to drop a bomb on him every chance I could. He accused me of not being appreciative.

"Luke, honey," I began, "you have this all wrong. I meant it in a fun, playful way."

He didn't see it that way. He walked into the living room, turned on all the lights, and blew out all the candles. The old Luke was back, the one that had too much to drink and just waited for one thing to set him off in a rage. He looked at me and commanded me to go clean up the messy kitchen. I just got up and did it. I refused to respond.

After I was done, I blew out the candles on the table and walked toward the bedroom. Luke yelled out not to forget my wine glass. I stopped and turned around and went to the living room to get my glass. I had a sip of wine left in it. He lifted it up and flung the wine in my face. I just took the glass from his hand and didn't say a word. I knew if I had stuck up for myself, there would have been a huge fight, and in his frame of mind I don't know what would have happened to me. I was afraid.

Luke was laughing very hard and loud, as if he couldn't catch his breath. I walked in the kitchen and put my glass on the counter and went directly to my room to use the bathroom and wash up and get ready for bed. The entire time he shouted that it looked like I'd been shot; how funny it was. I couldn't believe I was in this situation. And how effortlessly that "yes" had eventually slipped out.

Tomorrow was another day, just not the fresh start I'd hoped for. I set my alarm for the morning. I pulled the covers over my head.

I heard Luke laughing and screaming, calling me names from the other living room. Yelling as loud as he could about what a bloody mess I am.

I looked at the ring he gave me; I'm still not following my gut instincts. I don't know what is wrong with me. Am I stupid or what? When something is wrong, it's wrong.

I finally passed out to the sound of Luke's madness in the background.

CHAPTER THIRTY-THREE

I woke up to a new ring, and no evidence of my "fiancé" anywhere. Things were cleaned up and all traces of the previous night had been erased. When I checked my phone I saw a text message from Luke with a smiley face, and a wink. Creepy! I could not imagine being married to him. Why was my mind so messed up? I ignored my instincts constantly, and allowed a fuzzy head from wine and a great meal to actually get me to say yes to him. I couldn't believe it.

When I got to the kitchen I saw the ring box. I took the ring off and gave one last look at its magnificent beauty, and then set it back in that small velvet box, and put it on my dresser. I didn't want it. I felt so stupid, falling for his stunts again. There was no reason to take him at his word for anything good.

It was good that all the props from the night before were gone, because I was struggling. I got ready for work, checked on Feathers, and gave him fresh water. I grabbed my keys from under the rock and made my way to my car. Luke pulled up just as I was getting in. Instant relief flooded me that he hadn't seen my hiding spot for my keys. I took a deep breath and he rolled down his window and said a pleasant good morning. My lips didn't move and I gave him a puzzled look. He justified he was just playing around, and then looked at my hand and asked why I wasn't wearing the ring.

"Not now Luke, I don't want to be late for work. Let me put it too you this way: I don't want the ring, and I will never marry you."

He blew it off, saying I was just mad at him and I'd get over it. I didn't blame him for thinking that, as I'd shown that behavior. But I had to be strong.

"I'm going to work. If you want the ring it's inside on my dresser. You are right I'm over it. Find someone to give it to." This man is a truly heartless man, with no feelings for others.

I got into my car. I was glad to work today so I could stay away from him. Tomorrow, God willing, I could help him pack and get him out of my house.

Eager to flee, I sped out of the parking lot so fast I almost didn't stop in time for incoming traffic. *I need to slow down, take it easy.* My phone kept ringing and ringing. I didn't want to answer, it was probably Luke. There was nothing else to say.

Once I came to a light I looked to see who was calling. It had been Matthew. That's right, I was supposed to call him. I tried to ring him back but it went to his voicemail, so I left a message that I was all right and I'd explain later.

Then I began to focus on my driving. I was distracted and going too fast at times. I had to calm down before I got to work. The adrenaline inside of me was relentless, bombarding me with jumpiness.

All I could say to myself, over and over, was why did I allow this to happen? I knew he'd never change before last night, yet I was drawn in by what he'd done, and hoped for the best. It was so short lived. If I chose him to be my husband I had no reason to think my life would be any different than it had been the past two months. That was not acceptable. Fancy things didn't mean more than decency and self-respect. The price I would have to pay to have this life with Luke was too painful, too big. I would not do that to myself. I had to become stronger and let him go. I should have set boundaries from the beginning. I stayed silent and overlooked so many things to avoid conflict. I set myself up to be mistreated.

As I committed to myself about letting him go, I pulled into the parking lot. I just made it on time. I had to adjust my facial expression as I noted how stressed out I looked. I took my purse and ran to the club, put my things in my locker and punched in. I was right on time.

Then I saw Chef, who was assessing me. He asked if I was okay and I said I was, then I asked if he could see if there were things going on tomorrow so I could work some extra hours.

Chef said, "It's your time off to regroup, what's going on?"

I told him that I could use the extra money. Chef went to check the reservation book for me. The truth of the matter is I did not want that day off to be near Luke.

Pierre came into the kitchen, and said, "Chef told me you're looking for more hours, but there is nothing going on at the club the next few days. Sorry, I will let you know." I thanked Pierre.

Chef waited until Pierre left to ask me if there is something I need to talk about. That he's here for me. I told him I would explain everything at a later time.

"Chef, I really do need to talk. Can I call you tomorrow?" I asked.

"Yes, anytime," he said.

"Thank you!"

There were no reservations for today and I was working with Jasper and John, happy to see that John and Pierre came to an agreement. I walked in the dining room and said hello to everyone. No response from Jason; I didn't pay any attention to him.

I don't have time for his nonsense. He seems to be mad at us for doing our job, and he had to be spoken to for not doing his. I'm learning change is inevitable for a different outcome no matter what the situation may be. People should stop blaming the world for their mistakes. This is a choice, like everything else.

What concerned me was how slow it seemed to be. They weren't even opening the patio, and it was a beautiful day. Maybe they were watching costs more because of how slow it had been the past few weeks.

As the day went on, it grew more unbearable. I wanted to feel normal and be busy, but work wasn't allowing for that. I was wearing this fake happy face, and those who knew me best probably recognized how unauthentic it was. Plus, I was so tired from the stress. I just couldn't be home tomorrow. Even if I had to get a haircut, just to be out of the house. Then I could go to the beach. Luke didn't know I had tomorrow off, so I didn't have to worry about him doing anything to sabotage that—yet.

My phone was buzzing and I reached into my apron and pulled it out. It was Luke. I didn't answer. There were also several text messages from him that I hadn't noticed. There were emojis, x's and o's, and a request for forgiveness... Delete.

The mood at work didn't help the mood in my mind, either. Pierre was tense, watching who was doing what, like he'd been doing more. I hadn't been hungry for lunch, but now I was getting lightheaded. There was a bag of muffins in the kitchen, and fresh coffee made. I picked a corn muffin, cut it in half, and heated it in the toaster oven. I added some butter and had a cup of coffee. I began to feel better. It was so tasty. I peeked out of the kitchen. There were no tables for me at lunch.

Chef's kindness and worrying about me was the only real warm spot in my day. Finally, Pierre asked if he could see me. I nodded and we went to his office. He began by thanking me for always putting my best foot forward at work, consistently. The compliment was nice, and I appreciated it. What he said next, not so much. He told me to take the night off. I was working more than anyone else.

"But—" I began.

He didn't let me finish. He told me he had to be fair. I smiled, and I understood, but I did not want to go—at all. Pierre told me he wanted me to enjoy my time off and have some fun. I thanked him and headed out.

I stood to punch out and so many thoughts were in my mind. I felt like a rock was in my stomach. I couldn't help but wonder; if Pierre had known my situation, would he still have done that?

A big lesson unfolded: When there is something wrong, speak up. You have to let the people in your life know, so they can help you through it. You don't need to endure it all alone. I never should have pretended everything was all right when it wasn't.

The question is, now what do I do? It was unfair that I had to fear going back to my own home and just doing as I pleased because of Luke. I'd really made things difficult for myself.

I needed to call Matthew and explain what was going on in detail, not leaving out these little "inconsequential" parts, because all those little parts had led to a big mess, and an unhappy and unfulfilled me. The last time I didn't do what Luke said, he came close to hurting me very bad. I can imagine…what he would do when I tell him I really don't want him in my life.

When Matthew said he'd try to see if he could get to visit me early, I'd been excited, but then I told him to hold off. I thought that I could make it, but now, one week before Thanksgiving, I was worried about surviving the day.

The lies to myself and pretending I wasn't frightened had to stop. I was so scared. Chef's voice snapped me out of my trance. He asked what was wrong.

"Pierre gave me time off unexpectedly, and I needed to stay on. He wanted to be fair with everyone, and I understand that," I lamented.

Chef asked why I couldn't just go home and take it easy. He was very puzzled. It wasn't his fault he didn't know. He'd tried to help many times. Chef handed me a small container of lunch to go, and a bottle of iced tea. I thanked him. I had to get out of there. I felt like I was crumbling. I punched out, grabbed my lunch to go, and left before I broke down in front of anyone else. I just didn't want to risk it.

✳✳✳

I got into my car and started to drive. I felt so anxious that a tingling feeling came all over my chest. I needed to calm down, and I had to avoid Luke at all costs. Thankfully, I had a t-shirt in my work locker that I could change into.

When I was stressed or needed to figure something out, I headed toward the beach. I rolled down my window and allowed the fresh air to wash over me. The song, "Air I Breathe" came on the radio again and I sang it again, giving thanks to the good Lord for all his support. I needed His strength. Slowly, the anxiety lifted from me.

When I got to the beach I took my shoes and socks off and set them by some rocks, and then began to walk. I brought the lunch that Chef prepared for me, plus my phone, and found a spot as close to the ocean as I could get without getting wet.

I needed space to breathe. There I sat in silence, looking out to the most amazing view of the ocean. It was so clear, and seagulls were flying overhead. Seashells were scattered about the sand. Roaring waves were coming in, and splashing against the sand. What I loved most was how the sounds of the ocean naturally wiped away negative thoughts and replaced them with hope for me. That was what I needed, hope and strength.

I opened my container to see what Chef made me to eat. Wow, my favorite. He made me a Rueben sandwich and onion rings. Chef is the sweetest man I have ever met. He knows me so well. I took a bite and it was delicious. I opened the small plastic container that had ketchup in it, and dipped my onion rings. The sauce from the sandwich was all over my hands. I forgot to bring napkins, but it didn't matter. It was so good that I didn't set it down once. I ate it with delight and then washed my hands and mouth in the ocean water.

I went back to finish my onion rings, but that was not meant to be. When I turned around the seagulls had decided to eat them for their lunch. I couldn't help but laugh. After throwing my trash out I went to sit back down, and then took out my phone to see if anyone had called. No one had. It was the perfect time for me to call Matthew. His phone rang and rang. He didn't pick up, but that was okay. He'd see my calls, and call me back when he could.

Rolling my shoulders back and feeling the warmth on my face, I decided to lay down and then I drifted off to sleep to the lullaby of the ocean. I woke up to the sound of my phone buzzing. I glanced over, hoping it was Matthew, but it was Luke.

I noticed the time: 7:00 p.m. I answered and he started in. He'd called my job and they said that I'd left. Where was I? It was question after question, and I finally said I was at the beach when he took a breath. His next question was why I didn't come home, and I told him that I didn't want to. I needed to relax and be at a calm place. Then he told me to turn around. I did, and jumped. There was Luke standing above me with a scary grin on his face.

"What are you doing here?" I demanded. He just said he knew where to look for me when he couldn't reach me. That was disturbing, but it was no secret that this was my favorite place.

"Have a seat," I said. He didn't want to, he wanted us to go home. "I'm not ready to leave yet," I answered. "I came here to relax and enjoy the ocean."

He grabbed my arm and jerked me up and told me that we were leaving. I didn't look at him, but to the people a little further up, who had stopped, and were staring at us. I didn't want us to be a focal point, but it was better to have someone nearby, just in case.

"What's wrong with you?" I said. He responded by asking what was wrong with me.

"I don't want this relationship. It's more bad than good, and I'm not happy."

Luke said he was happy and he was not leaving. That we were together.

My phone started buzzing and I just knew it was Matthew, but I wasn't going to take it out of my pocket and risk Luke doing something like throwing it in the ocean. I'd check it when I eventually got into my car.

"Stop making a spectacle in public. Let's leave, my goodness," I finally said. Then he told me the next time I went to the beach I needed to ask first.

"Let's finish this fight at home," I said.

Which was the last place I wanted to be with him. I know what happens when we are alone at my house. There is nothing but heartache and pain.

He called me a bitch, along with all those familiar vulgar names he liked to direct at me, and I didn't even look at him. I just walked over to where my shoes were and put them on, and then walked to my car. I saw his SUV five cars away.

I began to drive away and then he sped off in a rage. It was time to call Matthew, as it would be the last peaceful moment I'd likely get for the night. He answered on the second ring, relieved to catch me. I was relieved to get to him, too.

"Matthew, love, I really need you to get home," I said. I wanted to sound calm, but I was in a panic. I had to explain how Luke would not leave, about the proposal the night before, and how I gave him back his ring. How my peace is gone, and he has me on edge. I kept rattling on, that I was at the beach, and Luke created a scene until I agreed to go.

I went on and on and on, and finally Matthew interrupted, saying he'd talk to his boss first thing in the morning. I had to calm down. He told me to stay quiet, and not to antagonize him tonight.

Then I began to cry, which made it worse, and my poor son apologized over and over that his hands were tied, he had to talk to his boss, and he'd do the best he could. I didn't want to hang up, but I knew I had to when I got home. Home, my beautiful home felt like hell more than anything for the past months. Matthew's one last question was about calling the police again. I reminded him what Luke said, that all his friends are police. Matthew told me that he'd do whatever it took to get him out of that home, and get me safe again. Just to keep my distance, and let him curse and do what he wants. He begged me to remain quiet.

Luke had beaten me home, and I glanced to make sure he wasn't watching for me through a window. I hid the car keys and then walked into the house, sliding my phone into my pocket. I was lightheaded and queasy from being so scared at that moment. I had no idea what was happening, but I felt trapped. I was worried for my safety. He's an alcoholic, and an angry man.

There was no sign of Luke so I walked in and shut the front door. He'd been hiding behind it. He jumped out lunging toward me, but before he reached me, I fell to the floor like a limp noodle. Passed out, everything went black.

***

My eyes blinked and I had no idea how much time had passed since everything had gone black. I got up and ran to the guest bathroom and threw up. I was a mess, and I glanced around and didn't see Luke anywhere. But my fear when I saw him lunging at me was vivid in my mind.

He must have gotten worried about what happened and fled. He would never know how to handle a situation like that. I could barely walk, I was so weak. I tried to change out of my clothes so I could take a shower. I was desperate to have it help me become more alert.

The water falling on me felt so good. I was glad to be alone, and hoped I would be all night. I didn't want him near me. I praised the Lord. I collected everything I could to have it near me, just in case. I went to check that the front door and windows were locked. I checked on Feathers, who seemed to be okay, and then turned off all the lights.

I went right to bed. My body was overcome with anxiety and fear that made me feel like I was unable to function. I woke up at three in the morning with a cold sweat all over my body. I went to the bathroom to splash some cold water on my face and get some relief. Then I went into the hallway and decided to take some NyQuil to help me sleep more peacefully. I needed something to help me fall asleep. I never had to take sleep aids but it was a must. My side of the bed was damp from sweating, so I moved over to Luke's side, and I can't remember what happened next, as I was asleep.

I woke up to a new day and it was eleven o'clock. I checked my phone and had several texts from Matthew, who was worried about me. I sent him a quick text that mentioned calling him later, and then I listened. I didn't want to get up until I could determine if I was alone or not.

It seemed I was alone, and I was grateful. My entire body was so sore though. I must have hit the floor hard. I got up and brushed my teeth, took care of Feathers, started some coffee, and then went to lie back down. My body was still drowsy—a combination of NyQuil and too much anxiety.

After another hour of rest I got up. Then Luke sent a text, asking if I was all right.

I didn't want to reveal anything so I responded with, "Yes, I'm much better this morning. I just got off the living room floor. What happened last night?" I asked.

What would he say? His response was unbelievable. He didn't know. He was leaving when I walked into the house.

I wasn't going to offer any satisfaction so I left it with an "okay." He responded that he'd see me tomorrow, that he had a very busy day. I didn't answer back. It was obvious that Luke was freaked out and scared, and I was glad that he was. He'd created a lot of problems. I'd allowed him to as well. I should have stood up for myself long before that.

However, he had me so paranoid that everything seemed suspicious, his response especially. The fact that he hadn't asked me about work today. He was so good at pretending nothing happened.

Until I got him out of my life, I had to keep him out of my mind. I called my stylist Bianca to get a haircut, and there was a three o'clock opening, which was great. Then I wandered around like a lost soul. I didn't want to cook or do anything, so I crawled back into bed to take another nap. Only I woke up at four thirty. I'd missed my appointment! I got up and opened the blinds, feeling a little hungry.

Bianca had called my phone. Matthew had been texting. My system was so messed up that I didn't even understand who I was. Luke had completely drained me. I immediately made a call to Bianca to apologize, saying I'd explain as soon as I could. She said she understood, and offered nothing more. Bianca and I spoke about the craziness that's been happening. She gets it.

I listened to myself speaking, and all I heard was me being a broken record. "I'll explain later," I said that over and over. The problem was that every time "later" came I kept putting it off. Maybe I was the insane one, not Luke.

I texted Matthew to let him know I was all right, and apologized for putting him in a tough position with his new job. But I did need him. I told him I love him.

Whatever happens to get Luke out of my life I will leave it up to the Good Lord Above! I miss my smile, and my laugh. Happy times with friends. I can't do this anymore.

A short time later Luke texted me a picture of himself. He was in his Escalade, wearing a navy blue button down collared shirt and a pair of jeans. His shiny Rolex watch was on his wrist, he didn't have a hair out of place, and he was smiling what I knew to be a slimy, fake charm smile. Under the picture he wrote "I love you," with a red heart.

I texted back: Luke, have a great time out. Enjoy yourself. He didn't respond, but how could he?

I had the uneasy feeling that he was on a date, and I felt relieved that I simply didn't care. He made it clear what he was doing. He never sent me a picture of himself put together as he is going out on the town. He wanted to get a rise out of me and that simply backfired. At this point I want my life back.

Unfortunately in my heart I knew what was going to happen next in my life was going to be ugly. He wasn't going to take his dismissal well at all. When it would take place wasn't for certain. Luke liked to spring his tirades on me, without warning.

He is so insecure right now that he doesn't want to be alone. Let me rephrase this: he can't be by himself. Luke needs attention around the clock. In the back of his mind he knows our relationship needs to come to an end, and it won't get any better. He has tried everything you can imagine to control me, belittle and curse me. As if I was worthless.

It is pretty sad he put me through all this torture, as if Luke needed someone to dump on. He really didn't want to be with me in the first place. He saw a kind loving person, and took advantage me. I should have followed my gut instinct and read all the warning signs before agreeing to this relationship. The first encounter I had with Luke and the disrespect he brought out into the open should have been enough for me to back away. I gave him too many chances, and I made to many excuses. I know this for the next time.

It's wonderful to be loved and adored. But the right kind of love and happiness is essential. Sometimes trying to compensate for everything that is going wrong is not love. I will never hide my feelings ever again, and make sure my self-worth will come first. Boundaries will be set. At this moment I would love for Luke to pack up and leave.

CHAPTER THIRTY-FOUR

I spent a bit of time thrashing out my thoughts with all the reasons that I'd been so stupid in this relationship with Luke. Always doing things that were against my instincts. Putting up with more than what was healthy for me. It went on and on, but I finally decided that I had enough of him being in my head at that moment. I knew what I had to do and would have to figure it out, regardless of how frightening it was.

When I glanced at my phone to see if Matthew had called, I saw that he hadn't. I wasn't going to keep bothering him, though. He'd call me when he knew what he could do. That would be good enough. I knew that I wasn't alone, and he'd never abandon me.

My stomach growled and I realized that I hadn't eaten in almost a day. I went to the fridge and there wasn't much there. I didn't want a sandwich, but that was my only choice. I made a salami and provolone on rye sandwich with mustard. I ate, grateful to have the opportunity. I made sure to sit near Feathers so I could hear him whistle and enjoy him being calm. The combination made me begin to feel better.

Feathers stayed as close to me in his cage as he could. He kept rubbing his beak against the frame and I knew he wanted to tell me something. I wished to God he could.

After I ate I made some iced coffee from the coffee that was left, and went to the living room to watch some television. I was flipping through the channels to see if there was a movie on so I could take my mind off all things painful for a bit. I needed a genuine reprieve. The movie I settled on was on Lifetime—a family going through very troubled times and how the mother tried to teach everyone to keep faith and know that they could overcome the darkness that had overshadowed the family.

The woman said, "Things might feel dark right now, but you will see all this will come to pass." Her family didn't want to listen and they were filled with negativity, but she was true to the course.

The movie turned out to be very inspirational and intense. At the end of the show the family embraced their mother, and wondered how she knew things were going to change. Their mother told the children, you should never lose faith. That's how come she knew.

I cried so much—I will apply this to my heart, and in my life. I thought about how I had loved Luke and would have stood by him through everything—until. I looked up and "Praised God."

I got up to go to the kitchen, Feathers was getting upset and chirping louder than I was crying. He knows there is something wrong. I opened his cage and put my hand in it so he knows I'm all right. My hand was wet from wiping my tears. Feathers rubbed his beak and face on it. He is very emotional right now. It's been very painful to be in this house.

I look at the time, and I can't believe it is already nine. It feels like midnight. I hope tomorrow is a day of clarity, better understanding, and the end of all this mess.

I took my hand out of the cage and closed it. I said good night to Feathers, turned off all the lights, shut off the television, made sure the front door was locked, and went into my room to get ready for bed.

I went into the bathroom to wash up. I looked in the mirror and said to myself, "I will get through this, stay strong. Amen." Then I set the alarm on my phone for five o'clock, put it into my pants pocket, and slid in under the covers and closed my eyes.

Morning came quickly. I turned to look at my phone. When I opened my eyes, Luke was storming into my room, slamming the door, and stumbling from being drunk.

His shirt was buttoned crooked, his hair was a mess. I knew what he'd been doing, it was obvious to me: He was out in someone else's bed. He thought I would come chasing after him with jealousy, professing my love for him, and that didn't happen. He knew by sending me the picture of himself all fixed up I knew what he was up to. I don't believe he expected that response from me.

I really didn't care who he was with or what he was doing. I wanted him out of my life. But why was he here? If it hadn't worked out that wasn't my fault.

He took my arm and pulled me out of my bed onto the floor and started to kick me in my side. I couldn't figure out how to protect myself. He was screaming that I wasn't good enough for him to marry, and I was a lousy bitch. He was going to show me who was no good now.

I pushed my phone down in my front pocket so he didn't notice it and then he stood me up from the floor and spat on my face, picked me up, and threw me onto the bed. The entire time he was cursing at me, calling me a fucking whore. *Thank you, Lord, I'll get through this*, I thought. I had to be numb so he couldn't hurt me more than he already was.

But how I cried. I was finally able to get up and wipe my face. I stood on the other side of the bed from him and stared in horror. I had three Mediterranean vases that my belated husband had purchased for me, and I treasured them. Luke took one vase at a time and began to smash them against the floor, breaking each one into a thousand pieces.

It happened so fast there wasn't anything I could do. He tipped my dresser over and everything I had on top fell to the floor like dominos around me. I had to be careful where I walked or I'd step on glass. I was trapped and he was a maniac.

He came after me and I fought back the best way I could. But it wasn't enough. He took me by the shirt and slammed my face against the wall and dragged my face across it. The pain and feel of raw flesh instantly stung. He was so vicious and strong at that moment that I couldn't stand up to him or do anything. I was powerless physically and all I had to rely on was my faith that I'd make it through.

Luke bent over and picked up the engagement ring box from the floor and held me against the wall. With his other hand, he flipped the box open and took the ring out of it. I watched the box fall onto the broken glass, and he turned to me and tried to force the ring on my finger.

I resisted, screaming, "I hate you! Leave me alone. You're a monster."

He continued to force the ring, and broke my ring finger in the process. I felt this pop on my finger and then a shocking pain traveled up my arm. My finger was swollen and deformed. I couldn't get the ring off, and I was crying. The desperation to stop crying so I could gain a level head was intense, and I was battling that just as much as I was Luke. How could I get out of the house? That's what I needed to figure out.

Luke released me for a split second, and I took off running into the kitchen, screaming for him to stop and leave me alone.

I was holding on to my hand as he got to me and grabbed me and kissed hard, biting my lips as he did it. I felt the tangy taste of blood in my mouth, and I was afraid to move, lest it be worse. Again, he began stating what he believed to be true. I was his, and I'd better get that.

Tears of pain and fear were rolling down my cheeks and I couldn't even evaluate all the different levels of pain running through me at once. It was too much, and I was losing faith that I could take it. I was so close to his face, I saw lipstick from his night out on his neck and the collar of his shirt. Feathers was screaming loudly, he was like a warning alarm for what was about to happen.

Luke held me by the arm and threw me on the floor in the living room, kicked his shoe off, and began to beat me with it. He beat me on my thigh so much that I went numb and couldn't feel the pain anymore. I had to get out.

My eyes stared at the front door, my exit, as I was getting beaten. My keys were under the rock just below the stairs. I had to get there, I needed to get away. I thought of Chef and the club right away. If I could get there he could help me and get ahold of Matthew.

Then Luke stopped beating me and charged into the kitchen. I tried to get up but it was so hard. I was dazed. He slung open the door to Feathers' cage, and Feathers began to peck at his hand forcefully. Luke squeezed his body and threw him against the wall in the living room as hard as he could. It made a loud thumping sound.

"Stop!" I screamed, but I didn't move. I didn't want him to come back at me again. I slowly tilted my head to look at Feathers. He was lying on the floor and twitching, barely able to move. He was alive, my poor Feathers.

Luke didn't see me move and he went to the bedroom. I jumped up with the ounce of energy I had left. I picked up Feathers and charged toward the front door and opened it up. I bolted down the steps and reached for my keys under the rock.

My car seemed like a mile away, but I sprinted as quickly as I could, blocking out the pain and running on pure adrenaline. Once I was in the car I put Feathers on the passenger seat and sped off.

I looked towards the house and saw Luke leaping down the stairs and chasing me. He was pounding on my driver's side window with such hate in his eyes. I sped up and fled, leaving him behind me.

CHAPTER THIRTY-FIVE

I drove as fast as I could to the club and couldn't stop crying. I was hysterical and out of control, hoping that God had the wheel and would get me to where I needed to be. I kept apologizing to Feathers for allowing this to happen. It was only eight and I was twenty-five minutes out. No traffic, thank goodness.

My concern briefly flickered on how busy the club might be, but this was a matter of life and death for me. I could not worry about that. My body was starting to bruise and swell. This made the task of driving much tougher. My broken finger made it hard to even wrap my hand around the wheel at all. The ring was also making me lose my circulation from the swelling. I needed to get it off. What would they say at the club? No one knew what I was living through.

My phone was in my front pocket and I could barely reach it. I wanted to call the club but I couldn't. I had to pee, but I didn't dare pull over and stop. What would people say? Would someone call the police? Luke's "police" friends! He said they would laugh at me. I became so bound to his words. I believed this was true because he was surrounded by people with influence. I didn't forget where we met. I'm a waitress, who would they believe?

I had to make it to the club. That was my only choice; at least there was an outside bathroom I could sneak into. Finally, the club was there.

I parked my car and headed to the outside bathroom in the back of the building. I rolled Feathers into my shirt in front of me, like a little pouch for him. I was barefoot and my feet had small cuts on them from glass. The stones of the pavement hurt them even more, and I was a bloody mess. It bothered me, although it hadn't been in my control.

So many illogical thoughts were running through my frantic mind. I just longed to piece it together and collect myself. It was strange how the pain wasn't bothering me anymore. I was still crying hard from fear.

I opened the door and slid into the bathroom, leaving a trail of blood on the floor from my feet. I tried to catch my breath, but my ribs were really bruised, maybe broken. I found a way to clean up, and then tried to help Feathers.

I ran my hands under the sink and filled up my palm to give Feathers some water. He was very thirsty, and took as much as he could. I was pretty sure his wing was broken, but I didn't know for certain.

As I did all this I avoided looking at myself in the mirror. I was so ashamed of myself, and how I'd allowed a man to do this to me. I walked outside on the beach afterward, and as the salty sand touched the bottom of my feet, it stung so badly. I sat down and allowed the cool air to wash over my face. I knew it was tattered, though I was afraid to look too closely. My eyes ached from crying, and my nose was stuffy from all the sobbing.

I looked to my left to see Chef walking towards me. I looked up at him and he ran to me, obviously startled, and asking what happened. Then he looked at Feathers and he was horrified. I didn't have to tell him, he knew.

All I could do was cry and say, "Police."

Chef grabbed his phone and called the police, telling them where we were. Then he gently took Feathers from my arms and wrapped him in a towel, and waited. He wanted me to go inside, but I just couldn't.

"Thank you, Chef," I said. It was so hard to look at him because I was so ashamed. He told me his name was Anthony, and to call him that.

"Anthony, can you call Matthew and let him know I'm here?" I asked. He took my phone and did that.

I just turned it over to him in that moment, because I was unable to do anything. Not only from broken and bruised body parts, but also because I couldn't even process the reality of what I was at that moment. A woman, broken and battered. Matthew was nearby and on his way to the club.

I looked at the ugly ring on my swollen finger, and asked Anthony to please find something to cut it off. It was cutting off my circulation; I didn't want to lose my finger. He handed me Feathers, and got up to go toward the toolshed. As he was coming back, Luke showed up, and I panicked.

"Anthony, keep him away please!" And Anthony did. I felt protected for the first time.

Anthony yelled at Luke, telling him to stay away from me. Then the police showed up and Luke said he could explain. Anthony was able to cut off the ring, I almost fainted. I needed to catch my breath. Matthew showed up. Anthony waved the police to where we were. Matthew said softly that the house looked like a warzone. We both began to cry.

"He beat me," I said. "Feathers is hurt too. I'm so sore, I need rest."

Luke was handcuffed and taken away. He was angry and screaming at the police.

"You have it all wrong, she is a lying piece of shit. How dare you do this to me! She is a lying whore. This isn't the last you've heard from me!"

They put him in the back seat of the police car. His voice became a whisper in the distance.

Matthew held me softly and sat with me on the sand. My Matthew.

"I didn't know you were coming today, you never told me," I said.

Matthew said, "I wanted to surprise you."

The police called an ambulance for me. I looked at Anthony who is so kind, and asked him to take Feathers to the veterinarian's emergency room. He told me that he'd take him right away. I had one more request, to please let Pierre at the club know what happened privately. I didn't want to lose my job.

"This was what I wanted to talk to you about once it was over. It's over now, and I want what happened to come from someone I trust." He nodded, and then he took Feathers, as he couldn't come in the ambulance.

Matthew began to cry and Anthony was so kind to him, telling him to stay strong for his beautiful, kind mother. Then he noticed the cut ring off to the side. Matthew called out for the officers to wait and handed them the ring—another bit of evidence.

The paramedics wheeled out the stretcher, and gently placed me on it, and put me in the ambulance. They took me to the closest emergency room. Anthony walked Matthew to his car. He was crying so hard. I didn't want my son to see this. I wanted this over to avoid any pain he would see.

Matthew looked at Anthony and said, "Look at what he's done to my beautiful mom."

Anthony wanted Matthew to stay strong. "What matters now is that your mom will get the care she needs, and Luke will never bother her again," Anthony affirmed.

In the ambulance, they began to check my vitals and do small things. I was so grateful to be alive and to feel free of Luke. Whatever happened next, I wouldn't have to go through it alone.

CHAPTER THIRTY-SIX

We arrived at the ER and the nurses quickly started an IV, washed my face, and checked all my wounds. They had me sit up and put my feet in a basin of warm water and soap. They wanted to make sure I didn't have broken glass on the bottoms of my feet. They lightly patted my feet dry, and didn't notice any.

After that I received a Tylenol injection for the pain and they put bacitracin on my scraped face and lips. They carefully and meticulously addressed all my swollen body parts, bumps, and bruises. After they were done Matthew came into the room. He leaned over and kissed me on the forehead, looking unsure of what to say or how to comfort me. Him being there was enough.

"Matthew, I'm so sorry you had to see this," I said.

He assured me that we'd get through this. He told me he loved me, and I thanked him. Then I yawned, and he said that he was going to go so I could get some rest. I reminded him to check on Feathers and he said he would, giving me a smile. Then he reminded me that after a bit I'd have to give my statement to the police, and he reminded me to tell them everything—emphasis on "everything."

I still had a few more tests to do after Matthew left. X-rays and such. When I heard Matthew speaking with the doctor I couldn't help but smile, even though my lips were so cut up. He was just like his father, kind and gentle and good. The doctor asked for Matthew's number, and said he'd call with results if anything came up.

Matthew called Anthony when he left and gave an update on what was happening with me, and later shared this conversation they had at that moment:

"Thanks for looking out for Feathers, Anthony. I need to go clean up the house. It looks like he went crazy. Luke made a mess out of things."

"He is crazy," Anthony said.

"There are broken vases and all sort of things thrown all over in my mother's bedroom."

"Listen, let's help her put her life back together. I will help you clean up and get things organized at the house. We will never know the pain behind those broken vases completely, but what we saw was enough to feel the hurt."

"You would really help me do this for her?" Matthew asked.

"Of course, Matthew. Your mom and I are really close friends. She kept this part of her life a secret. I believe she hoped that it would come to a close.

"Let's call the hospital and make them aware that she hasn't had anything to eat so they can give her lunch, while you and I will go to the house and clean things up. We also need to call the police and get his things out of her house. We can stop at the store and pick up some empty boxes that are being thrown out and we will pack his things up so he never has to return again for any reason," Anthony said.

Matthew asked, "Where will we put his things after we pack them?"

"We'll call the police and ask all those questions together, but we can start by putting his things in boxes," Anthony stated.

"My mother prayed that this day would come and something would happen, anything to get him out of her life. He is a mean, nasty man with one agenda, and that was to hurt my mom so she could feel his pain because of his own problems. She lived in hell. My mom paid dearly." Matthew began to cry.

Anthony told him to remain calm; that they had to stay focused.

"I respected her privacy and didn't pressure her. I figured that when the time was right she would let me know what was going on," Matthew said.

"Please, Matthew, don't blame her for trying to protect herself, and you. She didn't want you to be troubled, she didn't want anyone to be troubled," Anthony finished.

There is so much work to do.

CHAPTER THIRTY-SEVEN

I was healing and recovering as Matthew and Anthony were picking up the pieces of a painful time in my life. How blessed I was (and am) to have them.

The diagnosis for my injuries wasn't as horrible as it could have been. I didn't break any ribs, thankfully, but was very bruised. I'd need to see an orthopedic specialist to help with setting my finger. It was broken in two places, which was excruciatingly painful, even despite the pain medications I was on. My body was very swollen, and I needed a lot of rest. The doctor told me when the swelling went down, surgery for my finger was inevitable.

Dr. Hazel, who attended to me, was amazing as well with Matthew, and Anthony. It helped an extremely tough situation be more manageable. The kindness of people can mean more than any of us ever realize at times.

Matthew was upset and emotionally spent from the intensity of it all, and Anthony was such a strong, guiding force, a true voice of reason. The kindness of Anthony to help Matthew kept him strong. I was grateful he wasn't doing this alone.

The goal of Anthony and Matthew was to have all memories and things of Luke's out of the house before I was released. They knew they had time. This gesture was one that I was most thankful for. A surprise to Matthew and Anthony as they were putting things in boxes, was they realized Luke wasn't the only one I allowed to stay with me. They were confused and Matthew called me at the hospital and asked me if he should box all the children's things as well. He didn't ask me anything else beyond that. I stuttered and said yes, please. After they finished packing their stuff, Matthew called the police and asked what should be done with their possessions. The police told Matthew to leave them on the front lawn curbside and arrangements would be made to have their belongings picked up.

For Matthew, it was so hard to look at the house he'd grown up in, the house that he knew I loved, and know that such violence had taken place in its walls. Matthew never thought in his life he would see anything like this. To him it was something out of a scary movie. With Anthony's help, the two began to clean it all up. To this day, I'm sure they said more about Luke and thought more about him than they'd ever let me know. But what could they ever think or say that would shock me?

When it all became too much and Matthew broke down, Anthony was there for him, reminding him that the past couldn't be changed, but they could help be there for the future, in whatever way they could.

These were all things I knew as I lay in my hospital room, realizing that the wounds on my body would be long healed before my wounded mind, and heart. I still didn't understand how I'd lost control of so much…and so fast.

For the hundredth time, my thoughts drifted to how when trouble comes into your life, you should turn to people who offer to help. Even if it's just to listen, and they offer it, take it. It just might make all the difference.

***

I realized that I'd never mentioned the girls being at the house out loud to anyone, and it crushed me as it did Anthony and Matthew when they found out the way they did. There was no turning back at that point. No reason for an explanation.

They saw the signs of my secret in hindsight, recalling the hints. I wanted to work more, and I wasn't consistent with my correspondence. I didn't do as much with my friends, my natural cheeriness was stifled, and I became so distracted.

And then in a ceremonious gesture, with all the boxes of Luke's possessions on the front lawn as suggested, they opened up the windows to let the fresh air in, and let the negative energy out.

While they worked so hard to bring back a remembrance of the home I'd always loved, I gave my statement to the police about Luke and what he'd done. I wasn't allowed to go home that day, as they said a good night's rest was what I needed most. I wanted to go home, but they were probably right. The wounds of my last experience there were too fresh—physically and emotionally.

The last place that Matthew looked at, I learned, was in the kitchen. There were only two things that he found in there that he knew were not mine. Two huge wine goblets and a cast iron pan. He tossed them out without a second thought, he'd tell me later, and I smiled. Those goblets—they weren't the cause of my worries, but they certainly played a role in the turmoil.

I grew eager to see Matthew and Anthony again. I needed to thank them, despite my cut lips and medicated body. They had to know how truly grateful I was, and how truly sorry I was that I hadn't confided in them sooner. I don't know if it would have made a difference, but it couldn't have made things worse.

Visiting hours were approaching and I grew anxious, but it was a good anxiety, one of excitement for who was going to arrive.

CHAPTER THIRTY-EIGHT

From Matthew's Heart...

I *was so excited to drive and see Mom. We weren't going to tell her what we did and seeing her expression when she saw it would be won-derful. My greatest wish was that it would bring back that genuine, de-lighted smile she was so known for.*

Anthony suggested that I stay at his place that night, just to make it easier, and I was so grateful. I'd do anything for Mom, but finances were tight. Any kind gesture would be accepted graciously, especially from a man that I could see cared for my mother deeply. I did wonder how deeply those affections ran.

Anthony suggested I take my rental car back, get my belongings so I didn't have to worry about the added expense, and use his car for the remainder of my stay. We needed to get this done, before visiting hours. We hadn't changed the locks on the doors of the house yet. Anthony didn't feel comfortable leaving me at the house yet, until this was taken care of. I agreed. It was a bit much to take in.

As we were taking care of this task, he asked if I'd talked to my girlfriend yet. "How did you know I have a girlfriend?" I asked.

He told me how proud Mom was of me, and that she was always talking about how wonderful I was. It was good to hear, and while she always let me know, I guess I'd never realized how much she shared about me to others.

As we took care of some things, including dropping off my rental car, Anthony told me that he'd spoken to Pierre, Mom's boss, and explained the situation. Her job would be secure for her, whenever she was able to get back to work. I understand now the reason for all those hours. It kept my mom alive.

It appeared that everyone really liked Mom, which was no surprise, but it made me wonder why she'd been so resistant to open up. It could have made a difference. I could only sigh, because I couldn't understand in hindsight. For today, I was happy she was recovering and free of that monster.

We arrived at the hospital. Both Anthony and I were anxious to see Mom. We walked so quickly, making our way to her room—348A. It was six thirty on the dot, the start of visiting hours for the evening.

The doctor was coming out of her room. He told me that Mom would have her surgery tomorrow to set her finger. I must have looked very worried. The doctor reassured me that there will be no deformity, and it will look like it always had. There will be swelling, and it will take time to heal. It will be very important that she makes all her checkups. We were very happy to hear that.

Dr. Hazel told us that he would call as soon as she was out of surgery. He patted me on the back and said, "Don't worry son."

I thanked him, and walked into her room.

She was asleep and we sat there in silence, just watching her. Her feet were peeking out at the end of the bed, all bandaged up. I took the blanket, and covered them up. I pulled my chair close and gently reached for her hand. She opened her eyes and smiled.

"I love you both," she whispered. Then her eyes closed again.

Anthony and I looked at each other, and I started crying silently. I stood up and walked outside the room to breathe, unable to hold it in any longer. The thought of my mom almost dying in the arms of that monster pained my heart.

One of the nurses came over to see if I was all right. I told them yes, I just needed to walk away for a minute. I went to the bathroom and wiped my tears and blew my nose and went back to her room. Anthony was sitting in silence and when I sat back down he whispered to see if I was okay.

"Just a bit overwhelmed, that's all," I said.

The nurse came in to check my mom's blood pressure; she didn't wake up at all. She was so wiped out. And neither Anthony nor I left her side. I could tell he really cared for her, but I didn't ask him about it. I wondered if Mom knew, and I wondered if she cared for him, or had come to realize she did. I didn't in my heart think that this could have been on her mind going through this painful silence.

Anthony looked over at me and I saw such sadness in his eyes. I moved my chair close to his, and I put my arm around his shoulder and he began to weep. I got up and gave him a tissue.

"Do you want to go Anthony? Mom needs her rest, and I can leave her a note that we were here."

He nodded his head. Both of us were forced to acknowledge how painful it was to watch her suffer, and we would have done anything to ease her pain.... But we couldn't. All we could offer was support, just as the wonderful hospital staff had done when we weren't there.

We both stood up. Anthony leaned over Mom to kiss her on the fore-head and she raised her hand and touched his cheek. She didn't open her eyes, but I saw how she sensed the dampness of his cheek, and she began to wipe away his tears. He took her hand and kissed her palm.

After he stepped away I leaned in and kissed Mom's cheek softly.

"I love you," I whispered.

"I love you too," she said. We didn't have to leave a note. She knew we were there. Walking out was so tough though. It was so sad to see someone you loved in the situation she was in.

Once we were in the parking lot, we rode in silence back to An-thony's house. We got to his house and each just needed our space, a room to think and hopefully finally sleep. We were wiped too, not that we cared. Mom was most important.

Both of us drifted off to sleep for a bit, but at ten Anthony checked to see if I was awake. I was. He asked if I was hungry, and I nodded my head. I was a bit. He told me to get up and we could eat something. It sounded good.

I got out of bed and went to the kitchen where Anthony was. Anthony took out some already made dough from the fridge, a few containers filled with sauce, sausage, mozzarella cheese, mushroom, and onion. He said that we were going to make our own pizzas. I smiled for the first time since I arrived.

His kitchen turned into a pizzeria at that moment. Flour was on the counter and we began to knead and roll the dough. It felt good and made me realize that I had to be strong and in control in order to best help Mom in the days ahead.

I'm surprised Anthony doesn't have any kids. He seems to know what to do to keep things calm. I'm happy he's with me through this.

By the time we were ready to eat, I was quite certain I'd made the best pizza ever. It smelled so good. I couldn't wait to eat. After he took them out of the oven, and let them cool. He mixed a pitcher of lemon iced tea. Anthony poured us a glass, then we dove right in.

As we ate, Anthony asked what time I was going to arrive at the hospital in the morning.

"I was thinking ten thirty or so. I know Mom is going into surgery tomorrow, I didn't want to arrive too early. The doctor told us he will call. Can you come?" I asked.

He couldn't, and I could see it bothered him. He had a big meeting, he justified, but he didn't need to offer explanations. He'd done so much. Anthony suggested I drive him to the club in the morning, and take the car to go see my mom. He told me he'd give me the keys to his place just in case I needed to come back for anything. I thanked him for that. I forgot all about how I was getting to the hospital. My mind was spinning on other things.

After some food, delicious by the way, we both admitted that we were still exhausted. We both agreed that it was emotionally more than anything. We cleaned up and put everything anyway. I thanked Anthony again. We said good night. With that, we both went to sleep. I couldn't wait to see Mom in the morning.

CHAPTER THIRTY-NINE

Bringing Mom Home

Morning came. With a light tap at the bedroom door, Anthony said, "Good morning Matthew, it's time to get up."

I got up, and went to the bathroom to wash up. I got dressed and went to the kitchen. Anthony was there sitting at the table drinking his morning coffee, and reading the paper.

I said, "Good morning." He asked if I would like to join him in a cup of coffee. I told him I was a little nervous about Mom this morning. "Maybe after I drop you off at the club and I come back I will have some."

Anthony told me not to worry, that Mom would be all right. That she's in good hands.

It was time to go. Anthony handed me the key to the house; he told me to put it on my key ring so I didn't lose it. He grabbed his briefcase. We locked up and headed towards the club. On our way, Anthony asked me to kindly keep him informed about Mom. He would try to give an update about Feathers as soon as he got news. I asked him what time he would like to get picked up from work.

Anthony told me not to worry about that. "We will talk about it as the day progresses."

I pulled into the club. We gave each other a hug. Anthony told me to be careful. He'd call me later.

It was very early; I didn't want to go back to the house alone. I stopped at Dunkin Donuts. I went inside to sit down for breakfast. I ordered a sausage and egg croissant, and a cup of coffee. I texted Rachel to tell her I miss her and love her. She was texting me all sorts of questions, but my mind wasn't ready to answer. I was having a hard time absorbing all of this myself. I gently told her I'd explain everything when I saw her.

I was so eager to get to the hospital to see Mom that I arrived by ten thirty. I remembered that I forgot one critical thing as I pulled into the parking lot—fresh clothes for her. Well, the house was forty-five minutes away. It would take approximately two hours to get there and back. We'd figure something out. I wanted to be at her bedside when she got up.

The nurse saw me walking towards my mom's room, and told me to give her a few minutes; she was a little sick coming out of anesthesia. She asked me to sit in the waiting room. The surgeon came in to tell me that her finger was successfully set. I thanked him.

He explained that there would be a lot of swelling and discomfort. "I will give you written discharge instructions, and the prescription to fill out; the pain medication should only be given if needed. You can also make sure you have extra strength Tylenol in the house. Her arm should be elevated above her heart throughout the day, until she comes in to see me for her appointment, and I will explain to her the next steps towards healing. Your mom will be discharged today, as soon as she is feeling better."

I thanked the doctor for taking such good care of my mom. He told me I could go in to see her shortly.

After some time passed, a nurse came into the waiting area and told me I could go see my mom. I can't wait until this part is over. So we can put it to rest.

"Hi Mom," I said softly. Don't worry, I'm here."

She smiled. "Matthew darling thank you. I love you."

Her ability to shed her light in this dark situation amazed me. The nurses were removing her IV and sitting her up. They told us we were waiting for the discharge instructions, then Mom would be ready to go home.

Mom asked for some juice. The nurse brought her some apple juice with a straw. She just about drank the entire cup in one sip. I was happy to see that. Mom kindly asked the nurse to help her to the bathroom. The nurse turned to me and asked if I didn't mind stepping out for a moment. She was going to dress her as well. I left the room, and was asked if I could bring the car around to the front doors to pick Mom up.

I noticed they were bringing in a wheelchair. My timing was good. The doctor went in to speak to her. I ran down to get my car and waited for the nurse to wheel her out so I could take her home. The nurse helped me get Mom in the car and I buckled her in. I thanked the nurse for everything she'd done for my mom, and we left.

This was when Mom started crying. "I'm so sorry honey to put you through all of this. I tried to work things out on my own so I didn't have to bother you. It didn't work out so well, and I couldn't have handled it without you. Thank you so much for being here. It means so much to me."

"Mom, I will always be here when you need me, don't worry about all that right now, the most important thing is that you are all right. I'm going to call Anthony to let him know we are on the way home. I forgot to call him when I got to your room. There was so much going on."

I rang Anthony and it went right to voicemail. I left a message letting him know that everything was all right and we were on our way home. I'd call him in a bit.

"Mom, you can put your chair back and rest?" I asked.

"No, I'm fine, thank you. I feel much better today," she said.

I was so happy to hear that. I shared how helpful Anthony had been through everything and that I'd stayed at his house the night before. He didn't want me to be alone.

"He is an exceptional person. Anthony cares about me and my well-being. He is a kind and gentle soul," Mom said.

"Yeah, he is, and very generous," I added.

I pulled up to the front of the house and helped Mom in through the front door, so happy that the boxes were all gone. Once she was in, I said I had to move the car to a parking spot. She walked in and said she'd be okay. When I got back I saw Mom in her bedroom crying. My heart plummeted.

"Mom, what is wrong?"

She looked at me through her teary eyes. "The place looks great. Thank you for everything. This is so kind and amazing!" she cried.

"Anthony and I did it," I said. "Truthfully, I'm not sure that I could have done it without him."

"Matthew dear, did you change the lock to the front door?"

That was the one thing that I'd forgotten. "I'll get that done right away, but why did you ask?"

"He was in my room!"

"How do you know that?" I asked.

"The closet door is open and my dress hanger is on the floor. He took my elegant long black dress with beaded sides. Before he beat me up he was already dating someone else. Even though that dress was form fitted to me he must have given it to her as a gift, the tags were still on it. I worked very hard and many hours to buy that gown."

I understood, but I didn't get the full picture, I admit. "Mom, don't worry about that dress. The good Lord will give you plenty more beautiful dresses," I said.

"Please, get a locksmith here as quickly as you can," she said softly. I nodded my head.

Mom said she was eager to take a shower and clean up. She asked for a plastic bag so she could throw the clothes she wore away, and one to wrap her hand so it wouldn't get wet.

"I'm sorry I forgot new clothes," I said.

"You've done more than anyone could ever expect of someone else given the circumstances. I love you so much. I'm so proud of you," Mom said.

While Mom was in the shower, Anthony called and I explained about the locks. I was a bit panicked as well, because I didn't have the money for new locks. I hadn't even thought of it. We both beat ourselves up over it, especially realizing that he must have posted bail, and him coming in the house was really frightening. Luke was that type of man who didn't care about stay away orders or jail for that matter. If he wanted to get to you he would. He made it clear he wasn't afraid of anything. Which made me very nervous.

Then I remembered Feathers, and asked how he was doing. Anthony said Feathers was doing better, and he'd bring him over tonight. The sad part is that he has a broken wing, and would never fly again.

"How are you getting here? I have your car." He told me not to worry about that. He borrowed a car from someone else, and I could use his car until I went home.

After that I asked about the presentation Anthony had for work, and he said it hadn't started yet. He'd go, call a locksmith, and get me an update.

✳✳✳

I walked around the house while Mom showered and when she got out she asked about the locksmith right away. I told her he'd be here today. Not knowing for sure, but I didn't want to worry her.

She nodded, and then added, "After all he's done to me he came back for a dress."

I knew that added to the violation, but to me the dress meant nothing compared to her safety. "Mom, the good Lord will handle him in time. You have to stay strong and healthy. This is the beginning after; you're Picking Up The Pieces. I'm so happy he is gone and is someone else's problem, unfortunately."

"Yes, you're right, Matthew. I'm ready for a new journey full of love, faith, and happiness," she said.

"Sometimes people hide their inner demons and they surface when you least expect it. You are happy with who you are and there was nothing he could have done to bring you down, permanently. You're too strong for that. You have a good support group and you were smart to keep everyone away from him. You kept your personal life to yourself, as if you didn't have one," I said.

"I learned valuable lessons on how I don't want to be treated, and that I will never accept someone in my life that treats me badly again. Not even a second chance. I need to value myself and set boundaries for my self-worth. I let all my guards down and allowed someone to torment me, and beat me. This will never happen again, it won't ever be an option in my life going forward.

"I did keep people away from him. I didn't want them to be as dis-respected as I was when he lashed out. Anyone I cared for could have been his target," Mom lamented.

"That's the way he was, especially when he was drinking like that. Some people are happy and have fun. Not him, he became nasty and violent. Substance abuse will not be tolerated moving ahead in my life. This is an experience I will never forget or allow to enter my life again," she said.

Her spirit and determination were so powerful, because they were from the heart.

"I'm happy you're a healthy-minded person. The doctor who took care of you in the emergency room told me that you weren't crying vic-tim. That you understand what happened and how you got to where you are," I told her.

"Yes, I'm not an angel by any means. I made mistakes, too," she said.

I received a cell call from Anthony that the locksmith should be there at any moment, sorry for the short notice. I was so glad, I can't even explain how my stomach felt. I was in knots.

Then there was a knock on the front door. It startled Mom.

"This must be the locksmith," I told her. She breathed a sigh of relief, and I opened the door and found the locksmith sent by Anthony. I introduced myself, thanked him, and let him get to work.

I found Mom in the bedroom. "I forgot to tell you. Anthony is going to bring Feathers home tonight. He is fine but he has a broken wing," I mentioned. She was relieved that he'd made it. And before long the locksmith called out that he was done. That was fast.

I went out front and took the new keys from him. He handed me a receipt, told me to have a good day, and he was gone. The last piece was in place to protect Mom from Luke physically.

Mom yawned and she said she needed a nap. I made sure she got into bed okay, and then told her I was going to get some lunch, and a few things for dinner, and be back soon.

I locked the door behind me and left.

As soon as Matthew left my mind and body went right to sleep. I was mentally and physically worn out from this painful experience. I was doing the best I could keeping a stiff upper lip for Matthew and Anthony who tried so hard to help me find peace with something I did to myself. Soon enough my eyes were closed.

Waking up to screams of terror and gasping for air with sweat pouring down my face. It took me a moment to figure out where I was. Reliving the horror all over again. It seemed so real as if I felt him hitting me. I heard his voice clearly yelling, "You're a bitch and a piece of shit!" with the corresponding look of rage. I will never forget his eyes piercing through my heart. With seeing me in pain the only thing on his mind.

Tears rolling down my face in disbelief at what I let happen to me. I kept telling myself, *This was a nightmare you will be ok. Luke will never bother you again.* I repeated this over and over again. Until I was able to gather my thoughts and get a hold of myself. I got up, went to the bathroom and drank some water out of the faucet, wiped my face, and retuned to bed until Matthew came back.

CHAPTER FORTY

I heard Matthew come back in, and I called out to him. He was bringing groceries in and I slowly got up so I could help.

"Stay put," he said, carrying bags in. Not only did he go grocery shopping, he went to the pharmacy and had my prescription filled. So grateful for his love. It was funny to have him order me around like I was the child.

"Anthony taught me how to cook something last night. I'm going to make it for you for lunch," Matthew announced.

He told me to keep resting and that he'd get me when it was all ready. I was quite curious about it, but not that hungry at the time. Hopefully I would be by the time it was done. But truthfully, I would have eaten anything he made for me, because of the heart that went into it.

About an hour later he called me out to the kitchen. He helped me walk there and I smiled when I walked in. The table was set, it smelled fantastic, and he was grinning merrily. I grinned the same way.

"Wow," I said.

"I made Caesar salad and homemade pizza," Matthew said.

"Two of my favorite things," I said. I knew he knew that too.

"Anthony must be working today," I said after we sat down and began to eat.

"He has some food presentation today," Matthew said.

I forgot all about that and I hoped that tending to me yesterday didn't make that harder on him.

"This is really good, Matthew, you're a natural chef."

"If it's a two course meal every day, maybe," he said. We laughed. It was so good to have him home by my side. I knew that I'd missed him but at that moment I hadn't realized how much.

As we put together all the pieces of the chaos from the past days, both Matthew and I realized how much Anthony had done for us. Without him, everything would have been harder. The support in all areas, and even getting Feathers to the animal hospital were all so kind. His genuine goodness shined through.

After lunch, Matthew asked if I wanted to watch a movie, and I laughed about how spoiled I was getting. He told me he even bought popcorn.

"I have a few days Mom. Take advantage of it." He is so sweet.

✳✳✳

There was a knock on the door and I jumped. How long would it take me to relax? Matthew lowered the TV's volume and went to the door and asked who it was. It was Anthony. He opened the door quickly and I stood up from the couch and smiled.

Feathers was in his hands and he handed him to me. I thanked him with tears in my eyes for taking care of Feathers, and doing everything he could. I couldn't wipe away my tears, I had one hand. He then came to me, wiped my wet face, and kissed my cheek and asked how I was.

"Spoiled, thanks to you and Matthew," I said. "But how was your presentation today?" I asked.

"They loved everything!"

I was happy, and Matthew was too. Then he tossed Matthew his duffle bag that he forgot at his house.

Matthew smiled and said, "How did you know?"

"I went back to the house to take a shower, and the light in the guest room was on, and your bag was on the bed."

"Thank you so much for bringing it," Matthew said.

I glanced at Feathers' broken wing and Anthony apologized that they couldn't do more. No one could have done more. We decided it was best for him to be in his cage so he wasn't tempted to fly around. Hopefully his wing would heal in time. Matthew took him gently from my arms, and placed him in his cage.

"Would you like to watch a movie with us?" I asked Anthony.

He said he couldn't because he had a busy day tomorrow. So he gave me a gentle hug and then a gentle kiss on my forehead, which was nice, like good medicine. Then he told me to call him in the morning. Matthew and I stood at the door as he left; we waved goodbye as he passed.

After he was gone, Matthew said, "Mom, I really love that guy, he's great."

I smiled and sighed.

"You know what, I like him too. He's a very special man, an amazing friend." It was too early to think about anything like that, but I couldn't deny the existence of my feelings at that moment, either.

"How's Feathers doing?" I asked.

Matthew looked over at him and said, "He seems okay. I can tell that he's still in a lot of pain. I guess it'll take time."

I glanced at him, with the emotional feeling inside of me that has me thinking this is all my fault.

"He looks so dull, like there's no brightness to him," I whispered.

Matthew noticed my sadness as I was giving all my attention to Feathers. He came over and held me. He told me things would get better. He is just like his father, very considerate, kind, and so attentive to my feelings.

Matthew and I sat back down on the couch, finished watching the movie, and ate the rest of the popcorn. My hand started to ache. I got up and took my medicine; Matthew helped me open the bottle. I thanked Matthew for all he'd done for me. I told him I love him, to have pleasant dreams, and I gave him a kiss on his cheek. We said good night, and went to bed.

CHAPTER FORTY-ONE

Morning rolled around before I knew it. Sun was beaming in my room. I got up carefully to go to the bathroom. I straightened out my hair with my fingers; I only have one hand so it becomes a task even to put my hair back, but I managed.

I went to the kitchen to put a pot of coffee on. I looked over to see how Feathers was doing, and he was lying at the bottom of his cage. I screamed out to Matthew. He came running into the kitchen and asked what was wrong.

"Why are you screaming?!" he asked. Matthew looked around to see if there was anyone in the house.

"Look, look please look!" I cried, "Feathers is dead! He stayed alive long enough to come home and die here with us!" I continued.

"Mom, this is terrible. I'm sorry, I know you took care of him all these years after Dad passed."

We both started crying. Matthew held me up so I didn't collapse to the floor. I looked up and asked God to give me strength, I needed His help to get through this. I knew Feathers wasn't going to do well but I didn't think it would be this soon. I wasn't emotionally prepared for something like this. Time passed with thoughts of what to do with Feathers.

"I want to take him to your father's grave and bury him there. If it wasn't for Feathers watching over me and making a lot of noise, Luke would have kept beating me. Feathers was the distraction. I felt your father watching over me. Please Matthew get dressed and come with me," I said.

"Are you sure that's what you want to do?" Matthew asked.

"Yes, this is what we should do. Give Feathers a proper burial. He'd been in our lives for so many years. Can you call Anthony and let him know?" I kept crying and couldn't stop the flow of tears.

Matthew called and Anthony felt truly bad for us, especially when he heard me in the background crying so hard. I was truly heartbroken, although forever grateful to my courageous Feathers for saving my life.

I put on a clean kitchen glove and gently lifted him out of his cage and wrapped him in a flowered cloth. The anguish in my voice couldn't be consoled, and I didn't even try to hold it back.

"If I had spoken up this wouldn't have happened," I lamented.

Matthew wanted to help, but I had to do this. I felt so guilty about what happened to him, although it was not my fault.

I walked over to the front door and asked Matthew to open it, so I could set Feathers on the table outside. I took the glove off and dropped it. Then he closed and locked the door. I gathered all of Feathers' toys, and bells, and put them in a small box, so he'd have them with him in Heaven.

"God what has happened!" I screamed so loud. "Why didn't I speak up?"

Matthew stood in silence, as he cried watching me. He didn't know what to say. I looked up at Matthew, with a drenched face that blurred in my vision.

"I have to go get dressed. Please get changed, and get ready," I uttered.

I went into my room and slipped into a summer dress—that was the easiest thing to put on with one hand—and I put on a pair of flip flops. Matthew came out of his room and was ready to go. I picked up the box from the kitchen counter and handed it to Matthew. We walked outside on the porch. I kicked my glove out of the way, picked up Feathers, and held him close to my body.

Matthew locked up the house. I asked him to please get the small flower shovel I have under the porch. I was in such deep sadness. My thoughts were crushed. I had so many opportunities to end this nightmare. Matthew opened the car door to help me, and buckled me in. I put Feathers on my lap. As we made our way to the cemetery, we both were silent. Not a word, but quiet tears.

We reached the cemetery and parked. Matthew helped me out of the car. I walked with Feathers in hand over to my belated husband's grave, and Matthew followed behind me with the shovel, and the small box. I bent down in front of it. I placed Feathers down beside me, and Matthew handed me the spade, and put the box down near Feathers.

I began to dig and the tears were so uncontrollable. "What have I done?" I kept asking. There was no good answer. Matthew bent down, his own eyes filled with tears, and patted my back to console me.

I was gasping for air and then I began to talk to my husband. I told him everything that happened out loud and how Feathers protected me. I thanked him for giving Feathers to us.

I said, "Honey, you can rest now. I will be all right. I have learned and grown from this horrible experience and I will remain respectful of my true self and life."

Then I put Feathers into the hole along with his toys, and slowly patted down the dirt on top of his body. I paused for a moment and felt the tickle of tears rolling down my face.

I yelled out, wanting to be heard. "I love you with all my heart. Thank you for watching over me. Rest in peace, darling love."

Matthew bent down and took my arm. "It's time to get up now," he said gently. I stood up hugged him and told him I loved him. How could I ever thank him enough?

Matthew yelled out, "I love you Dad." And what a great dad he'd been, one who would be so proud of his son today.

I walked away that day filled with hope, and no regrets. It was not the time to quit or dwell, it was the time to move on from this experience. I'd learned lessons, and they were lessons that others could perhaps learn from too.

"LIFE BEGINS AFTER MANY LESSONS
HAVE BEEN LEARNED"
– AMILIA POWERS

ABOUT THE AUTHOR

Member: United Nations Association of the USA & UNA-Women

Amilia has a passion-driven focus to help others. She is a very active person who is highly committed in her role as an inspirational mentor. Through her mentorship, she works with clients in either individual or group settings, and forums to help them in their life's transitions. Amilia believes that there are no regrets necessary in life, only opportunities to learn from mistakes that are the result of challenging circumstances. With this at the heart of her inspirational healing and transformational practices, Amilia is committed to finding a way to reach out to anyone in need as they navigate through the challenges of their life.

"I stand behind my clients with encouragement to help them pick up the pieces and become stronger through their trials, improve self-awareness, increase selflove, so they can live a happier, and healthier life. I enjoy teaching individuals the importance of self-value; the understanding of how this can help you make better choices." Amilia says.

Over the years, Amilia has had many mentors who have taught her the valuable lessons and strategies about how to make a true impact on other people. Brian Tracy is one such man, and through his motivational speeches he has offered great insight on how to help people move past all obstacles and find success. This aligns perfectly with Amilia's vision and life goals. Every day is a chance for a new lesson and opportunity to extend my life experiences and commitment through inspirational coaching to someone in need.

Amilia is quite active in Toastmasters International, a wonderful nonprofit platform that trains individuals in public speaking, and how to present themselves with confidence. Amilia is formerly the club's President and Area Director, and continues her mentorship training.

I was recently interviewed on the TV show, *Times Square Today*. *Times Square Today* appeared on CNN, CNBC, and Fox News affiliates around the country. Amilia Powers was named America's premier expert in her field.

"I am passionate about the power of family, and cherish the opportunities to connect with my parents, son and daughter, and her five grandchildren, which are a constant source of laughter and joy for me. And to all who ask what my best nugget of wisdom is, I often say:

From Amilia,

To my wonderful readers, my name is Amilia Powers. I work one to one with individuals as a personal coach and teach important life principles. The number one lesson is the value of one's self is their key to personal freedom. I teach about developing boundaries and setting standards that are required for a healthy more loving and joyous life. These must be the nonnegotiable. These two keys set the stage for a more rewarding and fulfilling relationship. I help my clients create special strategies to develop the strength to stop making excuses, living in denial, and make the necessary changes to move towards a more positive and happy life. Last, and more importantly my clients are taught how implementing forgiveness allows them to find inner peace.

Love & Peace

Heed the warning signs.
The price you pay for not following your gut instincts
is one you wished you never made.

Contact Amilia Powers

Visit Me at

www.valueurself.com

www.coffeewithamilia.com

Follow Me on

LinkedIn, Facebook, Pinterest, and Twitter

Join Me at

amiliapower.blogspot.com

For more information on this subject,

and to read my latest articles

Made in United States
North Haven, CT
29 August 2022

23390029R00147